Please feel free to send me an email. Just know that my publisher filters these emails. Good news is always welcome.

Summer Nawaz - summer_nawaz@awesomeauthors.org

Sign up for my blog for updates and freebies!
summer-nawaz.awesomeauthors.org

I0618865

About the Publisher

BLVNP Incorporated, A Nevada Corporation, 340 S. Lemon #6200, Walnut CA 91789, info@blvnp.com / legal@blvnp.com

DISCLAIMER

BOUND

Summer Nawaz

BLVNP

ISBN: 978-1-68030-992-8

Table of Contents

Dedicated to Mama and Baba for being convinced I was talented before ever reading a word I wrote

Free Download

Get these freebies and *more* when you sign up for the author's mailing list!

summer-nawaz.awesomeauthors.org

Prologue

Kelsey

"It got too aggressive really fast, Kelsey. The doctors say I've only got a month—maybe two—left."

It felt like some sort of sick joke as the breath that I had been holding expelled from my lips, my heart dropping to the pit of my stomach as I fruitlessly tried to make sense of my mother's devastating words—words that easily crumbled my world.

Cancer.

Leukemia grew extremely aggressive over a short period of time, killing my mother and ripping her away from me. The thought of it sent shivers down my spine, accompanying the onslaught of tears that burned in my eyes.

My mother, the woman who raised me by herself because my father had died and she had no living relatives left, was dying. She was going to be gone, leaving me alone in a world that I didn't know how to exist in without her guiding me along.

My tearful blue eyes met her own, slowly shaking my head as I shifted on the couch to face her. If we had been standing, I was positive my knees would've given out, and I would've fallen into the physical embodiment of a crumpled mess on the floor. I knew I was feeling emotional.

"No, no. You're—you're kidding, right? Is this a joke?" Denial spilled from my mouth even though I knew the grim, heartbreaking truth in her words.

It intensified when she remained silent.

"You can't leave me, Mom," I whispered, my lower lip quivering, allowing the salty taste of tears to enter my mouth. I didn't even notice that I had begun crying.

My mother looked so beautiful but so sad, and if it weren't for her confession, I never would've guessed that she had been sick. Why didn't she tell me before?

She had just explained how she had been going to treatment over the past few months without telling anyone, and it seemed like they weren't doing her any good. She had refrained from telling me, her only child, and my mouth dried for not being able to detect something like this. *How could something like this happen right under my nose, and why hadn't I been able to pick up on it? Was she really that good at hiding the fact that she had cancer? Why just tell me now when all hope for recovery was already lost?*

Pulling me in for a hug, she wrapped her arms around my body as my own circled her waist, feeling her chin resting on top of my head as she muttered, "Please, honey, don't cry. You're going to be just fine without me."

My face was buried in her chest, wiping my tears on her shirt, and then I shook my head before pulling away to look at her. At that moment, I realized how tired she looked—bags under her tearful, dull blue eyes and her skin was paler than usual. Sniffling, I kept my arms around her as I managed to ask, "How? How am I gonna be fine *without* you?"

The grief on her face was now replaced with hesitation as she bit her bottom lip, cupping my cheeks with her bony fingers. "I've arranged something for you."

I wiped the remaining tears from my face while Mom absentmindedly played with a loose thread on her shirt. I sniffled once again, rubbing my hands against the material of my shorts, then frowned. "What?"

Mom took a deep breath, nervously running her fingers through her blonde hair, which only prompted the dread inside me to build up once again. Before she told me about her cancer, I knew something was terribly wrong at the moment I had seen her face when she said she needed to talk to me about something deliberate—apparently not as terrible as her having cancer but it was still something I wouldn't take lightly. She was now wearing an expression similar to that, which told me that whatever she was about to say, there was a chance that I wasn't going to like hearing it.

"I have a friend who lives in England." She began, her bony fingers wringing together on her lap. She glanced down at them before locking her gaze with my own. "She has a son and daughter around your age; they're such nice people. Good friends. And we've, uh…"

My eyebrows scrunched in impatience and worry, wondering where in the world she was going with this.

"We've arranged for you to go live with them."

It took me a moment to process what she said. I was staring at her in confusion until the words slammed into my mind like an eighteen-wheeler and it felt like someone dunked a bucket of ice-cold water on me. When the realization finally set in, I wrenched myself away from my mother and clambered to my feet, my eyes widening in incredulity. *Had I heard her right? She was shipping me off to another country to live with some people I'd never met?*

Unable to hear anything over the erratic pounding of my heart, I exclaimed, "Mom, are you crazy?" Her lips parted to respond, but I continued. "I can't—I'm not moving to England. That's insane. I have a life here, college!" God, I had so many more reasons to show how terrible of an idea that was, but my mind was going a hundred miles a minute. I kept stumbling over my words as my mouth tried to keep up with the swirling thoughts in my panicked mind. "I can't do that, Mom."

Mom remained calm and cool, though, staring up at me, still seated on the couch. This might have been her idea, but how could she possibly think that I would be okay with this? My entire life was in Florida, from the moment I was born to this very day and getting up and leaving wasn't something I was prepared for. I didn't want to move to England, I didn't want to live with some people I'd never met before. My mother was delivering devastating news after news. How could I leave the only place I've ever lived, the place where every single memory of my mother exists?

"Of course you can, sweetie," she replied, offering a small yet encouraging smile as she nodded— a lame attempt to convince me to accept this idea. "You're going to love England and you're going to love them. Her daughter is a little older than you but I know you'll get along well with her son. I wouldn't be doing this if I wasn't sure of that. Besides, you're only a part-time student. You're not quitting school. I'm sure you can transfer your credits after you move. If not, then you can still attend as an out-of-state part-time student."

I stared at her, my lips parting in disbelief. It seemed like she had everything figured out. Still, my incredulity and exasperation were ever present. "That's not the point, Mom." I argued, clearly frustrated. "You're asking me to give up my life here to live in a different country. With people I've never met. I don't care if they're your friends, *I've* never met them and you can't force a friendship between me and your friend's son," I added with a scoff. "I can't intrude on their lives and I sure as hell don't want to give up mine here." Mom sighed, standing up to her feet and grasping my hands in hers. They were cold, much like how I was feeling at this moment: grief, heartbreak, and pain over my mother's disease mixed with disbelief and frustration over the knowledge of being told I had to leave my home. These sent my thoughts and feelings to a frenzy that I couldn't even begin to understand. Mom was already planning for after her death and I still hadn't processed that she was dying.

"Please, Kelsey." She begged as her brows scrunched upwards in desperation that also colored her tone, making me clench my jaw tightly. "I want—" She choked on her words, inhaling sharply as her eyes glazed over, and then she squeezed my hands.

I felt a lump in my throat as a loud voice in my head obnoxiously reminded me of what ailed my mother, easily causing my eyes to burn once again.

"I want to be sure that you're going to be taken care of once I-I'm gone. We don't—we don't have any family left, and I know this one will take care of you."

My lower lip quivered as Mom slowly but surely began crumbling my resolve. "Why can't I just stay with Logan's family?" I muttered, shaking my head in desperation as I referred to my best friend of years. His parents were friends with my mom; it made so much more sense for me to stay with them. That way I'd get to stay with people I love and not have to leave Florida. "Why does it have to be *them*? Why does it have to be England?"

I guess a mother had her reasons because all Mom did was whisper another *please* as the tears in her eyes grew too much and began rolling down her cheeks. I knew then that I was defeated. Her reasons wouldn't be much help anyway because I knew I would start asking for reasons why cancer had to choose my mother, and I knew cancer didn't need a reason.

As much as I didn't want this, I knew I could do nothing about it at this point. It had always been just my mom and me, and I always did what she told me to because I had no doubt that whatever she decided was for the best. She was always looking out for me—that's what Moms do. Mom was always thinking of me and what was best for me, and I had never questioned her decisions before. I wasn't going to start now, not with the state she was in. I didn't want to spend whatever limited time I had with my mother arguing with her, even if I didn't agree with her decision on my life.

There was a lump forming in my throat as I miserably realized that this was, in a sense, Mom's dying wish. The ball of lead sank deeper to my stomach as my breath got caught in my throat, knowing that no matter how much I didn't want any of this—uprooting my life and my mother's sickness—I knew I had to go with it. And the absolute last thing that I wanted to do was disappoint my mother before she was taken away from me. At the thought of my mother not being around, bile rose up my throat.

"Fine." I finally agreed, swallowing down the acidic taste as Mom blinked in surprise as if she couldn't believe that I had given in so easily. I couldn't either, but I would do anything for my mother. Apparently that also meant giving up everything I knew here to live with a family I've never met. Taking a deep breath, I requested. "At least tell me who your friend is."

Mom squeezed my hands reassuringly. There was a smile of relief spreading across her own exhausted face as she admitted. "Her name's Amelia." Mom paused as a look of realization passed. "I think you may actually know of her son."

Of her son? I frowned. "What do you mean? Who's her son?"

"Cooper Shaw."

Chapter 1

"Hurry up, Kelsey! They're gonna be here soon!" Mom shouted from the living room, her voice ringing throughout the house, followed by coughing.

"Mom, just relax, alright?" I said to her as soon as I came to her view, shaking my head at her antics of trying to fix the couch cushions even though they were already positioned the way they were supposed to be. "Don't exert yourself too much, okay?"

"Yes. Yes, I know," she replied, finally sitting on the couch with the tired sigh that I had unfortunately grown accustomed to in the past few weeks. "But they're almost here, and we need to make sure everything's perfect."

I rolled my eyes, tucking a strand of my short blonde hair behind my ear.

Today was the day that Mom's friend and her family were coming to our house. It had taken them a little while to find the right time to come, because apparently Mom's friend, Amelia, wanted her entire family to come which meant waiting for Cooper Shaw to return home. The famous musician finally got some free time from his band expeditions and was able to make a trip here with his family to, well, meet his new housemate.

I had to will my stomach from twisting into uncomfortable knots at the mere thought of meeting someone famous. This was supposed to be exciting—not nausea-inducing.

It had been a little over three weeks since Mom told me about her cancer and about this arrangement, and we were finally seeing the family that was supposed to be taking me in.

Instead of letting my mind wander further, I kept in mind how Mom was growing weaker and that it was so visible. Her skin was getting paler by the day, and she couldn't stop coughing.

Much to my protest, she refused to stay in the hospital or even just to continue her treatment because she thought it wouldn't prevent her cancer from growing any harsher than it already was. Mom would much rather stay home with me than be confined to a hospital bed with several IVs stuck in her.

Either way, I wasn't leaving her side, mainly to make sure that she wouldn't exert herself too much. We even moved her to the guest room downstairs since going up the stairs had become a problem for her. At least that provided some distance from where my room was upstairs, where I spent nights crying in bed at the thought of my mother not being here one day. Pounds of makeup needed to be piled on my face to hide the bags that had developed under my eyes.

When Mom had told me that her friend's son was Cooper Shaw, I didn't believe her at all. But then she launched into the story of how she was best friends with his mother ever since they went to the same college back in the day, which was unbelievable since she never mentioned Cooper's mother before even though she was aware of who Triage was and how popular that band was.

Apparently, Mom had been friends with Cooper's mother, Amelia, for years even though Amelia moved back to England. And I hadn't a single clue.

It was insane because Cooper was obviously always touring and his band had come to Miami before—wouldn't his mom find it polite for him to visit mine? It didn't add up, and now I was beginning to wonder just how much I didn't know about my mother—first about her cancer and now this. I was still struggling to wrap my head around all of this, but Cooper and his family were flying here to Miami to meet us and the reality of the situation was slowly settling in my brain.

As we waited for them to arrive, I was on the phone with my best friend, Logan. I was fixing up the kitchen where Mom and I had put out a little dish of snacks consisting of some freshly cut fruit, and I was tempted to pick up a piece of cantaloupe and shove it in my mouth.

"This family better be nice," Logan said through the phone. "I don't want my best friend to get trapped with a stuck-up family of a stuck-up celebrity."

I chuckled, shaking my head at his words. Logan was always the protective type, but that was what made him such a good friend. The two of us had been friends for over twelve years now, joined at the hip.

There had been times when people assumed that we were together, but we were quick to deny that. I had only ever seen Logan as a friend and nothing more—anything more would get too complicated. My feelings for him were utterly platonic, and his were the same. It calmed me down whenever I remember that I always had him in my corner, especially during extraordinary circumstances like this.

"We'll see about that, Logan," I replied, resting my phone in between my right shoulder and cheek as I took two glasses from the dishwasher and put them inside the appropriate cabinet.

"So you're seriously going through with this?" he asked in a mixture of disbelief and apprehension, and I could picture him raising his dark eyebrows. When I had told Logan about my mother's illness and the big life decision that she had made for me, he was almost as heartbroken, shocked, and appalled as I was. There were some nights spent with me crying to him on the phone before falling asleep.

"I have to." I sighed, reaching up to hold my phone properly since my neck began cramping. "I—Mom's dying, Logan," I added in a hushed, shaky whisper. Saying it out loud automatically made my heart stutter and my eyes burn. "It's what she wants me to do, and I have to." I pursed my lips, leaning against the counter. "It's not like I want to; this whole thing can blow up in our face—I may not like them or they may not like me and Mom's plan could go to shit." I paused for a moment before sighing for the nth time and tilting my head back to stare up at the overhead lights on the white ceiling. "But I'm going to try and make it work—for my mom, I will."

Logan stayed silent for a moment. His breathing was the only thing that I could hear as we pondered my heavy words. Everything since the moment Mom told me about her cancer had been full of smothering dread and crippling fear of what was to come, enough to give me a consistent migraine and an erratically beating heart. "I guess you're right," Logan finally said with a sad sigh.

I nodded to myself, briefly biting my lower lip until I heard the bell ring. I stood up straight, and my eyes widened as I rushed out. "Shit. Logan, they're here. I'll call you later!"

"Tell me how it goes—" I heard Logan say before I hastily hung up.

As I made my way towards the front door, I stopped for a second to look at myself in the hallway mirror. I reached up to fix my wavy blonde hair, trying to make myself look presentable. I smoothed down my dark blue V-neck and white jeans, making sure my feet were comfortable in a pair of UGG slippers before quickly making my way down the hall.

I saw Mom standing up when I reached the front door. "Mom, sit down. I'm getting it," I said, shooting her a pointed look.

Mom sighed and sat back down without a fight.

I took in a deep breath before gripping the doorknob and pulling the door open.

And when I did, I froze.

Standing right in front of me was the startlingly familiar guy towering at over six feet, effortlessly dominating my small frame. Sunglasses covered what I knew to be green eyes. His lips were set in a firm line that accompanied the way his sharp jaw clenched under his dark stubble. Even though the first thing that I noticed was how tall and handsome he was, the very next thought in my mind was that this guy, just like me, wasn't happy about this situation at all. What the hell was *he* so angry about? I'm the one who had to move out of the damn country.

Still, I couldn't help but wonder how the pictures that I had seen of him online didn't do him justice—and he hadn't even taken his sunglasses off yet. However, the full sleeves of tattoos that decorated his nicely toned arms easily added to his wow factor— tattoos had always been something that I liked on a man. If I was going to be stuck with him, at least he was pleasing to the eyes.

God, I hated this.

I offered a small smile once I had gathered my wits, opening the door wider as I stepped aside. "Come on in," I said. As bitter and uneasy as I might have been, I still had to act like a civil human being.

Cooper Shaw merely nodded before walking in, and then I saw the three other people who were with him. They all looked familiar. Maybe because when you're a celebrity as famous as Cooper Shaw, you'll get to know what his family members look like whether you're a fan of his band or not.

A woman, who looked a few years older than me, followed Cooper inside—Cooper's sister, Alessandra.

An older man, who was taller than all of us women but was shorter than Cooper, followed suit. He had glasses on, and he had a balding head—Cooper's stepfather, Russell Travers.

The last person to enter the house was an older woman—Amelia.

Amelia stopped right in front of me. "It's so good to see you again, Kelsey." She grinned, looking absolutely happy to be here. "Gosh, you've grown so much."

I awkwardly smiled back since I had never met this woman in my life. *What should I say?*

As they walked in, I guided them to the living room where my mom instantly got to her feet, and I couldn't help but say, "Mom, relax."

"Oh, hush, Kelsey," Mom giggled, dismissing me as she walked over to Amelia. "Mia! I missed you."

"I've missed you even more, Klara." Amelia hugged my mother back. Since Mom's back was to me, I could easily note the look of grief and sadness that washed over Amelia's face when she hugged my mom, squeezing her eyes shut as the smile on her face slightly wobbled.

I looked away from their reunion, and my eyes landed on the tall boy next to me. He was standing with his sunglasses now folded, hanging from the neckline of his black Calvin Klein shirt. His green eyes were looking around our living room disinterestedly, making me wonder if he could look any more bored if he tried.

"You can, uh, sit down." I gestured towards the couch.

Once again, Cooper wordlessly nodded and sat down, Alessandra and Russell following his lead.

Mom and Amelia sat down on the two-seater couch diagonal to them, and then Mom's gaze landed on me. "Kelsey, get them some water, will you?"

Nodding, I spun on my heel and made my way to the kitchen, filling up five glasses of water and putting them on a tray before returning to the living room.

The only people talking were Russell and our mothers, playing catch up when I got there.

I offered the women water first before moving on to the rest. I gulped and stopped in front of Cooper, providing the last glass of water. The blood in my veins seemed to freeze as his green eyes flickered upwards to meet my blue ones in such a way that I felt as though he was reading me. It was nerve-wracking, and I tried not to show my relief when he wordlessly picked up the glass. He didn't even bother with a thank you. Then I stood up straight with the now empty tray in my hands.

The adults were busy talking as I awkwardly stood next to the couch.

At one point, Alessandra looked at me, her own green eyes meeting mine, although hers were much kinder than her brother's. She offered me a smile, something akin to sympathy and understanding, and I falsely returned it before turning around and walking out of the living room.

Depositing the plastic tray on the counter with a light slapping sound, I made my way to the hallway bathroom as fast as my feet could carry me.

I locked the door shut once I got inside the bathroom, then stared at myself in the mirror. My dark blonde eyebrows were scrunched together as I ran a hand through my lighter colored hair, harshly chewing on my lower lip.

I couldn't do this, no doubt about that, but I needed to stop being selfish. I had to do this for my mother. It was what she wanted, and I needed to deliver even though this had everything to do with my life. I knew my mom was asking a lot from me, but after everything that she had done, it just felt so wrong to not do what she wanted. I couldn't disappoint her, but the whole thing was making me incredibly anxious. I mean, it was one thing to live with another family but entering the life a guy who was in the world's biggest band? Yeah, right. As if anything about this was normal.

Bracing my hands on the cold porcelain counter of the sink, I shot myself a pointed look in the reflection before letting out a deep breath and exiting the bathroom. Returning to the living room, I noticed that Russell was gone. I furrowed my brows and asked no one in particular, "Where'd he go?"

Alessandra, who had been on her phone, put the device down on her lap and answered me in a sweet tone coated in an English accent, "To walk around for a bit. He's sick of sitting down."

I nodded in partial understanding until Amelia cleared her throat and spoke up. "We need to talk about the living arrangement." My gaze snapped to her in surprise, as if I hadn't expected for us to be talking about this already. "There seems to be a, uh, unexpected issue."

I saw the worry flood Mom's eyes before hearing it in her voice. "Everything alright?"

"Everything's fine," Amelia assured her with a squeeze of her hand. Her gaze flickered between my mother and I. "It's just— we experienced some plumbing issues in the hallway leading to the guest room of our house, which would've been your room, Kelsey," she added as she looked at me. "But it's flooded beyond belief and everything is destroyed. It's going to take a while for renovation so you can't move in there until it's done."

My eyebrows shot up, wondering if it was premature and overdramatic of me to want to pop open a bottle of Champaign. Did this mean I wouldn't have to move in with them just yet? "Oh, no," Mom worried and the sound of her voice made me feel a prickle of guilt for celebrating the snag in her plan.

"But we do have a solution." I tried not to show my disappointment at Amelia's words. Her eyes, a darker shade of green than her son's, met mine. "Cooper has his own flat in London, just a little ways away from our home. Kelsey is more than welcome to stay there while the house is being redone."

My lips pressed tightly together to stop myself from choking on my own saliva, not expecting those words to leave my mother's mouth—not that any of this had been expected. They expected me to live with some guy whom I didn't even know, at his apartment in a country that I had never even been to? I wanted to yell out that this was some sort of sick joke, but the cold realization was ever present. *Yes, this is some sort of sick joke, and I am the butt of it.*

My gaze flickered to the seated man. Cooper's expression was the same it had been since the second I opened the door, tight and annoyed and suddenly I understood why his expression held such irritation. He must've been already aware of this news and, just like me, he wasn't happy about it. Living with a newly introduced family was strange enough. But living alone with a man who had a larger-than-life presence, who had millions of fans all over the world, who hadn't evens said a word to me since entering my home, twisted my stomach into the tightest of knots.

It was obvious he didn't want me to live with him in his home as much as I didn't want to leave the United States, but Cooper remained silent where he sat. He didn't even bother jumping into fight the issue. Though, I'm assuming he already tried before they came here and it was a fight he already lost.

"I—" I tried to quickly form the words in my mind, staring at the two women almost helplessly. "Is there no other place for me to stay? I mean," I cleared my throat, trying not to show my panic as much as I felt it. "I wouldn't wanna intrude on, uh, Cooper's privacy," I added lamely, knowing that it was a pathetically feeble thing to say. I was intruding in on all of their lives, anyway.

"Of course not!" Amelia immediately denied with an easy laugh. She either didn't see my heightened discomfort at this turn of events or chose to ignore it. Her eyes flickered past me to where her son was. "Cooper's more than willing to have you in his home. Isn't that right, honey?"

I looked at Cooper, staring at him in mild dread because I really wanted him to argue with his mother, but the reluctant clench of his jaw told me that wouldn't happen. "Yeah," he spoke for the first time, his voice deep and slow, his British accent—much different than his mother's American one—adding a drawl to his tone that I had heard on TV and on the internet. Unashamedly, I found it so much more appealing in person. "It's fine with me."

I wanted to scoff. His expression said it was anything but fine, and the prickle of hatred I had with this arrangement intensified. The second Mom told me I'd have to live in England; I'd already started worrying about being placed somewhere I didn't belong. And now with Cooper's obvious distaste with the newfound plan of me living *with him* really did make me want to crawl into a hole. Could he stop playing along with this ridiculousness?

I studied him, watching him keep his bored gaze on the oak coffee table in front of him. For a second, I allowed myself to wonder how Cooper's rock star lifestyle would affect my own. He was always being followed around by paparazzi, fans tracking his every move from what I saw online. How would they take the news of their favorite musician living with a girl they'd never heard of? Even if it was an arrangement out of our hands? Would they care? Were they aware of this yet? Since Mom informed me about all of this, I hadn't spent too much time on the internet or watched any TV, but I did know that Cooper Shaw had some startlingly dedicated fans and every time he was spotted with a girl, which apparently didn't happen too much, the reactions were severe. Despite being one of the most sought-after men in Hollywood, Cooper, surprisingly, kept to himself most of the time and was rarely spotted out with a girl, unlike his band mates. He either was really good at hiding whoever he was involved with or the several rumors about him being a womanizer that would pop up every now and then were just that. Rumors.

"It's settled, then," Amelia smiled in satisfaction, her gaze reassuring to my mother.

My jaw tightened, teeth grinding together at the smiles on her and Mom's faces. Could they stop looking so happy? Did they not remember why this whole thing was happening in the first place? With a tight throat, I asked the dreaded question, "So, uh, when is this happening?"

Mom looked at Amelia as if she was silently getting her opinion before looking at me. "Well—" she cleared her throat "—the sooner—"

Crossing my arms over my chest, I didn't know whether it was defensively or timidly, but I cut in before she could finish, "Can't I stay here? Just—just for now." The last few words needed to be squeezed out of my throat because our *"for now"* was soon coming to a screeching halt.

Before Mom could answer, Amelia piped in. "Kelsey's right, Klara," she said, looking at Mom with a small smile. "You should spend some more time with your daughter." She trailed off, and her tone faltered because no one in this room missed the grim point that she was trying to make.

But Mom, ever the shining light, locked gazes with me and smiled. "Of course."

***

"So you're staying for a little while?" Logan asked as he crunched on salt and vinegar flavored Lay's chips, his hand immediately diving back into the family-sized bag on my lap.

I nodded and hummed in response.

He turned his head to look at me. "And you're seriously moving in with a guy you don't even know?"

My own head turned to shoot him a pointed look. "I was supposed to live with his family but I guess the universe decided that wasn't enough of a kick in the ass for me." I let out a dramatic sigh that I believed wasn't nearly exaggerated enough to show what I was feeling. "This is my new normal."

Logan scoffed, shaking his head as he returned his gaze to the TV that was showing old episodes of *Criminal Minds*. "This is such bullshit." He complained in disgust.

"Shut up," I said, frowning in mild annoyance. Clenching my jaw once, I continued in a gruff tone. "My mom's dying, Logan, and this is what she wants for me. I can't just say no. It's basically her *dying* wish." Dramatizing the word didn't feel enough for me to emphasize that this was what my life felt like right now—like some soap opera.

"Okay, okay, I'm sorry." Logan draped his left arm around my shoulders and hugged me sideways.

We fell into silence as we watched the show.

Unexpectedly, he muttered, "For the record, I think you're handling it really well. I know none of this can possibly be easy, Kels. With your mom and this England thing, how are you not a mess right now?"

I shrugged half-heartedly, eyes dropping to the half-empty bag on my lap. I tried to swallow the lump in my suddenly dry throat, but I couldn't. "Guess it hasn't really sunk in properly," I mumbled, once again, acknowledging the consistent pain that had made a home in the pit of my stomach, my chest, and my head. Every time the realization of my mom's situation dawned on me, it was like someone was ripping everything inside of me apart. I didn't even want to think about what it would be like when she was gone.

Suddenly, my dark thoughts were interrupted by the sound of the doorbell.

Logan groaned in annoyance and got up to answer the door. I tried to refocus my attention on the show playing in front of me until Logan's voice cried out, "Kelsey, it's for you."

Frowning, I placed the bag of chips on the table next to the couch and licked off the salt and vinegar powder on my fingers. Walking towards the foyer, I stopped dead in my tracks when I noticed who was on the other side of the door. "What're you doing here?"

"Your mum gave me the address," Cooper said in that deep accent of his. It would take some time to get used to; that was for damn sure. Once again, he had his sunglasses on, his lazy attempt at a disguise or just to shield his eyes from the sun; I wasn't sure. "She needs you to go home."

"Why?" I demanded, an instant flare of panic rushing through me as my heart began picking up its pace. "Is she okay?"

Logan worriedly glanced between Cooper and me.

"She's fine." Then the British rock star took a deep breath. "I was already in the area so she told me to come get you. She wants to get a head start in packing up your things."

My breath hitched when I heard his words. I ground my teeth together and felt the immediate tightening of the nervous knots in my stomach. I wondered if my expression looked as grim as Cooper's blank look, and I also wondered how he could seem so unaffected. I had seen this guy's interviews with his band—he was one of the most exuberant members. I didn't see any of those traits here at all. How could he not feel *something* knowing that me packing up my things meant I'd have to give up my life here? Did he have no sympathy?

I also tried not to focus on the fact that my mom was already making me pack my things up. We'd gotten boxes a few days before Cooper and his family arrived but they'd been piled flat in my room and every time I looked at them I wanted to throw them out the window. Now I'd actually have to start filling them. My life would be packed up, memories trapped in walls of cardboard ready to be picked up and taken to a place where I was expected to make new ones.

Taking a deep breath, I nodded at Cooper, feeling like I had just agreed to seal away my life. In a way, I think I had.

Chapter 2

I peered down at the silver diamonds on my wrist. They were glimmering against the sunlight, which was peeking through the blinds. It was a simple bracelet, a gift given to me from Amelia and her family which I was hesitant on accepting. It was unnecessary, felt almost like a bribe from them to get me to accept them as my new family. But some diamonds weren't going to do that. Not when the simplicity of the bracelet and the look of it was something completely my style, which told me they'd asked my mother's opinion on it. Their first gift to me reminded me of my mother. Utterly beautiful like her.

I wore the piece of jewelry as a sign of good faith, even if I really didn't have any. I wore it because my mom wanted me to. Still, that didn't mean I didn't feel my skin burn where it touched me, as if my body was just as unhappy about this situation as I was.

Well, I guess it didn't really matter what I or my body wanted anymore. I sighed as I looked at the bracelet. It felt heavy on my wrist, carrying the weight of the true meaning with them.

It's what she wants.

A sigh escaped my lips as I grabbed my phone and went on Twitter. I was scrolling through my timeline until something caught my eyes, making them grow wide in astonishment. I had gone from two hundred something followers to over seven thousand! *How in the world did that happen?* And when I clicked on my notifications, I saw they flooded in after Alessandra had posted a picture that I had been forced to take with her and Cooper, the three of us sitting on the couch with smiles faked genuinely—except maybe Alessandra's. If I didn't know any better, we looked like best friends, which was ironically hilarious. All the tweets in my notifications were filled with questions from people whom I didn't even know.

"They're from the fans." A deep voice startled me.

I looked up and saw Cooper sitting down on the loveseat across from me. He was clad in a plain dark gray shirt and a pair of jeans that, once again, put his intricate tattoos on display.

"Guess they found your Twitter."

"Guess so," I mumbled, locking my phone and putting it on the couch next to me. Alessandra hadn't even tagged me. "So what? Do your fans just end up finding and following everyone associated with you?" I scoffed slightly. "Kind of obsessive, isn't it?" Cooper frowned. "They're dedicated, not obsessive," he countered, clearly not liking my word choice. With a scoff of his own, he added, "They just like to know the kind of people I'm involved with. The kind of people I'm gonna *live* with." The pointed raise of his eyebrow irked me.

I rolled my blue eyes, leaning back on the couch and crossing my right leg over my left knee. "If you don't want me to live in your precious apartment, why'd you agree to this, anyway?" I asked him with narrowed eyes, finally uttering the question that I had been wondering about the most."

"It's not like I had a choice," he replied in a gruff tone, crossing his arms over his broad chest. "My mum basically forced me into this—saying how it'd make her best friend happy. I couldn't say no, knowing what was happening to your mum."

My face relaxed into a small yet grateful smile, but it quickly disappeared on account of his next few words.

"Plus, it helps that you aren't terrible to look at."

My expression turned into a glare. Exhaling sharply, I stood up and said, "Pig."

Cooper looked undeterred. "Not a very nice thing to say to your new roommate." He smirked and stood up as well, easily towering over me.

I flinched at that word, hating the way it rolled off his tongue so smoothly and tauntingly and the fact that it affected me that much. Scowling up at him, my icy blue eyes met his bright green ones. "Seven billion people in the world and I'm stuck having to live with you," I blustered, feeling very antagonistic towards him out of nowhere. A sudden dislike for this guy sparked within me, and I instantly knew that this wouldn't get easier any time soon.

Cooper's jaw briefly tensed before he replied, "No need to be a bitch, *roomie*."

I felt that spark of dislike flare into something bigger. He was patronizing me, and it was getting under my skin. "Don't call me that. It makes me want to knock you on your ass," I retorted, hands clenching into fists at my side. It may have been an overreaction on my part but he was genuinely pissing me off. "I think a black eye would go nicely with your rock star image."

Cooper rolled his eyes.

I walked past him and distinctly heard him mutter something under his breath.

"Bitch."

***

Cooper

"I don't know what to do, Julian," I whined on the phone. "This whole thing was so forced, and now we can't do anything about it."

Julian, my best-friend-turned-band mate, simply and unhelpfully laughed on the other end of the phone. "I've never heard someone complain about a roommate so much before in my life."

"Julian!" I yelled in exasperation and ran my fingers through my short hair, messing it up, but I didn't care. My eyes flickered to the door leading back into the house, harmless where it stood. "This is serious!"

"I know, I know. Sorry." Julian's laughter died down a bit. "But you've gotta cut her some slack, Coop. The girl's mum isn't well, so she's gonna be a bit on edge."

Another groan passed through me once again. "I can't even imagine what she's goin' to be like after," I said as I paced in the Ross's backyard, eyes trailing after a wilting bush of roses. I gulped at the sight of the dying flowers as a connection that I didn't want to acknowledge was made in my mind.

"Well, you know, while we're on a break you're gonna have to spend time with her. I've no doubt your mum expects you to look after her. She's part of the family now."

Family.

It wasn't a term I took lightly. My family meant everything to me, I always looked forward to seeing them when I got back to London or flying them out to whichever city we were in and I was missing them terribly. Mine never stopped supporting me in my endeavors, and I knew Mum reaching out to Klara and offering to take Kelsey in was no small feat. I felt terribly for Klara and I admired Mum for agreeing to Klara's wishes without a thought. But knowing I was to live with Kelsey in my own apartment left me uneasy, because that was to happen once we left Florida…after Klara passed away. There was no telling the state of mind Kelsey would be in, and I wasn't sure I was capable of helping her through it.

I shook my head, not only unsure if I could do that but if I would have the time. Although I risked sounding pigheaded, I was in the biggest band in the world, with many tours and albums under my belt and more coming my way.

Not to mention I now had to live with a girl I'd only met a few days ago. I hadn't lived with anyone since I was seventeen and I moved out because the band was finally taking off, with us always on the road and living out of suitcases for the first few years of our career. Hell, I hadn't even been in a proper relationship to live with another woman. And, sure, Kelsey and I living together was temporary until the house was fixed, but it was still something to be dealt with.

Besides, once people get wind of our living situation, I had no doubt that the media would misconstrue everything and the rumors of Kelsey and I would begin circulating. No doubt people would think we were together, that we were living together because that's the place our nonexistent relationship was. And dealing with that would be a headache on its own, I'm sure

"This isn't fair." I complained to my mate as I stopped pacing, looking up at the clear blue Miami sky. "I don't want to live with her." There was nothing I could do about it now, I know, but complaining to Julian was how I vented my current frustrations.

Of course, he chuckled. "How do you think she feels?" he questioned, and I could picture him raising his eyebrows. "From what you've told me, she's not too excited to be uprooting her life to move to England. Look, lad, you're not the only victim here. Neither of you want this; you both just got thrown into it, so now you have to come to terms with the fact that this is your new normal."

I briefly pursed my lips. "Doesn't give her the right to be such a bitch to me," I mumbled, thinking about our encounter after signing the papers a few days ago.

Once again, my best friend giggled. "Give her time to adjust, mate. She—"

"Mom!" I heard Kelsey's voice shout from somewhere inside, making me freeze at the sheer volume of her cry before I managed to swivel and face the house. "Wake up! M-mom, please. Mom! Oh, God, Amelia, help! Cooper!"

I knew something was terribly wrong when I heard Kelsey crying out my name. Without saying anything to Julian, I hung up the phone and ran across the yard and inside the house, following the sound of Kelsey's cries. I sprinted down the short hallway, my sneakers thudding against the hardwood floor as I made my way towards the downstairs room.

Reaching the room, I stopped short in front of the door where Kelsey's cries were the loudest. I looked inside, and my eyes widened as I expelled a deep breath.

Kelsey was sobbing on the bed, holding on to Klara's shoulders as she shook her mum's lifeless body. Then she lowered her head to rest her forehead against Klara's chest. "Mom, no. Y-you have to w-wake up, please." Kelsey's voice broke as she feebly shook Klara, fruitlessly trying to bring her mother back while her broken, loud sobs rang throughout the house. The sight of her grasping on to her mother and the sound of her heart-wrenching cries had my stomach sinking with dread.

Before I knew it, I ran to Kelsey's side and stood behind her. My eyes landed on her mum's closed ones, her blue eyes no longer in view.

Kelsey was shaking, face still pressed to her mother's unmoving chest as her wails escaped her.

Shortly, my own mother arrived in the room.

I glanced at my mother with a helpless look on my face.

Mum let out a gasp. "Oh no." Slowly, she walked to the other side of the bed, her hand shakily reaching out to grasp Klara's. "Oh, God. No…"

I watched as I felt my heart beat at a scarily steady pace, willing myself to remain calm when Mum's eyes began to water.

Kelsey lifted her head and shook it in desperation. "N-no, she's okay. She's alive. She—she has to be." She whimpered, trying so hard to convince herself and everyone else.

My heart broke. No longer did I care about her being rude and cold towards me for the past few days because right now, she was crying over her mother's dead body, and if I didn't try my hardest to comfort her at this moment, I wouldn't ever be able to look at myself in the mirror.

"Cooper, t-take Kelsey out of the room, p-please." Tears were pouring out of Mum's red-rimmed eyes.

My heart sank deeper if that was even possible. I was in front of two women who were utterly devastated, and it broke my heart—especially when I saw my mother's pained expression and because I knew there was virtually nothing I could do to make this horrible situation better.

I managed to nod at her words, biting my bottom lip as I held onto Kelsey's shoulders and gently forced her to stand up.

"No!" she yelled and thrashed about, trying to escape and climb back on the bed. "Stop! I can't go! Mom!" She wouldn't stop trying to wrench herself away from my arms, but my grip around her figure was tight.

"Kelsey," I whispered in her ear as she continued to struggle in my arms, wanting to be closer to her mother. She shouldn't be seeing her mother like this; nobody should see their dead mother lying on a bed.

"No, please." Tears ran down her flushed cheeks as another sob escaped her. "I can't leave her. No, I can't."

"Kelsey," I said, raising my voice ever so slightly to get her attention as her back pressed against my front, my arms still holding her. "Stop. Come 'ere, love." I begged, my tone growing soft in an attempt to soothe her in a situation that I didn't think was possible for her to do so.

However, Kelsey broke down, her sobs much louder. She tightly shut her eyes as her hands found my arm that was wrapped around her waist.

Mum just stared at Klara's lifeless body.

I held Kelsey up before turning her around to pull her into a proper hug. Her cheek rested on my chest, and I instantly felt her tears soaking through my shirt. My arms tightened around her as I rested my chin on the top of her head, and then I shut my eyes while she freely wailed for the loss of the most important person in her life.

I didn't know how long we stood like that. I was rubbing her back in soothing circles when I heard her whimper, "Mom," into my chest, followed by a sob.

"Shh, it's okay," I whispered in response as I slowly moved us out of the room.

Kelsey continued to cry as I took us into the hallway and up the stairs, eventually reaching her room. We sat on the edge of the bed, sitting so one of my legs was folded on the mattress so I could face her. Kelsey's face was still buried in my chest—sniffling, hiccupping, and crying—when she mumbled, "She's gone. My mom's gone. She's gone." She repeated the words like a broken mantra in numbing disbelief.

I swallowed the thick lump that had formed in my throat, my arms still around her as I clenched my jaw. Hearing her cry was a sound that I quickly realized was one that I never wanted to hear again because the utter heartbreak and pain that she was displaying was something that I would never wish even upon my worst enemy. I knew how I would feel if, God forbid, my mother passed away—I couldn't even begin to imagine the pain this girl was going through right now. It wasn't fair.

A few minutes later, Kelsey's cries grew softer and quieter until I was sure she wasn't crying anymore.

I slightly pulled away and looked down only to see that the poor girl had fallen asleep from exhaustion. Picking her up, I gently laid her down on the bed and let her sleep peacefully. I brought the turquoise-colored blanket up to her chest. Standing up straight, I gazed down at the blonde girl with tear-stained, flushed cheeks and swollen eyes. Biting my bottom lip, I walked out of Kelsey's room and shut the door before heading down the stairs of the now eerily quiet house.

When I entered the living room, I heard the hushed sounds of Mum crying on the couch as Alessandra and Russell comforted her. Walking over to them, I sat on the coffee table in front of them and grabbed Mum's hands, squeezing them reassuringly. "It'll be okay, Mum. Don't worry," I said, not knowing what else to say at this moment.

Mum sighed, returning the squeeze before taking her right hand to rub her face, then meeting my gaze. "How's Kelsey?"

I gulped. "She cried a lot, but then she fell asleep."

"This is just awful," Alessandra said with a disbelieving shake of her head. Her eyes flickered to all of us, showing the shock and grief that she held in them. "We didn't expect Klara to…give out so soon. I don't think Kelsey was expecting it to happen this quick either, the poor thing."

"I know," Mum said, leaning into Russell's side as he kept his arm draped across her shoulders. She took in a breath before continuing. "I'm going to take care of the funeral arrangements. After everything's said and done, Cooper, we're going to take Kelsey to London, okay?"

I nodded, inhaling through my nose. "Yeah, I know."

"And please, be easy with her when you get home." Mum pleaded. "She's going to be a mess. This is too much for her. Be kind to her."

"I know, Mum." I assured her, feeling my stomach lurch at this entire situation. I squeezed Mum's hand and lowered my head, remembering the promise that Kelsey and I had made to her mother. "I know…"

Chapter 3

Kelsey

Losing one's parents was a painfully numbing ordeal.

Being only nineteen and having lost both of my parents was something I never thought would happen to me. My dad passed away when I was younger in a car accident, and the fact that my mother was now gone was a newfound loss I hadn't wanted to experience for a long time.

After Dad's death, the two of us had gotten so incredibly close since we were all each other had. Now, she was gone, and I had never felt more alone in my life.

Cancer had always been something I, much like everyone else, wished never existed, and losing my mother to it only served to intensify my hatred for it.

Mom was such a strong person. When my father died, instead of locking herself in the room and wallowing in depression, she kept herself busy. She worked, cleaned, cooked, and looked after me by being more present in my life than she already had been. She kept herself together for my sake, and I became her number one priority. She was my hero with how she always remained optimistic and hardworking—and now she was gone.

The pain was unbearable. It was something that I had never experienced before, and it was eating me alive. My nose was perpetually red from how often I was blowing it, and my red-rimmed eyes were swollen. They were continually burning, too, with fresh tears gathering every time I thought I had finally cried myself out.

My mind would often flash to the moment when I found her lifeless body on the bed. I was unable to wake her up from her nap, and the mere memory of it had me wrapping my arms around myself and pressing my lips together in a feeble attempt to smother the sobs that were threatening to escape.

"You okay?"

Sucking in a breath, I turned around to have my blue eyes meet concerned green ones. Part of me was surprised that Cooper was worried about me, but then I realized it was common courtesy to be worried about someone after experiencing such a loss. Still, the genuine concern swimming in his eyes was almost endearing.

I shook my head to his question, feeling the tears pooling in my eyes once again as I looked up at him. Offering a pathetically sad smile, I turned back around to face the backyard. As I sat on the steps of the back porch, I noticed that the weather was beautiful today, but the flowers in the bushes were dead, and I tried not to think about its correlation to my life. "No," I answered. "But I guess I'll get there, one way or another."

Cooper released a sigh before I felt him sit down next to me. "I know everyone says this, but your mum is in a better place," he said, his tone quiet and understanding.

Glancing at him, I watched him keep his gaze out to the yard, slightly squinting against the sunlight that was peeking through the clouds. His feet rested on a step below mine while his arms rested on his thighs as he spoke, "When she was here, she was in pain, and I know you don't want to hear that, but it's true. She was— she was in pain, and she was hurting, Kelsey—hurting like none of us would be able to understand." I rolled my lower lip into my mouth, bowing my head as I shut my eyes. "She's…she's gone, but she isn't in pain anymore."

My brain soaked in Cooper's words of comfort, knowing that he was right. When Mom was sick, I knew she was experiencing a type of pain that I couldn't possibly imagine or understand.

Cooper is right; she may be gone, but she isn't hurting anymore. She's at peace now.

But it didn't make this any easier.

"She died a fighter."

A quiet sob escaped my lips as my hands reached up to wipe away the stupid tears that began to fall once again. I sniffled, briefly cupping my cheeks and feeling the cool material of my rings before looking at Cooper. He was offering me a small smile. Returning it appreciatively, I leaned forward and placed a soft kiss on his cheek.

"Thank you," I muttered once I pulled away.

I noticed his surprised expression as his lips parted and his green eyes widened when they met my blue ones. The surprise was quickly washed away when Cooper pressed his lips together, though they were tugged upwards, and gave me a small nod.

With nothing else to say, I took in a deep breath and stood up, offering Cooper one last smile before walking back into the house. I really needed to hear that, and thanks to Cooper, I felt slightly better than I thought I would.

***

"Are you ready?" Cooper asked, bringing the last of my suitcases down the stairs to join the rest who were already gathered by the doorway.

"Yeah," I answered, running my fingers through my hair as I glanced around. I had three suitcases full of my things, plus a carry-on and a duffel bag. The rest of my belongings had already been transported to Cooper's London address through FedEx over the past few days, which were helpfully received by Cooper's family since they'd flown back before us, and all that was really left in the house that I had grown up in was the furniture.

Before Mom's passing, we had sold the house and had been given time to pack up everything that we needed, and Mom had made it abundantly clear that she wanted her belongings to be donated to the Salvation Army. So with the help of Logan's and Cooper's families, we got it all done, albeit being one of the toughest things to do. Packing each picture of Mom and me came with a set of fresh tears to the point that I thought my eyes were perpetually puffy.

"When's the flight?"

Cooper checked his Rolex on his left wrist. "In two hours," he answered, "but we should get goin' now to avoid traffic."

I nodded, biting my lower lip.

Today was the big day. I was leaving Florida and moving to London.

Mom's funeral was four days ago, and as expected, it was full of uncontrollable tears. Saying goodbye to her, in an official capacity like the funeral, was heartbreakingly difficult; I wasn't even able to keep a brave face at the wake after the funeral when everyone was giving their condolences.

As if things weren't stressful enough, Logan and Cooper got to officially meet before the funeral. We were packing stuff at that time—since the only time that they had ever interacted before was when Cooper had shown up to Logan's house to pick me up to sign the papers—and the lack of friendliness between the two had become painstakingly obvious. And it became even clearer when Logan stopped by last night to say goodbye.

"I'll miss you, Kels," Logan muttered as his arms wrapped around my waist, pulling me in for a hug.

I hugged him back, my arms wrapped around his neck and my head rested on his shoulders. The scent of laundry detergent and his favorite Tom Ford cologne enveloped me, and I knew I was going to miss it once I left. "I'll miss you too," I replied. "You know I'll text and call whenever I can."

When the two of us pulled away, the sad expression on his face mirrored the tears that had pooled in my eyes. God, there hadn't been a day that had passed when I didn't cry.

Over Logan's shoulders, my eyes caught sight of the British man lingering by the kitchen entrance. "Kelsey, you need to finish packin'." Cooper hinted.

Clearly not appreciating our goodbyes being cut short, Logan's eyes flickered up to the ceiling in annoyance, not bothering to turn around when he retorted, "Hold on, man, we're just saying our goodbyes."

I furrowed my eyebrows at his tone, before my gaze flickered back to Cooper. I saw the way his eyes narrowed in a glare directed at my best friend, and the tension in the room was palpable. "I'll be up soon."

Cooper looked at me, expression relaxing as his scowl faded, then nodded before turning to leave the entryway and head up the stairs.

When I looked back at Logan, I gulped when I noticed him glaring at Cooper.

"I don't like him," Logan said, still looking towards the stairs.

I raised an eyebrow, mildly surprised at his easy admission. For some reason, I thought he would at least try to hide his dislike of Cooper. "Why?"

Logan shrugged indifferently, looking back at me once more. "Just because."

A short incredulous breath escaped me. "That's not a valid reason, Logan." I rolled my eyes, looking up at him pointedly. "And besides, I'm not asking you to like him. Just..." I shrugged before finishing. "Respect him."

A look of disbelief washed over his face. "Respect him?" He scoffed. "What happened to him being an asshole?"

I puckered my lips and shrugged once again as I shot him a somewhat defeated look. "That was before I realized he's a decent human being." Cooper had been nothing but a sweet gentleman since Mom's passing, all remnants of the rude guy from our first meeting disappearing without a trace. "It's not like you'll have to deal with him every day. Just be nice. He's a good guy."

Logan rolled his dark eyes, apparently not liking my idea. "Kelsey, do you hear yourself? You were dissing the guy just a few days ago—what happened to that?"

A sigh escaped me as I ran my hands down my back and settled them in the back pockets of my sweatpants. "He's—I have to live with him, Logan. He's my new roommate." I was unable to stop the slight, almost disbelieving chuckle that escaped me at that. "I'm going to have to get used to having him around at one point or another. He's been really nice to me. I—just give him a chance."

He merely stared at me for a few moments, his brown eyes looking at me calculatingly me in mild annoyance.

I offered a pleading smile.

Logan sighed. "Whatever."

I let out a light laugh, poking him in the stomach to which he squirmed at. "Come on, I don't want to leave Florida with you being upset. Smile!" I offered an exaggerated grin, completely cheesing. "For me?"

Logan was unable to stop the chuckle from escaping him at the sight of my wide grin.

I pointed to my dimples with my fingers before he shook his head in amusement.

"I'll see you soon, Kels." He promised, pulling me in for another hug.

Now it was time for me to say goodbye to Miami. Less than a handful of friends and memories were all that I was leaving behind, since I had no family left. I didn't even know if it was bittersweet or what.

Personally, I think a new start would do me some good, despite my initial protests at this arrangement. I could start a new life and meet new people because I knew my mom would want that for me. That was the point to all of this, right? Mom set this up so I could live a life that she knew I would enjoy, and although her death was still incredibly fresh, I was making it a point not to lock myself in my room and cry. For Mom.

"Come on, Kelsey." Cooper's voice pulled me out of my thoughts. "We should get goin'."

I pulled my lower lip into my mouth, watching him load my suitcases into the SUV, which was parked in the driveway. I nodded, then looked at the house that I grew up in—the house where every single important memory of mine had occurred, from my first steps in the living room to my first kiss on the front porch; where I found my mother's body, lifeless and dead; the house that was now just going to be another memory. Everything was still there except for the small decorations that made this house mine and my mother's home. They were either packed up to be taken to London or had been given away.

I felt my heart tug harshly as I gave a slight nod. "Let's go."

Chapter 4

The crisp air that surrounded me when I stepped out of Heathrow Airport forced me to wrap my arms around myself even though I was already wearing a jacket. I wasn't used to this cold weather; it was the complete opposite of the warm Florida weather.

The eight-and-a-half–hour flight seemed longer than it was, though I slept through most of it because it beat staying up and thinking about the state of my life at the moment. I briefly wondered how intense the jet lag was going to be, if at all.

Cooper and I weaved our way through the airport, keeping our heads down so Cooper wouldn't get recognized. Knowing how the paparazzi followed him like crazy, I was surprised and relieved that we didn't get spotted.

Out front was another black SUV waiting for us, and after all of our bags were loaded in the trunk of the vehicle, we got in, and the driver drove us to wherever Cooper's home was.

My forehead rested against the cold glass of the tinted window as we drove down the busy London streets while Cooper was quietly sitting next to me. The car was in pure silence except for the sounds coming from the other cars outside.

It was eight in the evening, and the roads were lit up by street lamps and bright signs of some stores. We drove past some landmarks that I knew of, like the London Eye and the Tower Bridge, and part of me was kind of excited about being able to actually visit these places someday. *I live here now. I can go see them whenever I wanted. Wow.*

I swallowed the lump that came with a new thought: *Mom would've loved it here.*

After about twenty-five minutes of driving, the car pulled into a gated parking lot. I peered out the window as we pulled up in front of a tall apartment building.

"Come on," Cooper muttered as if he didn't want to disturb the silence.

I followed his lead, unbuckling my seatbelt and stepping out of the car and into the cold air.

The driver, whose name was Dirk, walked to the back to pull out our suitcases along with another man who walked out of the building and towards us. He exchanged a few words with Cooper while I tilted my head back to look up at the building, probably being more than twenty stories at least, and let out a breath.

"Let's go inside," Cooper said.

My eyes landed on him, and finally, he wasn't wearing sunglasses. He buried the bottom of his face into the collar of his black coat when I nodded and followed him inside, carrying our respective duffel bags.

The lobby itself was high-class looking. It had black and white checkered marble floors, a sitting area with a couple of two-seater couches, and a middle-aged man sitting behind a desk with computers that, most likely, were for security reasons.

As Cooper and I walked in, the man behind the desk greeted us in a charming British accent—everyone's gonna have one of those here, aren't they?—and Cooper returned the greeting back kindly and introduced me to the security guard, Crosby.

I smiled at Crosby before Cooper and I walked towards the elevators to the right.

Neither of us acknowledged the deafening silence that was surrounding us, nor did we do anything to break it. We stepped into the elevator, and the steel doors slid shut.

Thank God this elevator doesn't play any annoying music or else I would've gone crazy.

Glancing at Cooper from the corner of my eye, I saw him busying himself with his phone, so I took the chance to glance down at my Converse-clad feet. It was awkward and somewhat tense because, of course, we were in a confined space. The mere thought of being stuck with him in the elevator only made me feel even more uncomfortable. We may be civil and respectful with each other, but we weren't exactly friends yet.

We hadn't talked much during the flight, which didn't really matter since I was asleep through most of it. But now that we were headed up to Cooper's apartment, where I was moving in, I hoped, for the sake of our sanity, that we could have some normal conversations.

The elevator finally stopped on the nineteenth floor. The steel doors slid open to a wide hallway with dark blue carpets, and gold-colored walls with the occasional decorative paintings hung up on the wall.

I followed Cooper's lead until we stopped in front of a door marked "1905."

He reached in the pocket of his coat, fumbling for a bit, before pulling out a set of keys. He jammed one into the keyhole and opened the door.

Just when the lock clicked, loud shouts took us by surprise, all of which were yelling, "Welcome home!"

I jumped a bit, startled at the sudden noise that killed the silence.

Cooper and I entered the spacious apartment, which was lit up by the in-ceiling lights that reflected off the large windows in the living room.

My eyes trailed over four guys and two girls who were grinning widely. I immediately recognized the four guys as Cooper's band members from Triage and the two girls who were occasionally seen around with them online.

The eldest member of the band, twenty-three-year-old Julian Finley, stepped forward and shouted, "Welcome back, Coop." Then he suddenly pulled the green-eyed boy in for a hug.

I couldn't help but smile a small smile since Cooper was caught off guard by the sudden gesture.

My previous shock was wearing off when he hugged back the blue-eyed guy with the spiky brown hair. "Good to see you too, Julian." Cooper slapped the other guy's back as they hugged.

The rest of the group took turns to greet Cooper. A clamor of greetings filling the air until their attention turned towards me.

I fidgeted uncomfortably in my spot at the feeling of all their gazes, and it was especially nerve-wracking to know that the eyes that were staring at me belonged to Spencer O'Leary, Rafael Ricardos, Miles Adler, and Julian—Cooper's equally famous and good-looking band mates.

Cooper, realizing that everyone was staring at me and was, most likely, waiting to be introduced, cleared his throat. "Uh, guys, this is Kelsey." He was awkwardly rubbing the back of his neck, and his uneasy demeanor was something that I hadn't expected—not when I had seen the videos of him during his band's concerts. He was like a totally different person. "My, uh…"

I couldn't blame him for trailing off like that. But, once again, I was kind of surprised. When we first met, he had thrown around the term *roomie* in my face, and while that wasn't too big of a deal, it was still something neither of us was fond of. But now, things had changed. The reality was setting in, and we had no idea how to act.

"Roommate." One of the girls finished it for him with an easy smile on her delicately shaped face that reached her hazel eyes, not finding the term as unusual as Cooper and I did. Maybe we were just being overdramatic. Through the media, I knew she was Julian's longtime girlfriend. "It's so nice to meet you, Kelsey. I'm Dawn."

The other girl, taller with darker skin and curly hair tied into a bun, stepped forward and offered a smile as well. "And I'm Noelle. Lovely to meet you."

I returned their smiles, trying my best to hide my shyness as I stood in front of these two gorgeous women—I probably looked awful because of my red-rimmed eyes and messy hair—and the entirety of one of the biggest bands in the world.

The other four members of Triage were, as expected, much more handsome in person. They all stood tall with facial features and bodies that made me think that god took his time in making them. No wonder most of their fan base consisted of girls lusting after them.

"Nice to meet you, guys," I said, hoping my voice didn't give away the nerves that were twisting up my insides. Or the fact that a wave of exhaustion just washed over me, making me want to do nothing more than climb into bed and sleep until tomorrow morning. I guess my nap on the plane wasn't enough.

Cooper glanced at me, and our eyes met.

I was hoping that he would notice the tiredness in my eyes.

After a moment, he cleared his throat and nodded towards a set of stairs that led up to the second floor. "Come on, Kelsey, I'll show you to your room."

***

Cooper

My sneakers padded against the stairs as I headed back down to the living room. All of my friends were, as usual, making themselves at home as they lounged on the couches. "Hey." I sighed as I sat down next to Dawn, leaning my left elbow on the armrest.

Spencer, who had taken control of the remote, flipped through the channels, then glanced at me. "Where's Kelsey?"

"Asleep," I answered as I ran my fingers through my short hair, messing it up a bit, and leaned back on the black leather couch. "Jet lag caught up with her, and she needed rest."

Miles nodded, sitting in between Noelle and Rafael as Spencer finally landed on a football match. "That's good," Miles mumbled. "She should rest after everything she's been through."

Everyone else nodded and murmured their agreement.

I pressed my lips together and agreed with the rest.

It was silent for a brief moment before Noelle spoke up. "You've been nice to her, right?" she asked, prompting me to stare at her. She shrugged at my taken aback expression. "Well, you were complaining nonstop every time we spoke with you on the phone."

I groaned, glancing at everyone else, though they were no help since they nodded their agreement. Huffing, I crossed my arms over my chest and glared at Noelle.

"I'm bein' honest, Coop. The poor girl's mum passed away, and now she's living with you without a choice. I can't even imagine how overwhelmed she is—not to mention, she's definitely going to be introduced to your world if she lives with you, and that's something that's going to take time for her to get used to. You need to help her with this transition."

"Noelle's right." Rafael acknowledged, my eyes now flickering over to him as my friends decided to dump unwanted advice the day I got back. "You know your mum is counting on you for this. You've gotta make things as easy as possible for Kelsey. This lifestyle isn't somethin' someone easily adjusts to. You know that."

I let out a sigh, leaning my head back on the couch because even though they were right, they were only spewing out things that I already knew. My life was dramatically different than Kelsey's, much more fast-paced and continuously watched by millions of people around the world. So far, Kelsey hadn't had any firsthand experience with the paparazzi, fans, or the media, and I had no doubt that would change too soon just by her association with me. It would be more intense than any of my friends would have to face because she was a girl who came out of nowhere and was now living with me. We could tell the world she was a family friend all we wanted, even if it was the truth, but they would always be looking for something more.

Dawn, noticing the tension that I was experiencing, just rubbed my shoulder comfortingly, making me let out a heavy sigh. "All you have to do is be patient."

Chapter 5

Kelsey

I woke up the next morning blinking the sleepiness away, utterly confused at my surroundings. The king-sized bed that I was slumbering on wasn't my bed, and the light gray walls weren't the same as the baby blue ones in my bedroom. I sat up, the blanket pooling at my hips, and looked around the dark room with eyes heavy with sleep.

Suddenly, I remembered exactly where I was: in London, in Cooper's apartment, in the guest room.

It was confusing waking up here, in a completely different place, and the reminder of *why* I was here in the first place wasn't gentle. I was here because Mom died. I was here because she wanted me to be here.

Reluctantly, not quite ready to face the day ahead of me, I slowly got out of bed and walked out of the room in my tee and pajama pants, my bare feet tingling at the cold floor as I headed down the stairs.

As I descended, my eyes wandered to the living room where, through the dark, I saw Cooper's sleeping figure on the sofa bed. The soft snores escaping him confirmed his presence.

I bit the inside of my cheek when I reached the floor, noticing the guitar that was propped up against the couch Cooper's too-tall figure was sprawled across. It didn't even look that comfortable. *Had he been playing at night and fallen asleep?* I heard his band's tour schedule was rigorous, so it was surprising that he'd give up any night of sleeping on his own bed to be on the couch.

The fact that I was even considering Cooper's sleeping habits had me shaking my head quickly.

Sighing quietly, I continued walking and entered the kitchen, switching on the light above the stove because the main ones would probably wake Cooper. Then my eyes flickered to the clock on the stove. I suppressed a frustrated groan when the time read "6:08." No wonder it was still dark out—it may be morning, but the sun hadn't even risen yet.

Cursing the jet lag, I began looking through several stainless steel cabinets that matched the fridge and appliances, looking for something to prepare breakfast for myself while my stomach quietly growled in hunger. Eventually, I found a bowl and spoon and a box of Coco Pops cereal. Sitting down on the small circular glass table in the corner near the entryway that spilled into the living room, I quietly ate my cereal, making sure my spoon didn't clink against the ceramic bowl.

Just a few minutes later, I glanced up and saw Cooper walking into the kitchen, harshly swallowing my mouthful of cereal because the guy was wearing nothing but a pair of red and black flannel pajama pants while his arm reached up to rub the back of his neck. No matter how difficult it seemed, I tried my hardest not to stare too obviously.

Honestly, it wasn't a surprise that the twenty-year-old musician's body was as toned and as lean as it was. He also had tattoos made up of skulls and roses and even what looked like a pirate ship snaking along his arms. If that wasn't enough, his pants hung dangerously low on his hips, and I made it a point to keep my eye level above his chest.

Knowing I was there, Cooper glanced at me and dropped his arm, giving me a single nod. "Good morning." His accented voice was thick with sleep.

I swallowed another mouthful of cereal. "Morning," I replied, watching him walk across the kitchen.

He turned the water faucet on and grabbed the tea kettle, placing it under the water.

Eyes on his muscled back, I absently twirled my spoon around in my bowl of milk and cereal bits. "Why'd you sleep on the couch?"

Cooper turned the faucet off and faced me, shrugging as he held the kettle in one hand. "Didn't wanna play in my room. It's right next to yours, you would've woke up."

That bit of information was surprising yet also sweet, honestly, but it still made me feel bad. "You didn't have to do that." I stood up and walked towards the sink. "It's your house—you can do what you want where you want." Really, I felt weird feeling the need to tell him that, because I didn't think it'd be necessary. *Why was he living like a guest in his own home?* Someone as dedicated to music as Cooper was, I wasn't surprised to know that he spent odd hours of the night playing his instruments.

In fact, his love for music was all over the apartment. From what I briefly saw, he had a shelf in the living room that displayed all the awards that the band had won along with their discography framed on the walls.

If he wanted to play music in his own room, who was I to stand in the way of that?

Cooper merely puckered his lips in thought, then nodded before putting the tea kettle on the stove and switching it on. I was washing my dirty bowl and spoon when I heard him ask, "How'd you sleep?"

"All right, I guess." I shrugged as my eyes stayed on the task at hand. "Until jet lag decided to wake me up so early." I smiled faintly, glancing over my shoulder to see Cooper cracking a lazy smile as well. "Same for you?"

"Partially." Cooper nodded and leaned back against the granite counter in between the stove and the fridge, arms crossing over his bare chest.

I forced my gaze not to flicker to the way his biceps flexed.

"I've also got to get to the studio in a couple of hours, so I guess it works out."

I nodded as I put the wet bowl on the drying rack. I was about to grab a dish towel to dry my hands when the tea kettle began whistling.

Cooper poured hot water into a mug that already had a tea bag in it before moving around the kitchen to get some milk and two teaspoons of sugar.

Awkwardly, I remained by the sink, watching him take a sip of the hot drink before his green eyes flickered to meet my gaze.

"If you want, I can give you Noelle's and Dawn's numbers, and they can, like, come over." He shrugged, trying to appear nonchalant. "So you won't be alone in the flat."

Being alone would definitely stir up thoughts concerning my mother, assuming that I ever stopped thinking about her in the first place. Grateful for his thoughtfulness, I smiled and nodded. "Sure, sounds good."

***

Cooper had left for the studio over an hour ago.

I was sitting on the leather couch with my phone on my lap as my fingers absently twirled the rings on my finger, my lower lip stuck between my teeth. I hadn't called Noelle and Dawn yet because, honestly, I was nervous and conflicted about having them over. I didn't know the two girls, but making friends with them would be a good idea since they were dating two of the Triage members and I was, for the time being, living with another. As hard of a pill as it had been to swallow, my life now involved Cooper and his family, who kept texting and calling to check in on me, which was sweet. But I had no doubt I would be spending time with Cooper's band mates, so, with my mind made up, I typed a new text message for Dawn.

Hey, Dawn, it's Kelsey. I'm at the apartment by myself and was wondering if you and Noelle wanted to come over?

Once I hit send, I only had to wait a moment or so until my phone vibrated with a new message.

Absolutely! I'll call Noelle, and we'll be over in a bit! XX

I smiled at her text, surprisingly feeling a bit excited as I stood up from the couch. Since I had already taken a shower, I had already changed into a pair of sweats. But since I had to wait for the girls to arrive, I changed again to look more decent, settling on an oversized red sweater and a pair of black leggings.

It was cold out on this March day, and despite the heater inside the apartment, I still couldn't bring myself to get warm. I tried not to think that ever since Mom left, so did the warmth.

Twenty minutes later, the knocking on the front door pulled my attention away from the TV, where I had been watching a random show on Netflix. I knew that it was the girls since Cooper had told me before he left that for security purposes, only a few people were allowed up straight away and didn't have to be buzzed in—Dawn and Noelle were two of them.

"Hey." Noelle smiled when I opened the door.

"Hi, guys." I stepped aside to allow them to enter, then closed the door and followed them towards the couches, nervously rubbing my hands together. "Thanks for coming."

Dawn grinned as the girls shrugged off their coats, draping them on the arm of the couch. "It's not a problem." Her hazel eyes glimmered with delight. "We're glad you invited us over."

I sat down on the couch next to the wall while they settled on the other.

Noelle untied her hair from its bun to allow her curls to come undone. "How're you likin' London so far?"

A chuckle escaped me, either because of their adorable accents or because of my answer. "I haven't seen any of it yet. But looking out the window, the city does look really beautiful."

Dawn leaned against the couch on her right side to face me, and then nodded. "It is." She agreed. "You should definitely go to the London Eye or Buckingham Palace. They're tourist type spots but worth it."

I grinned. "I've always wanted to go there."

Our conversations flowed nicely as we munched on some chips—or, as I learned, they were called crisps here in England.

I got to know Dawn and Noelle a bit more. They told me their jobs—Dawn worked at a fashion magazine while Noelle worked as a dance instructor—and how Dawn was born and raised here in London while Noelle grew up in a town a few miles away from here that I definitely wouldn't be able to pinpoint at a map.

Noelle, who had moved on from chips to Oreos, spoke up, "Mm, you should meet Heidi sometime—you know, Rafael's girlfriend."

"She's in Manchester visiting her family, but she should be back in a few days," Dawn said as she removed her boots and sat with her legs folded beneath her. "The four of us should go out for lunch."

I smiled at the idea, nodding as all previous nervousness disappeared, now replaced with excitement at the prospect of meeting Heidi.

Noelle and Dawn had only been here for a few hours or so, but chatting with them came so easily and naturally, which wasn't a surprise since they were so sweet.

As we continued our conversation, my phone vibrated with a new text message, and I blinked in mild surprise upon seeing that it was Cooper who messaged me.

Everything good? Are Noelle & Dawn over?

For some reason, I felt a small fond smile tug at the edge of my lips as I looked at my screen. It was sweet how Cooper showed his concern even if it was just through a simple text message. Both of us knew he didn't have to, but it was nice that he did anyway.

"What's the smile for?" I glanced up and saw Noelle staring at me before looking back at Dawn, who was smirking knowingly. "You have a boyfriend we don't know about?"

I just laughed nervously.

Noelle lightly swatted her friend's arm before looking back at me, quirking a perfectly plucked eyebrow. "Is it Coop?" The way she asked suggested that she already knew the answer. Then the two girls exchanged knowing looks, making me roll my eyes.

"Maybe," I mumbled as I quickly sent a reply to Cooper.

Yeah, they're here. We're hanging out.

I locked my phone and dropped it next to me on the couch, then looked up and saw Dawn and Noelle staring at me with smirks dancing on their lips. Honestly, I had no idea why they were staring at me like that, so I just laughed. "Please stop, you're freaking me out!"

The two of them giggled in response, and before it died down, Dawn's smirk was replaced by a genuine and kind smile.

"He's a really great guy, Kelsey," she said, her voice taking a more serious tone as she slightly sat up. "Cooper may have that—" Dawn paused, eyes flickering to the ceiling as she thought for a moment before looking at me and continuing "—that rock star attitude, but he really cares about all of his friends and family."

Noelle nodded in agreement, looking at me with a smile. "And I have no doubt that includes you."

Chapter 6

"What're you cookin'?" Cooper asked, prompting me to turn around from where I stood. He entered the kitchen, clad in a Guns N' Roses shirt, with a leather jacket on top, and black jeans. He offered me a smile as our gaze locked. His jaw was sharp and smooth since he had shaved yesterday.

"Spaghetti," I answered, giving the pot of noodles one last twirl with my fork before turning the stove off. "Want some?"

Cooper grinned, nodding. "Yes, I'm absolutely starvin'."

I chuckled as I drained the water from the pot, and then put the spaghetti back in the pot.

Cooper was kind enough to take out two bowls.

I put some spaghetti in the bowls before joining him at the glass table where he had already placed the pasta sauce.

The two of us sat together, eating in silence as neither of us attempted to make conversation. It was awkward because Cooper and I really had nothing to talk about. Apparently, we were still trying to adjust to this situation, which was now our new normal.

I hadn't really gone out since we got to London almost a week ago, but I knew the frenzy going on in the media, thanks to

Twitter and every other social media. Triage fans were going crazy over the fact that the front man of the band suddenly had a new housemate, and I had to turn my Twitter notifications off because I kept receiving new tweets every few minutes. I found it crazy how everyone felt like they were owed an explanation, trying to find out what could possibly be going on. I had already seen a number of tweets by people speculating I was involved with Cooper, but I stayed silent. I didn't want to feed into it.

It was also why I was scared to be seen in public, and perhaps that was why I stayed inside this apartment where Cooper and I were still trying to adapt to everything. I mean, I was still unpacking my things and making sure that I didn't break down into tears every time I thought of my mom.

Every time the thought of her crossed my mind I had to hold back tears or lock myself in my room. I didn't want Cooper's sympathy, didn't want to make him feel as though he had to console me. Dealing with Mom's death was something I would have to go through for the rest of my life. Cooper and I were still too new to each other for him to feel the obligation to comfort me.

We didn't talk too much while we were in the apartment, just passing his and hellos and how was your days. We'd eat breakfast together but it was a silent affair, the clinking of utensils against plates only adding to the tension.

One morning he woke up earlier than me, and I was so relieved because I didn't have to deal with the weirdness of sitting through breakfast with him.

While he was gone, I kept myself busy by unpacking my things, trying to make his apartment feel, even for just a bit like mine. I placed my clothes in the drawers of the dresser and hung them in the closet. My bedside table now held a couple of photo frames of my mom and me, and every night before I sleep, I would look at the pictures and remind myself of how and why I was here. But that, of course, wasn't going to help me with my situation with Cooper.

We were two people with entirely different lifestyles who had been thrown into this unwanted arrangement. Conversations between us were stilted and awkward, so we still hadn't got to know each other well, but here we are—living together while telling his mom that everything was as normal as could be every time she called.

Even when we were together, we didn't know what to say to each other because it seemed like we would forget common social interaction methods; it would just get weird and awkward, and I was growing tired of it especially since I was beginning to get used to seeing him around the apartment. I wasn't going to lie; sometimes I expected to see my mom come around the hall like she had never left. But every time reality sank in I had to swallow the lump in my throat and remind myself Mom wasn't here. Cooper was.

Suddenly, our silence was broken when my phone began to ring. Without checking the caller ID, I answered, "Hello?" I felt Cooper's eyes on me. Granted, I responded so damn fast because the tense silence was beginning to make me twitch.

"Hey, Kels!" My best friend's deep voice rang, and I couldn't help but smile at the familiar tone.

Leaning back in my chair, I twirled some pasta around my fork. "Hey, dude, what's up?"

"Nothing." Logan's tone allowed me to easily picture him shrugging lazily. He proceeded to tell me that he was bored and wanted to talk to me, and then he asked me how the city was.

I laughed lightly, eyes on my plate of half-eaten pasta. "It's good," I answered with an absent nod. "Ridiculously cold though. How're you doing?"

He complained about how boring home was without me, which brought a smile to my lips. Then he asked, "How's your new roommate?"

I snuck a glance at Cooper, who was drinking his water, then looked away before I had a chance on keeping my gaze on the way his throat moved. "He's sitting right next to me."

Cooper's gaze snapped towards me, eyebrow shooting up in a questioning look while I just shrugged nonchalantly.

"Oh," Logan replied with distaste.

I let out a frustrated breath before saying his name in a warning tone. "Logan."

"Okay, okay, sorry."

Rolling my eyes, I muttered that it was fine before continuing our conversation.

He told me about how classes were keeping him on his toes while I told him about how my credits had fortunately transferred to a local university in London and that I had already begun my courses. They were all online courses, for now, and I figured maybe next year, I could become a full-time student and actually go to class.

Speaking of which, after fifteen minutes of chatting, Logan said, "Alright, I have to get ready for class. I'll talk to you later. Bye! Love you, friend."

I chuckled, then bid goodbye. "Love you too."

As I twirled some spaghetti around my fork, I noticed Cooper glance at me with a quirked brow. "Who was that?"

"Logan," I answered, lifting my fork as I quizzically looked at him. I had said Logan's name during our conversation. Surely Cooper knew about him. "You remember him, right?" I asked before biting into my food.

"How could I forget," Cooper muttered as he took a bite of his own food, tearing his gaze away from me.

I shot him a questioning look since I detected mild irritation in his tone, but Cooper had already refocused his attention on his food, putting an end to the conversation.

***

Cooper

Just take her out for dinner, honey. You're going to have to get to know her at one point or another. Stop skirting around one another!

I puckered my lips as I read Mum's text. I was standing in the middle of my bedroom, thinking of what to do.

Mum had been on my case for a few days because she knew Kelsey and I had yet to actually sit down and have a proper conversation. Since she was a two-and-a-half hour car ride back home in Birmingham, she couldn't precisely chastise me in person, and I was sure she would really do that.

Glancing up from my phone, my eyes landed on a picture on Kelsey's bedside almost immediately, making me swallow the nonexistent lump in my throat.

A smiling picture of Kelsey and Klara stared back at me, a young Klara holding a five-year-old Kelsey on her lap as they both smiled for the camera.

I expelled a deep breath, then made a quick phone call. Afterward, I tucked my phone into the pocket of my jeans and left Kelsey's room realizing she wasn't there, and walked down the stairs and into the living room where Kelsey was watching a television program.

She immediately sat up when she saw me descend the stairs.

"We're going out for dinner." I didn't leave her any room to argue, which only made me mentally curse at myself because I probably sounded like a dick.

Kelsey stared at me in startled wonder. "We are?" she asked.

I nodded.

"Where?"

"A restaurant called The Cut." I smiled encouragingly, hoping she would agree even though my words had sounded like a demand. "It's a lovely place. You'll like it. I've already made the reservation for us at 7:30."

Much to my relief, Kelsey nodded, albeit hesitantly. She shut the TV off, then glanced at the time on her phone as she stood up. "Okay, I'll go get ready."

I nodded.

Kelsey walked up the stairs, not sparing me a single look.

I settled on the couch where she had been sitting. I was already dressed in a black sweater with a jacket on top and jeans, so I merely busied myself with my phone while waiting for her to get ready. But bringing my attention to the millions of tweets that I was receiving was proving to be difficult since a part of my mind nagged that, technically speaking, Kelsey and I were going on a date. It would finally give us the opportunity to sit down and have a conversation with each other—nowhere to duck and hide. But the more sensible part of my head just assured that were just doing this to get to know each other, like Mum said. Like Kelsey's mum would want us to.

Not to mention, this would be the first time that we would be seen together in public, and I could only hope that we didn't get interrupted by paparazzi. The last thing any of us needed was Kelsey being overwhelmed by cameras being shoved in her face because of the obnoxious paparazzi.

While I waited, my mind ran with dozens of thoughts a minute as I tried to relax for this dinner. *Why was I so worried?* Never in my life had I ever been this anxious about going out to dinner with a girl, so why should this be any different? Sure, Kelsey's and my circumstances were unusual, but it shouldn't warrant such nerves.

Thankfully, she came back down twenty minutes later, much quicker than I expected, and when I glanced up from my phone, I couldn't help the way my eyes widened at the sight of the blonde girl.

Kelsey came down, heels of her short boots clicking against the stairs. She was dressed in a yellow blouse and a pair of white skinny jeans. A black jacket draped over her right arm as her left hand gripped her purse.

I stood up, almost like I was in a daze because truth be told, she looked beautiful. Admittedly, Kelsey was a pretty girl with big blue eyes and faint freckles that dotted the bridge of her nose and some on her cheeks, but this was the first time that I saw her all dressed up. It might take me a moment to get used to it.

She came to a stop in front of me, offering me a shy smile.

I cleared my throat and let out the smile on my face. "Ready to go?"

She nodded, her smile slightly widening as she shrugged.

Kelsey and I exited the flat and headed towards the elevators. Offering Crosby a two-fingered salute, I stepped out of the building with Kelsey and walked to the closed parking lot where my black Audi S8 was parked. My security detail, Dirk's SUV, was there as well.

"Evenin', Dirk." I smiled at him as I dug my car keys out of my pocket.

My bodyguard returned the greeting, then went inside the SUV, ready to follow us.

The drive to the restaurant was silent but surprisingly comfortable. The only sound came from the radio, playing a Maroon 5 song, and the low hum of the engine.

During the fifteen-minute drive, I couldn't help but throw occasional glances towards Kelsey, who peered silently out the window. She was watching the streets we drove down and the buildings we passed by. I made a quick mental note to take her out to see the city since I knew she hadn't done so yet. It was not that she wasn't capable of exploring London by herself; I just didn't want her to feel alone in a city so big. God knows that's how she must already be feeling since the loss of her mum.

We got to the restaurant soon enough, but just as I pulled up in an available parking spot, camera flashes began blinding us, startling Kelsey as she gasped from the unwanted attention.

I cursed under my breath and killed the engine of the car. I looked at Kelsey, who was shielding her eyes, and said, "Don't get out yet."

She nodded.

I glanced out my window and saw Dirk already standing by the door and making sure the paparazzi kept a distance. Throwing open the door, I tightly clenched my jaw in annoyance even though I was already used to the flashes and constant shouting that blended together.

Dirk helped me out and guided me towards the passenger door.

My ears were full of the familiar sounds of the paparazzi yelling out my name, trying to get me to look at their cameras for a picture, but I ignored them.

I opened the passenger door and saw a worried looking Kelsey, who was still trying to shield her eyes with one hand as she stepped out of the car.

Closing the door behind her, I took a step closer to Kelsey and whispered, "Keep your head down." Then we began making our way through the crowd of photographers.

Instinctively, my right hand reached and grabbed one of Kelsey's, ignoring how warm her hand felt. I realized how small her hand was compared to my own when my fingers and rings grazed the ones decorating her own. I held her close as the paparazzi followed us across the parking lot and towards the front entrance of the restaurant, my patience thinning like it usually did when paparazzi found me at times when I wished they wouldn't.

The first time I was out with Kelsey, and we were already bloody hounded. Although I wanted to curse at everyone for badgering us, I kept my lips tightly pressed together and let Dirk do his job of safely guiding us instead.

Finally, Kelsey and I stepped into the warm restaurant, away from the photographers.

Dirk stayed outside once we were in.

Letting out a breath, I didn't dare spare Kelsey a single glance as we approached the host in front. "Reservations for Shaw."

The uniformed guy took a look at me. When realization dawned on his face, he quickly nodded and picked up two menus. "Right this way, sir."

Kelsey and I followed him, our hands still joined. I noticed a couple of patrons at their tables do a double take as we passed them. However, I kept my attention on anything but them, focusing on the white curtains and the red walls which were decorated with pictures, until we stopped in front of a small circular table with cushioned white chairs. Kelsey and I sat down across from each other as the guy gave us our menus and announced that our waiter will be joining us shortly.

Throwing another glance at her surroundings, Kelsey mused. "Fancy place."

A fond chuckle escaped me at that. "Yeah," I said before my smile slipped from my face. Then I cleared my throat, sitting up. "Look, I'm sorry about what happened outside. I didn't think—"

"Don't apologize." Kelsey interrupted, her blue eyes holding nothing but sincerity.

I stared at her in genuine surprise.

She shrugged, picking up her menu. "I mean, it's something I'm going to have to get used to, right? Might as well start adapting now."

I gave her a small smile, a bit shocked at how understanding she was. Truth be told, I figured that she would be utterly overwhelmed by her first paparazzi experience, or even be openly annoyed, but she seemed to be handling it well. Undoubtedly, that was a relief to both of us.

As we looked over our menu, a redhead waiter came by to ask us for our drinks, then left with my order of ginger ale and Kelsey's Pepsi.

Once he was gone, we spent some time looking over the menu as the low hum of chattering in the background filled the silence to not make this date awkward.

"So, Kelsey." I glanced up at her, meeting her questioning gaze. "Tell me a bit about yourself."

A smile tugged on the corner of her pink lips. "There's honestly nothing to tell," she replied, closing the menu and setting it down. I guessed she had decided on what she wanted. "I'm your normal nineteen-year-old who likes to read and draw. Though, I *do* hope to become an artist someday."

"Really?" My eyebrows shot up at the last bit of new information, not completely expecting that. "D'you have, like, a sketchbook or somethin'?"

Kelsey nodded as her smile spread into a full grin, showing off the dimples that I never really got to see. It was a welcome sight. "Yeah, I love to draw scenery and people." She briefly bit her lower lip before continuing. "Back home, I used to go to the beach because there would be so many people around. I would just sit down and draw them for hours."

I smiled as I nodded along to her words, realizing that this was something that we could relate to. We were both lovers of art, she with her sketches and me with my music. There was some common ground between us after all. "I'd love to see your sketches someday," I found myself saying, hoping I wasn't intruding and that my tone displayed how genuine I was feeling.

And I guess it did because she smiled and nodded just as the waiter returned with our drinks and asked for our orders.

When the waiter had left, Kelsey and I returned to our conversation, unrushed and gentle, and I was grateful that there weren't any awkward moments of silence or pauses between us.

Kelsey told me about the different art competitions that she had won and how she was majoring in art history, and then she asked me about my own music and career, looking genuinely interested in what I had to say.

Some people in the restaurant were trying to take photos of me from their seats, but I didn't care since I found myself immersed in my conversation with Kelsey. We were finally having a real conversation that filled the awkward silence that we usually found ourselves in, and it was a much-needed relief.

She was in the middle of telling me about her first time in driving a car—I didn't know how we got to this topic—when the waiter returned with our food. Nonetheless, she still continued on telling me how she didn't know which pedal was which and how she accidentally reversed when she was supposed to go forward.

We laughed for a bit until the smell of our food finally caught our attention.

My steak was massive, and it had steam coming off it as it was placed in front of me.

Kelsey's eyes widened as she laughed. "Have fun finishing that."

I picked up my fork and knife, quirking a playful eyebrow. "You can always help me with this."

"I'm good with my own food. Thanks." Kelsey giggled, picking up her sandwich with both hands, then took a bite out of it.

I shook my head and chuckled before cutting off a piece of my steak.

Kelsey took a sip of her Pepsi, then hummed. "You know, I have to compliment you on your restaurant choice. This place is great."

I smirked, proud that she was enjoying her meal. I was also glad that this dinner was going a lot better than I thought it would. All of my initial fears of it being dreadfully awkward and tense were thrown out the window.

We continued talking as we ate, and this time, I started the conversation with a story about the night the band and I partied too hard after winning our first Brit Award. Much to my pleasure, Kelsey looked genuinely interested in what I had to say, and I felt strangely pleased every time I made her laugh—so much better than occasionally hearing her cry whenever she thought I couldn't hear her.

Once we had finished our dinner, I finished off the rest of my drink before asking her, "D'you want dessert?"

Kelsey shook her head, eyes slightly widening as she put her napkin down. "God, no. I'm so full—I won't be surprised if I fall asleep in the car."

Chuckling at that, I signaled the waiter for the check, which he brought over promptly. Before paying it, I texted Dirk that we would be out in a minute. Then I handed the black folder where the check and my credit card were—to the waiter.

Kelsey and I put our jackets on and waited for the waiter to return. Once the waiter came back with my credit card and receipt, I placed my card back inside my wallet, and then we went to the front of the restaurant. Unfortunately, once we stepped out into the night, we were swarmed by the paparazzi that hadn't left.

"Cooper! Cooper!"

"Smile for the camera, lovebirds!"

"Kelsey, love, look here!"

Several more things were being shouted at us as Dirk demanded them to stay back.

My hand, once again, found Kelsey's as we walked towards the parking lot. My teeth ground together, and my brows furrowed against the flashes as we approached my car.

Kelsey used the clutch in her free hand to cover her eyes more effectively, keeping her head bowed and just looking at her feet as we walked.

Feeling a surge of guilt for something I knew I couldn't control, I squeezed her hand reassuringly, then felt a small sense of relief when she surprisingly returned the gesture.

As soon as we were near the car, I opened the door for Kelsey, allowing her to get in the car first, before swiftly making my way to the other side as I ignored the constant shouts and flashes.

Starting up the car, I let out a frustrated breath and glared at the photographers who were still gathered around us outside the windshield.

Hmm. How big of a scandal will it be if I run over some of those bastards?

With a quick shake of my head, I pulled out of the parking lot—with no photographer getting stuck under my tires—and swallowed down my annoyance. "Sor—"

"Don't"—Kelsey interrupted my apology, causing me to glance at her and see the small amused smile growing on her face—"even think about it."

Chapter 7

Kelsey

After having dinner with him, Cooper proved my quick and harsh judgment wrong. The annoyance that I had initially felt towards him when we first met mixed with the opinions of some of the media outlets that labeled him as an egomaniac who only cared for himself, was a false judgment of character on my part.

He continually apologized for the swarm of paparazzi that had found us. It wasn't his fault, and he couldn't control other people's actions, but his commitment to apologizing was endearing.

My initial grievance towards Cooper when we had first met was quickly washed away as I realized how sweet he was; not to mention that after losing my mother, his true caring nature came out of the woodwork.

Cooper was at the studio again today. The band was working on their third album, so I was, once again, by myself.

After finishing my assignments for my classes, I figured I had nothing better to do since I had finished unpacking over the past few days, so I decided to head out.

With sunglasses shielding my eyes from the surprisingly sunny day, I left the enclosed courtyard and parking lot, then began walking down the sidewalk. I headed towards the Starbucks around the corner, which I had gone to a bunch of times already.

I had grown to like London quicker than I anticipated. Despite being used to the warm Florida weather, the cold atmosphere here was comforting, and I quickly began to like it.

Although I had only walked around a couple of blocks away from the apartment, the chatter of the people around me always brought a smile to my face because of their accents. Well, I guess I was the one with the accent around here.

The people at the Starbucks and the little bakery on the other side were so pleasant as well, which was something that the people back in my hometown weren't that keen on being. Now I knew why that rude American stereotype came to exist.

As I entered the brewery, the fresh smell of coffee greeted my nose and made me smile. I stood in the relatively short line before paying for a frappuccino.

Walking down the sidewalk, I sipped my beverage through a straw and kept my gaze to my left, watching the cars drive by. I hadn't been paying attention to where I was going, causing me to accidentally bump into someone.

My eyes immediately widened, startled at the sudden impact. "Oh gosh. I'm so sorry!"

"No worries."

I looked and saw that it was a brunette whose hair barely brushed her shoulders. She seemed to be around my age or maybe older.

She squinted. Her hazel eyes looking me over, while I stared back in mild nervousness and confusion. Then she gasped as her eyes widened. "Wait! You're Kelsey, right? Cooper Shaw's girlfriend?"

My eyes widened behind my sunglasses, shocked at the fact that she recognized me so quickly and that she had assumed I was his *girlfriend*. I figured Cooper's fans would be kind of confused as to who I was, and from the paparazzi interaction we had I could see how our affiliation could be misconstrued, but someone actually saying it to my face was different. I ignored the blush I could feel rise as well. Cooper and I were barely even friends, so someone thinking we were more than that was just ridiculous to me. "I—uh, um…" I was holding my drink so tightly that I thought the plastic cup would burst under my grip.

The girl grinned as if I had actually confirmed her question. Well, I guess I had. "It *is* you!" she shouted, earning a few questioning gazes from the pedestrians. I wanted to tell her that while it *was* me, I was most definitely not Cooper's girlfriend. "I'm a massive Triage fan. You have no idea. Can I please get a picture with you?"

I blinked in confusion as my lips parted in wonder and puzzlement. Was she serious? "W-why would you want a picture with me?" Bewilderment was evident in my tone.

"Because you're Cooper's girlfriend." She shrugged as if it was the most obvious thing in the world. The grin never wavered from her face while I was still struggling to make sense of this. "Please? Just one picture?"

My mind was telling me to just take the picture no matter how strange this encounter was because if I had said no, I knew there was a chance that I would come off as rude. The last thing I needed was to have a bad first experience with one of Cooper's fans. So, forcing a smile to hide my uncertainty, I nodded. "Sure."

The girl's grin widened as she pulled her phone out. She came to stand next to me while I placed my sunglasses on top of my head, and then she put her arm out to snap a picture with me. .Smiling at the picture, she said: "Thank you so much!"

A breathy chuckle escaped me, still confused on what was going on. "It's no problem. But, uh." I bit my lower lip before telling her, "I'm not Cooper's girlfriend. We're friends." Not entirely true, but not a lie, either.

The girl's eyebrows rose at that. "Oh." She then pocketed her phone before smiling. "Either way, it's still brilliant to meet a friend of Cooper Shaw's." I thought it was weird. "Well, I best be going. Thank you again."

I nodded and returned the smile, watching in mild curiosity when she paused and met my gaze once again.

In a soft and genuine voice, she said, "I'm really sorry for your loss."

Blinking in surprise, I managed to offer a small smile before she walked away.

I was really taken aback at her words. That wasn't what I was expecting, and for a brief moment, I was confused on how she knew about my mother's passing. Then I realized that I had posted things on my social media, and if Cooper's fans began following my accounts, they would certainly know. Still, it was sweet of her to offer her condolences even though she didn't have to.

As I walked back to the apartment, I silently hoped that any future interactions with Triage's fans went like this one.

***

Cooper

Sitting on the comfortable leather couch in the studio, I scrolled through my Twitter and interacted with fans. I was reading their tweets to the band or to me and responded to some of them. As I did so, much to my surprise, I came across a new post from a fan who tagged me in it. I blinked at the tweet, mildly taken aback. Apparently, this fan had bumped into Kelsey earlier today and was able to take a photo with her, making me wonder how that must've been like for Kelsey. No doubt that she was bewildered during the encounter but by looking at this, I smiled in relief when I realized that Kelsey's first encounter with one of our fans was a pleasant one.

"Coop, if you're done smilin' at your phone like some nutter, you're up." Rafael's deep voice resonated through my mind, pulling me out of my thoughts.

Looking up, I tuned back to the present and hastily shoved my phone back in my pocket.

Julian, who was on the other end of the couch, raised a questioning eyebrow.

I ignored him and stood up, walking straight to the carpeted recording booth. I put the headphones on and looked at the lyrics of the newest track, which Miles and I wrote.

Nate, our sound tech, gave me a thumbs-up as the tune of the song began playing, and then I began singing at my cue.

When I was finally done, I hung the headphones up on the microphone stand, then walked out of the booth. I fell right back on the brown couch next to Spencer while Rafael and Miles were talking with Nate.

Just as I settled next to Spencer, his blue eyes met my green ones. "You never told us how your dinner with Kelsey went."

Suddenly, all eyes were on me while Nate excused himself out of the room to make a phone call.

"It went well," I answered with a shrug.

Miles leaned back against the soundboard, crossing his arms over his chest. "Did you find out anythin' about her?"

"She likes to draw," I replied without hesitation, comfortably leaning back against the couch. "Used to go to the beach just so she could draw people, spent hours doin' that. Studyin' art history in uni."

I gave some other smaller details, nothing too personal because it wasn't my place to tell my band mates. Still, they all looked impressed with what I had learned from Kelsey.

"Sounds like you really got to know her." Julian proudly smirked.

"It was just one dinner."

Rafael raised an eyebrow. "So what? You just go out on one dinner, and you think you're fine for the rest of your life?"

"Of course not." I seemed defensive, though I wasn't exactly sure why. "It's obviously goin' to take more than one dinner to get through to Kelsey, you wanker. She's incredibly...guarded— it's hard to just get her to smile."

Spencer snickered. "D'you blame her? She's gotta live with you."

I glared at him while the others fell into a fit of chuckles.

"What Spence means is..." Miles quickly jumped in, cracking his tattooed knuckles out of habit. "This whole situation is strange for both of you. It'll take a good while to get used to."

"Plus, you're not just *some guy*," Julian said, pointedly raising his eyebrows. "You're Cooper Shaw, front man of Triage. Your fame follows you around, and she's not only going to have to adjust to you but the fans and the paparazzi as well."

Squeezing my eyes shut, I let out a groan and tilted my head back, my hands pressed against my face. "She's going to face so much shit." My voice was muffled by my hands before dropping them to look at my friends. "I mean, Heidi, Noelle, and Dawn have to put up with so much from some fans because they're your girlfriends. No one even knew about Kelsey, and all of a sudden, she's living with me? Some of them are furious, and at some point, Kelsey's gonna be confronted by one of 'em." I was no stranger to some of our more extreme fans harassing people, especially the women, we were seen out with. Whether they were dating us or we were just friends, it didn't matter to them. Already there were rumors of Kelsey and I being together circulating, and according to our management it was better if we just left it alone and didn't speak on Kelsey's behalf. It didn't mean I didn't feel at least a little bit worried if she was getting harassed online.

Sympathetic and worried looks crossed their features before Rafael spoke up. "It's your job to help her through it, mate."

I couldn't resist a scoff from escaping as I muttered, "Easier said than done."

Julian, who was tapping his notebook on his lap with his fingers and was never unable to refrain from producing a beat, muttered, "Oh, hop off it. Kelsey doesn't even seem that bad."

"She's not." I sat up, earning questioning expressions from the boys. "It's just hard to get her to talk. At first, I thought it was 'cause she didn't like me, but now, there's barely any conversation between us since her mum passed."

Spencer patted my back. "It'll take time for her to open up to you, Coop."

Suddenly, Miles's face lit up as he held his hands out as if he just had the most wicked idea. "How about we all go to dinner tonight? Nothin' fancy, just Garfunkel's. Noelle and Dawn too."

Rafael patted Miles's shoulder in agreement. "Heidi too." Then he grinned towards the rest of us. "She's back in town."

The rest of us murmured our consensus.

Maybe this would be good for Kelsey. The more she got along with my band members, the better.

Miles, happy with our answers, nodded. "Brilliant! We'll meet at Garfunkel's at Trafalgar Square at eight. Tell your girlfriends." Then his grin turned into a teasing smirk as his brown eyes met my green ones. "And your roomie."

The conversation ended with me grabbing the pen on the table next to me and tossing it at our bassist's face.

Chapter 8

Kelsey

Even though I would be with friends, my nerves were jumping with anxiety at the thought of having dinner with Cooper's band members and their girlfriends. This was a group of friends that were incredibly close, and their relationships and friendships went way back.

Despite the warm welcome that I had received, I knew the way my mind worked, and I knew I would feel like an outsider among them. The dramatic side of me wanted to feign illness and back out from this dinner. Nonetheless, I swallowed my nerves down and proceeded to get ready, taking calming breaths while simultaneously telling myself that I was worrying for no reason.

Once I had pulled on my jeans and blouse and finished my makeup, I gave myself a brief once-over, not wanting to spend any time fretting over my appearance—it would just make me even more nervous—before heading down the stairs.

Cooper was waiting for me, already dressed in jeans with a black and blue flannel. He offered me a smile and asked if I was ready to go.

The two of us got in his car and headed towards the restaurant while Dirk followed behind.

A familiar silence fell upon us once more. The radio was playing songs while my fingers twisted the rings on my finger, a new nervous tick that I might've recently developed. Then I wondered if Cooper felt the same pressure that I did to break the silence that existed between us and if thinking of a conversation starter seemed as awkward for him as it did for me.

Despite the enjoyable dinner that we shared a few nights ago, it still wasn't enough for the two of us to be completely comfortable around each other. We still couldn't just start talking randomly as if we were friends. We were still two strangers living together, practically walking on eggshells in each other's presence and too hesitant to fully commit and adjust to this dynamic. And I guess I was too busy thinking of what to say to Cooper because, within ten minutes, I realized we had already reached the restaurant.

Unsurprisingly, my eyes caught sight of the paparazzi before their cameras even began flashing, and from what Cooper had briefly mentioned before we got in the car, the others were already here. The photographers must've shown up when they did and decided to wait outside, which I found ridiculous. *Don't they have homes to get back to?*

Once again, Dirk guided Cooper and me through. He was assisted by a couple of burly looking men, who I assumed to be the other members' security details.

Entering the restaurant, I glanced around and saw the looks that the people were giving us. Some seemed surprised while some focused on the boisterous group in the corner.

Cooper led me to the group's table when I heard Julian's voice. "Look who decided to join us." His accent seemed posher than any other British accent that I had heard so far, and it was nice.

I stood next to Cooper, though much shorter because of his towering height.

Everyone looked up and greeted us with smiles.

There were only two seats available, which were on one side of the table, because the other side's bench that lined up with the wall was already filled up.

I sat down between Cooper and Noelle, right across a girl with long blonde hair and big green eyes that were a shade darker than Cooper's. She was sitting next to Rafael.

"Kelsey, this is Heidi, Rafael's girlfriend." Cooper took it upon himself to introduce us, nodding at the girl sitting across from me.

I offered a smile.

The girl held her hand over the table, which already had bread baskets, then beamed when I shook it. "Lovely to meet you, Kelsey."

I returned the sentiment, picking up the laminated menu book in front of me as everyone, once again, dissolved into a conversation. As I looked over the options, I occasionally glanced around, trying to keep up with what they were talking about. Something about an upcoming concert for the guys and a recital that Noelle was preparing for her students.

Everyone's voices were lapping over each other's, and my grip on the menu tightened as I, for some reason, began feeling a sense of uneasiness for being unable to participate. I wasn't sure whether it was because of lack of confidence or because I genuinely had nothing to say.

Maybe it was because a part of me knew I didn't fit in here, with this group. The guys had known each other for years. They grew up together, and their relationships with the girls had been going on for years as well.

Never mind the fact that these people were friendly, trying to include me in their conversations as the dinner went on. I just couldn't shake the feeling of being out of place. Not to mention, I could hear the murmurs and feel the stares of the other customers in the restaurant, but it seemed like they didn't even exist to these guys. *How was it so easy for them to ignore the holes being burned into their backs?*

Even when our food arrived and when everyone dug in, the chatter and the laughter around me didn't stop. Of course, that wasn't the problem at all—the problem was me. I felt so awkward, like the odd one out, even though the people surrounding me were talking to me to make me feel like I was a part of the conversation and a part of the group as possible. However, all I did was smile as if I belonged, as if I wasn't unwillingly forced into all of their lives, and as if it wasn't like they had any other choice but to accept me because of a promise the mother of one of their friends made with mine. Part of me was aware I was probably being dramatic, letting my overanalyzing mind get the better of me, but there wasn't a switch to turn these nagging musings off.

I could feel a pair of eyes staring at me as I cut a piece of my chicken, which was barely eaten. I glanced up and met Dawn's eyes.

She was sitting on the other end of the table. She had stopped eating her fish, offering me a concerned and questioning look before subtly nodding as if she was asking: *Are you okay?*

I nodded, hoping that I had masked the uneasy expression on my face and praying that she would believe me. Then I placed my napkin next to my plate and stood up.

Cooper glanced up at me, looking away from his conversation with Spencer and Heidi.

"Excuse me." I offered a forced smile before walking towards the bathroom at the back of the restaurant. I glanced back for a split second and saw that the only people who had seemingly noticed that something was wrong were Cooper and Dawn.

Clenching my jaw, I walked to a narrow hallway and stepped into the ladies' room. I approached the sink, then stopped to stare at myself in the mirror, bracing my hands on the porcelain counter. Peering into my blue eyes in the reflection, I pursed my lips as I sharply exhaled through my nose. Shaking my head, I couldn't help but mutter under my breath. "What's your damn issue?"

I was quickly growing tired of the anxiousness that I had been feeling throughout the night, which was now being accompanied by tears of nothing but frustration pooling in my eyes. There was no one else to blame for my uneasiness except me because the group I was with were some of the nicest people I had ever met—you wouldn't even think that some of them were members of the biggest band today. They were friendly and kind, so why was I making it so difficult for myself to feel good around them?

Tears escaped my eyes, wetting my cheeks. I instantly wiped them away as my lips parted to take a breath. This wasn't what my mom would want for me; she did this because she was sure I would be happy and okay, but here I was, unable to keep my word to her. The thought of disappointing my mom made my eyes burn once again.

The bathroom door suddenly opened. Dawn entered, seeming hesitant yet concerned as she shut the door behind her. She took a step closer to me, making me gulp, then asked, "Are you okay?"

I let out a breath, and then my lips pressed into a pathetic smile. "I don't know what I'm doing." I confessed as a short and humorless laugh escaped me. Then I felt fresh tears leaving my eyes. I wiped them away and inhaled a shaky breath as my eyes met

Dawn's hazel ones. "I feel completely out of place out there. It's not fair to you guys, but I feel alone here, I guess. I'm so—it sounds stupid, I know, but I just feel like I don't belong." I hugged myself as if I was trying to comfort myself for feeling the way I was.

Dawn's shoulders sank as she let out a breath, shaking her head before approaching me. "It doesn't sound stupid at all." Her voice was soft, and the smile on her face was comforting. "And you're not alone."

A light scoff escaped me before I could stop it. "But it's how I feel, Dawn. I mean, I feel so weird when I'm around you guys, even Cooper. And it has nothing to do with you all—it's just *me*. I was forced into all of your lives, especially Cooper's." I briefly bit the inside of my cheek. "I don't know. I feel like a burden, I guess."

Much to my surprise, Dawn pulled me in for a hug, engulfing me in her fruity scent.

My eyes briefly widened before returning her hug and realizing that it was much needed.

"You being a burden is absolute rubbish; no one thinks that—not even Cooper." She squeezed me as she said this.

"You don't know that," I retorted as we pulled away, her hands still on my shoulders.

"I know Cooper." Dawn had an encouraging smile on her lips. "And believe it or not, he's a sweetheart. And the rest of us? We're just a bunch of twenty-year-olds tryin' to live our lives as the world watches. It's not easy, but you've got us. You're going to be just fine."

Dawn's words comforted me more than she would understand, making me smile gratefully at the brunette girl. It was beyond sweet of her to come in here and check on me even if she didn't have to.

After we spoke, she went back to the table once I assured her that I would be out in a minute. Then I turned to my reflection when she was gone to make sure I didn't look like the mess that I had been feeling. Taking in a calming breath, I made my way towards the door but stopped short when it swung open. My eyes widened when I saw who was entering.

"This is the girls' bathroom—I hope you know that." I warned, though my shocked expression probably betrayed my tone.

"I know," Cooper replied, his Adam's apple bobbing nervously while his green eyes looked so bright under the lights of the bathroom. "Just wanted to make sure you were alright."

A smile tugged at my lips. "Yeah, I'm fine."

Cooper didn't look entirely convinced, taking a step forward. "Are you sure? D'you want to go home?"

I shook my head before mustering up a playful tone. "I haven't even finished my dinner yet."

Cooper let out a breathless chuckle as his fingers raked through his short dark hair.

I stood there, idly picking at my unpainted nails as I kept my gaze on him.

He looked away, absently staring at the closed stall doors to his right for a few seconds before his gaze locked onto mine. "You're not a burden, y'know."

I blinked, taken aback at his words, wondering how in the world he knew that. Heat flushed across my cheeks in embarrassment. He wasn't supposed to hear that—oh my god!

"I heard you and Dawn talking," he said with a slight smile, confirming my thoughts of him overhearing.

The heat on my face intensified. *Goddamnit, he must be thinking that I'm overdramatic, which I couldn't entirely blame him for.*

"But honestly…" He, once again, took me by surprise by giving me a friendly grin, showing off his annoyingly perfect teeth and shoving his hands in the front pockets of his jeans with his thumbs popping out. "I know we got rushed into this unexpectedly and unfairly, but I also know that if we tried to get to know each other a bit more, we'd be able to get along. Maybe this wouldn't feel so awkward by then."

His words sank into my mind as I continued to absently pick at my nails, staring at him in something akin to admiration. Who knew he would be the one to finally bring up this much-needed conversation—especially in a girls' bathroom?

He took two steps forward. "I know you're not too happy about this: bein' stuck with someone like me and all, but—"

"Someone like you?" I interrupted, taking a step towards him as he nodded. "Look, Cooper, this really doesn't have much to do with you personally—I'm positive that I'd still be this awkward even if it were any other guy I had just only met. It's just that your life comes with lots of changes to mine."

Cooper sucked in his bottom lip, his upper teeth digging into the flesh.

I offered him a reassuring smile, understanding that I wasn't the only one struggling with this. "I'm just gonna have to get used to your lifestyle and everything. It might take a while, but I'll eventually get used to it." I hadn't realized that we had gotten literally close to each other until there was only a foot or so separating us.

Cooper's hands suddenly enveloped my smaller ones and gently squeezed them, making me feel a sudden warmth on my skin and in my chest when a smile appeared on his lips. "Take all the time that you need."

Chapter 9

Kelsey

It was already one o'clock in the afternoon, and Cooper still hadn't shown his face. I realized that he wasn't going to be up anytime soon on his own.

The band were doing a sound check for a concert that they were putting on later tonight for a charity, not to mention a meet-and-greet with fans, but Cooper was still snoring in bed when I checked on him.

With a shake of my head, I let out a breath, knowing that I would've to wake the musician up. He was sprawled out on his stomach, buried under the comforters. Approaching his side, I pulled the comforter off him and revealed his short and messy dark hair tousled atop his head. A small smile tugged at my lips when I noticed how peaceful he looked. Soft snores escaped his parted lips while I gently shook his shoulders. "Cooper, wake up."

He just mumbled something under his breath.

"Seriously, you're going to be late."

Cooper grumbled some incoherent words.

I rolled my eyes, realizing that I wouldn't be able to wake him up in a civilized manner. So I stood up straight with a huff, hands on my hips, then glanced around the room to see if I could wake him up some other way. For a brief second, I considered pouring some cold water on him but decided that may be too extreme. So I crouched down near him once again, taking a deep breath before screaming as loud as I could. "Cooper!"

As expected, the musician shot up from the bed so suddenly that his legs got tangled up in the sheets, dramatically tumbling down on the floor next to me.

I jumped to my feet as I laughed uncontrollably. While I was laughing, I noticed the wild and alert expression on his face when he sat up on the floor and leaned back on his hands, looking at the blankets that were bunched around him. Then his gaze flickered up to me.

Oh my god! I think tears were coming out of my eyes as I gasped for air—I couldn't even remember the last time that I laughed this hard.

"Bloody hell, Kelsey!" Cooper yelled as he struggled to stand up.

At this point, I was sitting on the edge of the bed and was laughing like there was no tomorrow.

Cooper stared down at me in bewilderment. He was finally free of the blankets when he crossed his arms over his chest, trying to keep the irritated expression on his face. But I knew he was struggling because of the way his lips were twitching.

"S-sorry." I was wheezing as my laughter slowly died, leaning back a bit to look up at him. The guy was tall enough already, but when he stared down at me while I sat, I felt like I was only two feet tall. "You wouldn't wake up, and I needed to take drastic measures."

Cooper huffed as his hands reached up so his fingers could push his unruly hair back.

I stood up after finally sobering up from my fit of laughter. This little interaction seemed to make my day, which was a pleasant change from previously feeling awkward around Cooper. "Get dressed. You have sound check."

With a roll of his eyes, Cooper turned to head towards the bathroom. "Yes, Mother."

I couldn't help but smile when I exited the room and went back downstairs, my grin widening as I thought of the improvement between our recent interactions. Cooper and I had been getting along over the past couple of days, and I found myself starting conversations with him instead of avoiding him whenever he came back. We weren't best friends by any means, but it was a start.

Cooper wanted this thing to work out between us, and he knew it would take me some time to adjust. Besides, being friends with the person you're forced to live with, whether or not it's temporary, should be an essential factor in making things work, and that was what we were focusing on now. Becoming friends would surely help us out in the long run.

While Cooper took a shower, I settled on the couch and grabbed my laptop to continue writing an essay for my Shakespearean Literature class.

Only fifteen minutes had passed when Cooper came down the stairs. He was dressed in a vintage band t-shirt and in his usual jeans while his dark hair was still damp. "Are you comin' to the concert tonight?" he questioned as he reached the last step.

My attention went from my homework to him, raising an eyebrow. "I don't know, should I?"

"It'd be cool if you did. Dawn's comin'."

I thought for a moment, contemplating the offer. By the time that I had to leave for the concert, I would undoubtedly be done with my homework, so I really didn't have any excuse not to attend. "Sure, I'll come."

"Sick." Cooper triumphantly smirked, making me wonder if that was the smile that had swept his fans off their feet. "There's an extra ticket and VIP pass in my bedside drawer. Make sure to grab 'em."

My eyebrows shoot up at the information as I giggled. "Do you always keep extra passes lying around?"

His smirk only widened as he walked towards the table behind the couch to my left. "No—those were especially for you."

For some reason, heat flushed my cheeks as I laughed. "Alright, I'll see you there."

Cooper grabbed his car keys from the little bowl on the table, twirling them around his fingers. "I'll send a car for you," he said, already making his way towards the door. "Bye!"

***

A couple of hours later, I was at the arena where the concert was being held. Dirk was by my side to take me to my seat.

The atmosphere was already buzzing with excitement as people of all ages—mostly teenage girls—filed in the area, bouncing with enthusiastic energy to see their favorite band. Many of them were wearing shirts with either the band's name or the guys' faces on them.

Dawn had texted me, saying that she was already in our seats, which were around the middle section of the floor. As I got there, I saw just how good the view was. I could see the stage right there, about ten or so rows ahead.

Spotting Dawn was easy. She was sitting in her seat when she looked up and grinned as if she sensed me approaching. She was wearing the same VIP tag around her neck like me.

We exchanged greetings and hugged each other as Dirk stood nearby.

"Are you excited for your first Triage concert?" Dawn asked.

I let out a breathless laugh as we sat down. "I think so, but I don't think I'm ready for the screaming fans."

Dawn's hazel eyes twinkled. "You'll get used to it."

As we waited for the concert to begin, I noticed the girls who were seated around us, pointing towards Dawn and me and whispering things to one another, but I followed Dawn's lead and paid them no attention. If they approached us, fine. Otherwise, I wasn't going to initiate an interaction.

Fortunately, the concert started as the lights immediately turned off, enticing ear-piercing screams from the thousands of fans surrounding the arena, their attention solely focused on the stage.

The sound of a guitar played through the speakers as a fog machine blew some smoke on the dark stage before the bright white lights went on to reveal the members of Triage up the big stage: Julian was on the drums on a platform higher than the stage in the back. Rafael was on the keys to the left. Miles was on the bass in front of him. Spencer was on the guitar to the right, and Cooper took center stage with a sleek black guitar of his own. They dove into their opening song right away as the beat of the drums resonated in my chest.

I got to my feet, and my eyes widened in wonder and excitement when Cooper's lips parted as he began singing. My eyes remained on him as he sang, looking entirely at home up on stage while playing the guitar.

The band's dominating genre was a mixture of pop and alternative, heavy on the guitar and bass. They sang songs everyone else did—love and heartbreak with some self-discovery in there as well.

The show they put on had me dancing and singing along with Dawn and the other attendees who weren't a stranger to their music. I even stared in amazement when they each had a couple of their own instrumental solos in some songs. Cooper was just fantastic with the guitar.

They stopped in between some songs, taking the opportunity to welcome everyone to the concert and thanking them for attending since all proceeds went to a charity that helped children in third world countries. Then they would launch into another song, and I couldn't help but notice how some fans would throw things onto the stage—phones, stuffed animals—*was that a bra?*

When the concert ended about an hour or so later, Dawn grabbed my hand and said, "The lads are waiting for us backstage."

The arena was full of the chattering of fans as they left and was full of blue and white confetti that littered the ground as well.

Dirk had arrived to get us, and Dawn and I followed him through the arena and towards the backstage, entering a space where everyone was moving around quickly and purposefully as they wrapped everything up. Instruments were being moved around as well as other items that were used on the stage. Dirk led us down a wide hallway where people were also busy doing one thing or another.

Finally, we reached a door labeled "TRIAGE DRESSING ROOM" for tonight. When we walked in, I noticed the guys lounging around on the couches and the chairs, happily chatting as they hydrated themselves with water bottles and used small towels to wipe their faces and necks that were drenched with sweat. Despite witnessing them jumping around on stage, I was still kind of surprised to see them so sweaty, a result of them giving it their all on stage.

Noticing Dawn and I entering, the guys voiced their greetings and waved from where they sat.

Cooper sat up from a green couch with a white towel draped around his neck. "How'd you like the show?"

I walked closer to where he sat across the room, passing a table that was full of snacks for the guys to indulge themselves and a few racks were some of their clothes hung, which were separated by papers that read each of their names. "It was amazing," I answered.

"Wasn't that the best concert of your life?" Julian grinned as Dawn came to sit on the armrest of his chair.

I offered a teasing grin as I sat on a chair next to the couch where Cooper and Miles were occupying, and then I shrugged nonchalantly. "I don't know about that. The Drake concert that I went to last year was unbelievable."

Julian playfully glared at my words as the rest of the boys chuckled in good nature. They relaxed for a bit, winding down after an exhilarating concert.

I pulled out my phone, furrowing my brows when I saw I had a couple of missed calls from Logan. As the others took part in idle chatter, I called him back.

He picked up on the third ring. "Kelsey, hey."

"Hey." I furrowed my brows in concern as I stood up.

Cooper shot me a questioning glance.

I gestured to excuse myself for a minute, then walked towards the door. "What's wrong? You good?"

Logan let out a short breath as I left the room and walked to the hallway. It wasn't as bustling out here as before, only the occasional person passing by. "Yeah, I'm fine. I tried calling you before."

"Yeah, sorry about that." I leaned against the white-tiled walls in the hall. "I'm at the boys' concert."

"The boys?"

I shifted my weight from my right leg to my left. "Yeah, you know—Triage."

"Oh," Logan muttered, making me frown at the noticeable drop of tone. "Anyway, I called to tell you that there's a box of your mom's things that we found that she had given us for safekeeping. Do you want me to ship it to you?"

My breath hitched in my throat as he said this, my free hand rubbing down my clothed thigh. *Did I want it?* The memories that were sure to be brought up once I opened the box would be like stabs to my heart. These were reminders of the woman who's not here anymore. But I didn't ever want to forget my mom or the person she was, and having some of her belongings would help keep her memory alive—not that there would ever be a threat of me forgetting my mother.

Gripping my phone tightly, I sighed. "Yeah, send it over."

"Okay," Logan replied before, thankfully, changing the subject. "How are you over there?"

I couldn't help but smile lightly as I leaned my head back against the wall, staring up at the brightly lit ceiling. "Really good. Cooper and I've gotten to know each other, and we're becoming friends, I think."

"Good to know." The blunt flatness had returned in his voice, making me furrow my eyebrows at the fact that he wasn't even attempting to hide his disdain.

"Logan, are you okay?" I asked despite knowing the answer. I wanted to give him a chance to express it.

"Yeah, I'm fine." He cleared his throat. "Look, I gotta go now. I'll ship the box over tomorrow."

My lips pressed together, and then I forced a small smile on my face to convince myself that things were fine. "Okay. Thanks, Logan."

We bid each other goodbye and hung up before sliding my phone back in my pocket.

Instead of going back into the dressing room, where I could hear the sound of everyone chatting through the door, I stayed leaning against the wall. I was going over the fact that I would soon have to open another box full of Mom's things that would, no doubt, bring back the tears that I hadn't shed for the past few days. Sure, there had been times when I would find myself crying, typically when Cooper wasn't home and especially when I was in the shower, but I was getting good at not crying so much anymore. That would most likely change upon the arrival of this box. The ever-present ache in my chest at the knowledge of my mother not being around anymore was sure to intensify as well, stirring up the nausea that seemed to rise every time I thought about her.

Another sigh passed my lips just as the door opened. Cooper stepped out. "Hey, all right?"

I nodded, straightening myself. "Yeah, I'm good."

Cooper absently nodded, shutting the door behind him as he shoved his hands in his jeans pockets and went to lean against the wall across from me. He didn't look as sweaty as he was before, though his hair appeared a bit damp since some of it stuck to his forehead. Still, he looked every bit like the rockstar he was, with his tattooed arms on display and his dark stubble adorning his jaw.

I watched him glance down the end of the hall, where people were still taking the stage apart and whatnot.

"I need to talk to you," Cooper said, turning his head to meet my gaze.

I splayed my hands against the cold wall behind me, leaning my lower back as I slightly tilted my head. "Sure, what's up?"

Cooper brought his right hand up, fingers clad with chunky rings that rubbed at his jaw as he mirrored my position directly across from me. "I've wanted to tell you this for a few days, but things had been goin' on, and there never seemed to be a right time to bring it up."

I furrowed my brows in both curiosity and concern, wondering what he was on about.

Cooper briefly stared up at the ceiling, releasing a breath before meeting my gaze once more. "The lads and I—we're leaving for tour in 'bout a week."

I inhaled a soft breath as his words registered. *A week? We were just starting to properly get along, and now he was leaving?* In the back of my mind, I figured I could've maybe known about the tour if I had just gone online, but schoolwork had kept me busy. I had deserted my social media for a while and stayed away from entertainment channels that may possibly report this type of stuff.

A sinking feeling in my chest went along with the sudden dryness in my throat as I mustered up a smile, trying to make it seem as genuine as I could. "That's great, Cooper. You guys must be so excited."

Cooper let out a soft chuckle, and for some reason, he looked amused, making me narrow my eyes at him. "I know what you're thinkin', love." I pressed my teeth together as the term of endearment easily slipped past his mouth as if he didn't even notice. "You're not goin' to be here by yourself."

"I'm not?"

He snorted, shaking his head before smirking. "Of course not. You're comin' with us."

My eyes widened at that bombshell, nearly choking on nothing but my own spit as my back went ramrod at his words. *Is he joking? He has to be. Am I even allowed to come along?*

"What?"

Cooper nodded, smiling as his green eyes gleamed under the bright lights. "I talked to our manager and the rest of the team, and they don't see any reason for you to not be able to come." He shrugged. "I figured you could come with us on the European leg of the tour, and when we leave for America, you come back here. You still have school, after all, to keep up with. Plus, the tour bus has six bunks, so there's an extra one for you." He playfully smirked. "I mean, if you don't want, you also have the choice of staying back here with my parents and Alessandra, but I just figured you'd like a chance of getting some traveling in." He raised his eyebrows as if he was asking: *What do you think?*

My lips parted in surprise as I let out a short breath of disbelief. Going with Triage on tour meant that I could see parts of the world that I never thought I would get a chance to visit. I knew I was just beginning to adjust to London, but this was my place of living now, and I would come back to it later. Saying no to visiting other sites in Europe would be a tremendous missed opportunity on my part. Living my life, being happy—isn't that what Mom wanted for me? "Yes." I agreed with an excited laugh, nodding. "Definitely, yes. That sounds amazing. I'm in."

***

Two days later, I got out of the shower, then donned a shirt and a pair of sweats. I was drying my wet hair using a towel when I walked out of my room to head downstairs. I walked by Cooper's room where he sat on the bed with his laptop in front of him. I tried not to think about how snug he looked in the sweatshirt that he was wearing.

He glanced up at me just then and said, "There's a package for you downstairs."

I briefly raised my eyebrows at that, then headed downstairs. I caught sight of a FedEx box in the living room. I checked the label, and it was from Logan, immediately realizing that this was the box of Mom's things that he promised he would send over. Gulping, I headed to the kitchen and pulled out a pair of scissors from the drawer before sitting on the ground in the middle of the living room. I cut the tape and opened the flaps of the box.

My breath hitched in my throat when I saw the first thing that was staring up at me. It was a picture that I hadn't seen in years—of a newborn me cradled in the arms of my mother who was sitting ona hospital bed probably moments after I was born. My father sat next to her with one arm wrapped around Mom's shoulder and his free hand holding Mom's hands that were cradling me. They were smiling at me, not even paying attention to the camera, and it was crazy yet believable how quickly the tears burned my eyes.

Setting the photograph aside, I looked through the box, realizing most of the contents were pictures of Mom and me along with some of her old jewelry that had her birth stone, a green peridot, and her copy of *The Count of Monte Cristo*, which was her favorite book. I could feel my breathing grow heavy and my tears soak my cheeks as I held each item in my hands.

The reality of my mom not being around anymore hit me like a train once again. She was nothing but a memory now, both in my mind and in these material possessions of hers, and only being able to hold her things, even if it wasn't her, was enough to have me drop them back in the box with a *clunk* and release a gasping sob. I covered my mouth, trying to smother the sounds as I squeezed my eyes shut, but the action only caused more tears to leak while my other hand tightly gripped the edge of the box.

I shook my head, using both hands to wipe my face and simultaneously sucking in a breath to steady my overactive heart. Breaking down wasn't going to do anything for me except give me puffy eyes and a red nose that would make Rudolf jealous, so I bowed and shook my head, repeatedly telling myself to relax and that it was all right.

In between my methods of calming myself down, I guess I hadn't heard Cooper coming down the stairs because his voice startled me as he put his hand on my shoulder. "Kelsey, are you okay?"

I lifted my head and saw him crouching down to my left with his right hand on my shoulder. His brows were scrunched upwards in concern as his green eyes looked over my face. I probably looked like a mess. "Yeah." I sniffled as I wiped my cheeks for any remaining tears. "It's just—these are some of my mom's old things."

Cooper's gaze flickered to the box in front of me, his hand dropping from my shoulders as he lowered himself to sit cross-legged.

My fingers fiddled together as I watched him pick up one of the photos from the box—my mom and a six-year-old me at the bottom of a slide. I was so grateful that someone was able to capture this beautiful moment of us laughing.

"She was beautiful," Cooper mumbled.

My gaze flickered to his face, and my expression softened at the fond look that he was wearing, which I didn't even think he realized.

He was still staring at the picture. "Mum's mentioned on more than one occasion of how good of a person Klara was."

My eyes welled up with tears as I nodded. Then I kept my head bowed and my gaze on my fingers. "She was." I bit down on my quivering lower lip as memories of her being an active member of my school's PTA, planning fun birthday parties for me, and taking me trick-or-treating when I wasn't old enough to go by myself whisked around in my mind.

"Come 'ere." Cooper sighed, and before I knew it, his arms wrapped me in a hug as he pulled me into his chest. Within seconds, I deflated into his arms and my cheek pressed against his chest as the rush of emotions came flooding back, quiet sobs involuntarily escaping from my mouth. This time, instead of feeling embarrassed about being so emotional, I felt nothing but comforted by Cooper's soothing voice. "It's okay, Kels. Everythin' will be okay."

Chapter 10

The first stop for the Triage's tour was in Glasgow, Scotland, where they would be playing two shows before heading off to the next destination. The near seven-hour drive was spent in the band's large tour bus, fully equipped with six bunk beds, a bathroom, couches that lined up most of the middle of the bus, and a kitchen area where the guys had stacked their favorite food. In the corner on the slab of wood that separated the driver's seat and the rest of the bus was a mounted TV, providing us with entertainment. There were a total of five buses: one for the band, three for their road crew and team, and one for the band that was opening up for Triage called Brick City.

In the seven hours that we spent on the bus, I realized that it was surprisingly big enough for the six of us, but that didn't mean that living here with five guys was going to be an easy feat. And because I had come to know them so well, I didn't feel uncomfortable or nervous to be here with them—if anything, I was kind of excited. The irony wasn't lost on me, though. I had been so hesitant, so nervous and bothered about having to live with just Cooper in his apartment. But now I was with him *and* four of his band members in a space significantly smaller than his London home yet those worries were nowhere to be seen.

When we got to Glasgow by mid-morning, we checked in at a hotel and settled into our rooms. The boys used the little free time that they had to unwind after being stuck on a bus for hours.

Just as I exited the en-suite bathroom, my stomach let out a mortifyingly loud growl, and my cheeks heated up when Cooper turned to look at me with the most amused expression on his face.

"Hungry?"

I pressed my lips together, embarrassed, as my cheeks heated up. "Little bit."

Cooper's grin widened, his green eyes dancing with mirth as he shoved his wallet in the back pocket of his jeans and shrugged on his favorite black leather jacket. "C'mon, we'll get some lunch. I'm hungry myself."

The two of us left our hotel room after I pulled my sneakers on, walking down the carpeted hallway as my stomach let out another mewl.I wrapped my arms around my stomach and muttered, "Holy shit, shut up."

Cooper let out a loud hearty laugh as his right arm draped across my shoulder, comfortingly rubbing my upper arm. "Don't worry, love. We'll get some food in you quick."

The sudden contact heated up my cheeks once more, my heart doing a strange leap in the confines of my chest—both things I chose to ignore.

Upon reaching the lobby, I saw Dirk already there waiting for us. Cooper and I put on our sunglasses as we left the hotel. Not a lot of fans were out here, but since there was a handful, Cooper motioned for me to head towards the rented SUV, which was waiting directly out the front, while he took some pictures with the fans.

I watched through the window as Cooper interacted with them. He had a genuine smile on his face when he took the selfies, signed the autographs, and even hugged some fans. The reactions that he was getting from them were so sweet; the girls were utterly mystified by his presence as they stared at him like he hung the moon. It was actually kind of cute.

Cooper soon climbed into the back with Dirk joining the driver in the front seat, and then we were off to grab some lunch at a Scottish restaurant that I couldn't hope to pronounce the name of, though we were seated quite quickly. The rest of the day passed that way as well—quickly.

Cooper and I left to go back to the hotel after we finished lunch, and soon enough, we all left for the stadium so they could have a sound check.

Before I knew it, I was sitting at my seat at the end of the row on the floor—I wanted to be in the audience for, at least, the first concert—as Brick City opened the show. The Scottish fans were literally partying in their seats. This band was relatively new, but their insane talent had gained them quite the following as everyone in the audience screamed their lyrics while I was still trying to learn them.

There was a brief intermission when the Brick City stage was deftly taken apart so the Triage one could be set up. The lights in the stadium turned on as the air was filled with the low murmur of chatter. People were taking this opportunity to rush to the bathroom or get food from the kiosks. Meanwhile, I just awkwardly stood there by myself. I didn't have Dawn next to me to keep me company this time, so I busied myself with my phone while I was waiting for Triage to come on.

Standing to my right was a group of fans who had been minding their own business until one of them recognized me, I guess, because she suddenly demanded in a Scottish accent, "Aren't you Kelsey? The bird living with Cooper?"

I blinked at her in surprise, taken aback by her tone, which told me that this conversation wasn't going to be as friendly as the first fan encounter that I had.

"Um…" I stammered out like an idiot, taking in the scowl that she was giving me before my brain functioned normally again. "Yeah, that's me."

Her dark brown eyes gave me a distasteful once-over before she scoffed, apparently unimpressed with what she saw, which only made my throat tighten. "He's a decent lad for letting *you* live with him" She smirked. "He probably did it out of pity."

My eyes widened, and my jaw slightly dropped at her bluntness, incredulous at how someone could be so downright rude to another person. She didn't even look regretful for her hurtful words. I stared at her in disbelief, feeling a surge of anger and shame rush through me. How rude of a person do you have to be to use someone else's parent's passing as a not-so-subtle insult? Not only that, but the mere way she spoke clearly insinuated that she didn't think I was good enough for Cooper's company. Like I didn't deserve to live with him. Her words were unwarranted and incredibly hurtful. Suggesting that Cooper opened up his home to me because of my mother's passing—which, in a way, was true—was incredibly heartless and most demeaning.

The girl next to her gave me an apologetic look and mouthed, *I'm sorry*, on behalf of her friend, who had already turned her back to me as she went back to her conversation with her friends.

Gulping, I offered a half-hearted smile, then faced the stage just as the lights dimmed. Excited screaming ensued as tears pricked my eyes. A harsh reminder of my mother being gone ripped the excitement out of my system in the blink of an eye.

A part of me told myself that it was okay for me to cry because of what happened to my mother while the louder part of me was screaming at myself for being so damn sensitive and for taking what people said to heart—especially since I didn't know them. Unfortunately, I just wasn't the person who didn't care what other people thought of her.

***

Cooper

Our concert in Scotland, the first to kick off our tour, had ended, and I still felt the adrenaline rushing through my veins when I returned with the lads to our dressing room. I caught the towel that our manager, Anthony, tossed at me and used it to rub my face and neck, which had a layer of sweat. Downing water from a bottle that I had picked up from the snack table, my eyes flickered towards the door that had just been opened by Dirk, who held it open for Kelsey to walk through.

She gave us all a smile, congratulating us on putting on a fantastic first show to start off the tour before settling on the couch. She put her left elbow on the armrest as she leaned her head against her hand.

The lads and I, who had just put on an hour and a half long show, were jumping around the dressing room and recalling the best moments from the stage while Kelsey was sitting down as if she was the one who was exhausted.

Taking a step towards her, I glanced down at the blonde girl and muttered, "All right?"

She lifted her head to look up at me, offering a tired smile. "Yeah. Just a little sleepy, I guess."

I didn't buy it. I didn't know when I had learned to read Kelsey, but my gut was telling me that she was lying, and I figured it was better to ask her when we were back at the hotel instead of when we were around everyone else. So I bit my tongue, despite feeling uneasy in seeing the tired expression on her face, and went on Twitter as my band mates either raided the snack table or, in Rafael's case, sparked up a conversation with Kelsey. If I talked to her now, I had a feeling that I would start prodding about what put off her mood.

As I leaned against the wall and used the towel with one hand to rub my neck, my eyes landed on a series of posts on Twitter that miraculously told me everything that I needed to know. Our band had fans on Twitter who took it upon themselves to inform other fans on updates concerning things the band or its members. Honestly, it was a great thing, and sometimes, these people knew what the band was involved in before any of us knew it.

However, this particular account spoke of something that occurred during tonight's concert, which had me clenching my phone so tightly that I feared it might break.

Apparently, from what these posts read, Kelsey had an encounter with a fan during the show that had said some completely unnecessary harsh words to her, words that sparked anger in me that I didn't see coming.

My jaw clenched tightly at that speck of information as my eyes trailed over to Kelsey, who remained seated across the room. No wonder her face appeared so crestfallen; the last thing she needed was an opinionated fan making her feel like shit.

Things were already rough for Kelsey. She had just lost her mother and now this? She was already getting used to the significant changes in her life, and while I knew she was going to have to brave some harsh fans at some point, I honestly hadn't expected it to be on the first night of our damn tour.

The fact that the person who had made Kelsey upset was someone who listened to our music made my stomach twist uncomfortably. My jaw clenched tightly, feeling my teeth grind together as I stuffed my phone in my back pocket. I was trying to stay calm, not wanting to draw the attention of Kelsey and my band mates. I could hold off until Kelsey and I were alone.

Usually, the night of the first show always warranted a celebration from the guys, but because we had just gotten to Scotland earlier this morning, we decided to put a pin in the celebrations for now. I was more than content with that decision since I needed to talk to Kelsey. And also because we had returned to our hotel at around 12:30AM since the show ended around eleven and we wanted to make sure the fans had cleared out before we left.

Finally, when we entered my hotel room, since Kelsey's was next door joined by another door, I barely shut the door behind me and said, "I know what happened at the concert, Kelsey."

Her shoulders dropped, and her head tilted back in defeat pausing on her way to her own room before straightening and turning to look at me. "And? There's nothing that we can do about it, right? What's done is done. It's over." She continued to her room.

I blinked. "No, it's not," I retorted, frowning, then followed her into her room. I was mildly surprised at her dismissal of the situation. I watched her sit on the edge of the bed as she took her earrings off. "Kels, you can't let what people say get to you, yeah?" My feet walked without the consent of my brain, bringing me to stand in front of Kelsey's seated figure before I crouched in front of her. My hands grabbed hers, squeezing them in what I hoped was a comforting manner. "I know this is hard, but I'm here for you, I swear."

I noticed the way her lips tugged into an appreciative smile when she glanced up, her blue eyes glancing at our joined hands.

My own gaze followed hers, admiring the way our hands seemed to fit together nicely. Her hands were small in my own, but I couldn't help but notice how comforting the touch seemed to me. I wondered if she felt that way, too. My lips rolled into my mouth as the bracelet Mum had given her glimmered against the light of the bedside lamp, feeling a lightness in my chest when Kelsey hesitantly questioned, "We're in this together?"

A breathy laugh escaped me as I reassuringly nodded at her. "Promise."

Chapter 11

Kelsey

After the Scotland shows, the next tour stop had been in Wales and then Ireland. We were currently at the venue in Dublin. Brick City just recently walked off the stage after finishing their sound check, and Triage was up next.

I walked into the arena through one of the back doors, spotting the group of VIP fans all the way in the front as they watched the guys play around rather than rehearse for the show tonight.

Lingering in the back, I took a seat in one of the chairs in the last row, humming along to the songs that they were playing, which echoed throughout the empty arena.

Suddenly, I felt my phone buzzing in my pocket. It was Logan calling me, and I answered by greeting him cheerfully.

"Hey." I could sense a smile from his voice. "What're you up to? I hear music."

"Oh, that's just the guys rehearsing." My eyes were on the band as Julian performed an awesome drum solo. Even in sound check, they give it their all. "We're in Ireland right now. It's pretty cool here."

"I bet. Any plans of visiting Florida?"

I briefly bit the inside of my lower lip, then sighed. "I'm with them for the duration of their European tour. That's four months long."

"And then what? You're going back to London?"

Shrugging, I leaned back into the plastic chair with my phone pressed to my ear. "Yeah, probably." I looked at the ceiling, and it had so many lights and wires hanging from it. "I don't know if I'm gonna be back in Florida any time soon."

"Why not?" Logan sounded both confused and surprised.

My free hand ran through my wavy hair, pushing it out of my face. "It'll be too hard. I mean, I grew up there, I know, but my mom did too," I answered, hoping that my words made sense. Florida had been my home—it still was—for a long time, but that was when I still had my mom with me. Being there when she wasn't didn't seem doable at the moment. "It's just too much right now."

"You have to come back at some point, Kelsey," Logan retorted, and I knew him well enough to know that he was trying his best to control his tone even though he was starting to get annoyed. I didn't want to upset him, but I couldn't lie to him either. "We all miss you here."

"*We* as in you and your parents?" I sighed. "You guys are the only people I have there. I just can't, Logan. At least not right now." I really hoped he would understand. It wasn't like I was telling him that I was never gonna come back to Miami—I just didn't want to right now. Maybe if more time passed since Mom's death, it would be easier to go back, but not enough time had gone by yet.

"Is this you talking or your new *friend?*"

I blinked at the accusation. "Wha—Cooper?" I was bewildered, my eyes flying to the man in question, who was now sitting on the stage with his guitar on his lap and Spencer next to him. His long legs dangled off the edge as they conversed with the girls who were standing there. "Why would you even think he has anything to do with this? He doesn't control me, Logan. I'm my own person."

"I'm just saying." Logan sighed, sounding both flustered and irritated, which indicated that my previous hope of not upsetting him had gone out of the window. In my defense, I was only telling him the truth. "I can barely get a hold of you these days, and now you're sticking to Cooper's side even though you told me he was infuriating when you first met him." The accusatory tone in his voice did nothing but exasperate me as well.

Now, both of our moods were off all because of what I thought to be something utterly ridiculous. All of this wasn't coming from him because I said I wasn't ready to go back to Florida—his dislike of Cooper was seeping in as well. "You have to understand the time difference." I rolled my eyes even though we were talking on the phone. "And I told you that when I *first* met him. He's not like that, and it's my choice to stay here, not Cooper's. Stop being an ass about it."

"Whatever, I have to go," Logan said and ended the call before I could even say anything. I guess he had enough of me and our conversation.

Dumbfounded, I stared at my phone, letting out an incredulous scoff at his childish antics. He was blowing this whole thing out of proportion and expressing anger where it was unnecessary. And insinuating that I wasn't going back to Florida because of Cooper was beyond ridiculous and entirely not true. If he couldn't see that, then that wasn't my issue. Instead of feeling bad about Logan being upset with me, I could only say the feeling was now mutual.

Right before Triage's sound check ended, I headed backstage and towards their dressing room, passing the boys of Brick City and having a brief conversation with them before they were ushered off to do some dressing room interviews. I was now in the Triage's dressing room by myself for a couple of minutes until they came inside, accompanied by their hair and clothing stylists who began working on their looks for tonight.

I was sitting on the couch, leaning back and crossing my leg over my knee.

Cooper approached me, quirking a questioning eyebrow as he came to sit down next to me. Even though we were seated, he was still startlingly taller than me. "You all right?"

Why was he always asking me that? Actually—why was I still giving him reasons to ask me that? How needy.

I smiled and nodded. "I'm fine."

It was like nothing got past him because Cooper merely chuckled and slid down on the couch a little, still taller than me but was now seated more comfortably. "Every time someone says they're fine, it doesn't take a genius to know they're not." He turned his head to the right to look at me. "Come off it—what's wrong?"

My lips pursed at his curious expression while his green eyes silently prodded me to confide in him. Finally, I gave him a half-hearted shrug. "It's just Logan." I admitted, my eyes flickering at Rafael being sat down by their hair stylist, Marianna, in front of the mirror to fix up his dark curly locks. "He's angry because I said I won't be coming to visit any time soon."

Cooper hummed in understanding as his arms loosely crossed over his chest and his long legs splayed out in front of him. "Because of the tour?"

"That, and because I don't think I'm ready to go back just yet." I confessed, briefly puckering my lips. "It's where my mom grew up—where I grew up with her. I just know it's too soon for me to go back because I won't be able to handle it."

"I understand." Cooper nodded, offering me a friendly smile, then leaned sideways closer to me. "You don't have to go back if you're not ready yet. Only you could know how to take care of yourself best—if staying away, for now, is what you have to do, then do it."

My eyes remained on his bright green ones as a small smile grew on my lips.

Cooper offered me one of his own and squeezed my knee before standing up to talk to Spencer, leaving me to sit on the couch and soak in the warmth of his words and the touch of his hand on my knee.

My eyes trailed after him, unable to tear my gaze away while he stood with his friends, talking animatedly about god knows what. I couldn't understand what anyone was saying anymore as I took in the sight of Cooper.

For the first time, I let myself admire his physical features. He stood tall at well over six feet, lean with just the right amount of brawn that didn't make him seem overly muscular. His short dark hair was messily tousled atop his head, giving him that rock star look which he had the confidence to wear and the voice to match. The bright green of his eyes and the genuineness of his smile just wrapped up the deal with a sweet bow, honestly. He was, from what I had read, one of the biggest musicians in the industry today, but you would never guess that he unabashedly had a heart of gold.

***

The taste of the Fiber One chocolate brownie was lost on my cold-ridden taste buds, yet I continued munching on it as I lay all alone on the bed of my hotel room. The boys had a concert, which should be long over by now, and I hadn't attended because standing in the middle of thousands of screaming girls wasn't something that I was up for today. That, as well as the fact that I was fighting off a cold and a sore throat, was most definitely the cause.

The digital clock on my bedside table read 1:12 AM.

The boys should be returning soon.

My bedside table was also littered with a glass of water and the medicine that the boys' manager, Anthony, had picked up for me from a nearby pharmacy.

I had managed to take a nap after taking some medication, so my sore throat was now dying down a bit, although it still hurt when I tried to talk or even when I just tried to swallow water. This made me briefly wonder if this was how the fans' throats felt after continually screaming during a two-hour concert.

Smothering a groan that I knew would kill my throat, I lay on my stomach and buried my face into a pillow. Though that was interrupted because I heard the door opening, followed by footsteps and a familiar British voice.

"You feelin' any better?" Cooper knew I was awake since I had just responded to his text a few minutes ago.

I lifted my head and rolled over on my back to look up at him, trying to sit up straight. He was in his usual shirt-leather jacket-and-jeans getup, and he was looking at me with a concerned expression. "A bit," I replied, my voice unsurprisingly hoarse. I sounded like I smoked three packs of cigarettes a day.

Cooper's eyebrows shot up, shrugging off his jacket as he shot me a look. "You don't *sound* any better," he said, draping his jacket over the back of the chair. "Have you eaten anythin'?" He made his way over to my side, the back of his hand grazing my forehead as he felt for my temperature. I brushed off the shiver that ran down my spine at the touch, chalking it up to my cold rather than Cooper's skin innocently against mine.

Leaning back against the mountains of pillows, I said, "Not really. My throat hurts too much."

"You know what you need? Soup. Hot soup."

I ran my fingers through my hair, pushing it back and away from my face. "I don't want to eat or drink anything, Cooper."

He was already reaching for the telephone on my bedside. "Do you want to get better or not?"

I remained silent.

"I'm orderin' you some soup." Cooper picked up the phone and ordered some chicken noodle soup, and then he hung up and shot me a triumphant look.

I rolled my eyes. "How was the concert?" I sounded like I was whispering.

"Good. I got a bra thrown at me."

I snorted, utterly unladylike, but sick Kelsey couldn't care less.

"Has Logan called you back?"

My expression dropped at the mere mention of my best friend's name, who refused to speak to me for reasons that I, personally, thought were ludicrous. I had called and texted him for the past few days, but he never responded, so I stopped after a while. There was only so much that I could do to get him to answer me. "No, he's ignoring me."

"He'll come around." Cooper reassuringly smiled as he pulled his wallet and phone out and placed it on the other bedside table. "He's your best friend."

I slightly smiled, hoping he was right.

Moments later, someone knocked on the door, and Cooper went to answer it. He thanked whoever was at the door before returning to my line of sight, carrying a tray that had a steaming bowl of hot soup.

Damn, that was fast.

Cooper set it down on my bedside table, instructing me to eat it while it was still hot.

I thanked him and he smiled in return. Cooper then pulled out some clothes from his bag and without a single word, disappeared to take a shower. There had been a mix up when we arrived to the hotel early in the morning, the manager informing us they had overbooked and they were a couple rooms short. So some people had to double up and after reassuring Cooper multiple times I was okay with it, the two of us ended up in a single room.

The bed was huge and while I hadn't been really thinking about the fact that Cooper and I would have to share it earlier, it was now on the forefront of my mind and suddenly my face was heating up. It was definitely not because of the cold.

I shook my head, reaching for the soup and hoping that it would take my mind off the fact that I would be sharing this spacious bed with Cooper.

As I ate my soup, I knew it was doing wonders to my throat because I had managed to finish it in record time. Placing the tray back on my bedside table, my eyes flickered to my phone to see if I had any new messages.

None.

My jaw clenched in irritation, releasing a huff as I leaned back against my pillows.

Logan and I didn't argue much, so this was effortlessly annoying the shit out of me. As much as I wanted the two of us to get past this and makeup, the more stubborn part of me was saying that the next time he called—*if* he called—I was going to ignore him. Call me petty, but he should get a taste of what he was dishing out in the first place. I knew it completely went against patching things up between us, but serving him a taste of his own medicine wouldn't hurt.

Trying to get my mind off Logan, I turned the TV on and propped up on a dresser, flipping through some channels.

A couple of minutes of aimless channel surfing later, the bathroom door opened and Cooper stepped out. He was now in a white shirt and a pair of gray sweatpants while he used a towel in his hand to dry the back of his head. His bare feet padded towards the small vanity while I tried my best not to focus on the way his shirt fit him so snugly. The thin material showed off every ripple of muscle every time his tattooed arms flexed when he reached up to dry his hair.

Swallowing inaudibly—and then wincing at the mild pain that was still in my throat—I shut the TV off and made my way towards the bathroom to get myself ready for bed and to stop staring at Cooper. I stared at my reflection in the mirror, shaking my head in contempt at myself—not because I found Cooper attractive but because I was unashamedly checking him out. *What if he saw me?* That would be horrifying.

I returned to the room. My breath now smelled like mint, and the only source of light was the bedside lamp. I approached the bed, and Cooper was already under the covers. The closer I got to the bed, the more I could feel my heart picking up its pace at the notion of having to sleep next to Cooper. The bed was big enough so I doubted we would come anywhere near touching, but it was still nerve wracking to share a bed with a guy I wasn't *with* like that. I knew Cooper wasn't the kind to try anything, God no, but the whole idea had me holding my breath.

Climbing under the covers on my side, I lay down and switched the lamp off just as Cooper shut his. The room was enveloped in complete darkness until my eyes began adjusting to some of the moonlight that filtered through the curtains, illuminating the room in a soft glow. I closed my eyes, and despite being in a pair of flannel pajamas and being under layers of blankets, I couldn't bring myself to feel warm, helplessly shifting and folding myself to preserve some body heat.

"Are you cold?"

My eyes blinked open, quickly adjusting to the little to no light in the room as I instantly found Cooper looking at me. He was lying on his right side, facing me with his left arm above the comforter while I mirrored his position as well. "A bit," I mumbled, pursing my lips for a second.

Cooper shifted a little, and to my utmost surprise, I felt his arm slide across my waist under the covers, pulling me in and tucking me into his chest.

My eyes widened at the sudden contact, and I was prepared to push him away, partly because I didn't want him to get sick and partly because this was exactly what I had been anxious about in the first place. But the warmth that he emitted was instantly comforting as it spread through me like a tamed fire, and the musky scent of his body added to the soothing gesture.

If I wasn't so tired and sick, I was sure my heart would've gone into overdrive at this new position that Cooper and I were in. Neither of us was used to this closeness, and I wondered what possessed him to do this since neither one of us ever initiated a gesture such as this before. It was unexpected and different. But really, I wasn't entirely put off by it. Stunned and slightly overwhelmed but not put off. So I did what any other girl would've done when they were being cuddled by Cooper Shaw: I snuggled up next to him and shut my eyes as his soft, buttery smooth British voice whispered, "Better?"

I smiled against his chest, sleep bulldozing me. "Much."

***

The next morning, we were on our flight to Spain, which had gone more smoothly than I anticipated. My throat was gradually getting better, but I paid more attention to my excitement over the fact that I was headed to Spain. The boys had a day off before their concert in Madrid, and all I wanted to do was explore the place since I had apparently never been there before.

The drive to the hotel itself was beautiful. I was sitting by the door, peering out the window to look at the sights of Madrid, which consisted of beautiful parks and stunning buildings. The little kid tendencies sparked up within me since all I wanted to do was jump out of the car and explore the city, and I couldn't wait until it was time for me to do so.

After we checked into the hotel, Cooper and I went to our adjoining rooms—I found myself enjoying us having rooms together—while the others went to theirs. When we got in, I walked over to the window and looked down at the beautiful city since our floor was high up on the building. My eyes widened as I watched the cars and the bicycles that rode by beneath us, making me jump on the balls of my feet.

"You seem overly excited," Cooper said.

I turned around and saw him smiling at me at the doorway connecting our rooms as I raised my eyebrows. "It's *Spain*!" I screamed, and my voice was slightly raspy as I threw my hands out to gesticulate my enthusiasm. "Not all of us have been here before, Mr. Rockstar."

Cooper genuinely laughed, staring down at my much smaller figure. "You want to go out, explore the city and stuff?"

My eyes widened comically as I eagerly nodded.

"I'll let the security guards know."

I happily smiled, and while Cooper made some phone calls, I grabbed my coat and slid it on, picking up my purse and untucking my hair from the collar of the coat. Then I followed Cooper out when he was done with his phone calls.

Like magic, Dirk had appeared as well, along with another security detail named Paul, and then the four of us made our way down to the lobby through the elevator.

With sunglasses on our faces, I watched Cooper pull out a gray beanie from the pocket of his leather jacket. He pulled it on his head, hiding his dark hair.

As we stepped out of the elevators, I asked, "Are we driving or walking?"

Cooper hummed in thought. "Let's walk. A better way of takin' in the sights, ain't it?"

I hummed in agreement as Dirk and Paul nodded and led us to the back exit where there weren't any fans crowding it, and then we set out for an afternoon in Spain.

It was a bit cold outside but nothing unbearable since I put my hands in the pockets of my coat, hoping I wouldn't get sick all over again. Knowing my luck, I wouldn't bet on it. "Where are we headed to?"

"Buen Retiro Park," Cooper answered with a smile, turning his head, and I assumed he glanced at me from behind his sunglasses. "It's a beautiful place. We visited it last time we came here."

We walked for about ten minutes before finally reaching a gorgeous park with a body of water in the middle where people were on little canoes. There was also a place where it looked like a monument was built. I wasn't knowledgeable about the history of this place, but it was a beautiful park with so much greenery and flowers.

As I admired my surroundings, Paul asked, "You two want to get a boat?"

Cooper looked at me for approval.

I shrugged with a smile.

Cooper looked at Paul and said, "Yeah, that'd be sick."

Paul nodded and said something to Dirk before walking away. Minutes after he disappeared, I saw a small blue canoe being brought up in front of us on the bank of the river.

I watched Cooper get in first before holding out his hand for me to take.

Accepting the offer, I felt the warmth of his hand against my skin, creating a flush to my cheeks that reminded me of the other night when I was sick and he had literally cuddled with me before going to sleep. Unfortunately, we had woken up the next morning on either side of our beds as if what occurred before we fell asleep never happened. But we both knew it did.

The blush, it seemed, never stopped appearing on my cheeks every time Cooper touched me in even the most innocent of ways. It was a development of our progressing friendship that I wasn't quite sure how I felt about yet.

Cooper sat on one end while I sat on the other end of the boat. He took charge of the oars and began pushing us away from the bank where Paul and Dirk stood in their black shirts and black pants, looking burly and intimidating to anyone who would dare glance at them.

As Cooper and I floated along the lake, it was quiet; the only sound was from the water that lightly splashed against the oars and from the distant sounds of the birds chirping and the people chattering. Trees lined up some parts of the bank of the lake, and I couldn't help but stare around in wonder and awe because of how peaceful it was. It was definitely a change from attending concerts almost every night for the past two weeks.

"I like it here." I absently voiced my thoughts, looking up at the clear sky and hugging my coat to my chest as a light breeze blew by. "It's peaceful." Looking back at Cooper, I saw the smile on his face, so handsome and charming.

"Me too." He agreed, gently rowing the boat. "If I lived in Madrid, I would come here all the time."

I returned his smile and met his content gaze, understanding the sentiment as the water barely splashed under us.

Suddenly, the sound of my phone's shrill ringing ruined whatever moment that we had. I sighed as my gaze dropped from Cooper's, digging my phone out of my purse. My lips turned straight when I saw that the call was from Logan. I furrowed my eyebrows, remembering the petty promise that I had made to myself about Logan calling me.

Do I want to answer or do I want to unnecessarily drag this out because he hurt my feelings?

Swiftly, I declined the call and put my phone back in my pocket instead of throwing it to the lake like I was tempted to.

Cooper slightly jutted his chin at my purse. "You don't have to get that?"

"Not at this moment."

Chapter 12

I was with Cooper yesterday when Logan kept on calling and texting me even after I rejected his calls. I had chosen to ignore him even though it was bitchy move. I figured I would call him back after ignoring him once, but the stubborn and petty side of me won and decided to let him have a taste of his own medicine. If it was okay for him to ignore me for the past days because he was angry at me for no reason, then I could also ignore him for acting like a jerk. It was ridiculous of me, I know. I was well aware because he was my best friend, but I was in no mood to be the bigger person. If Logan thought it was reasonable for him to ignore me as if I had done something wrong, I could do the same—in my mind, I had a probable reason. It may be backwards and going completely against my initial desire of wanting to make things right between us, but I was too stubborn for my own good.

We were now in Verona, Italy, and just like Spain, it was absolutely gorgeous. At the moment, the guys were messing around as the stage crew set up for sound check, and I roamed around the huge amphitheater, looking up to see the clear blue sky. I found myself enjoying walking around the empty arenas as the guys did sound check, the spaces seeming so much bigger when they weren't packed with hundreds of thousands of fans, producing intense body heat. Open arenas like this, however, did wonders in reducing the hot atmosphere during the concert.

I had gone backstage to go to the bathroom and came back out when the band finally began sound check, seating myself in one of the back floor seats once again as I watched them. Their second song in, my phone began vibrating in my hand, and I raised my eyebrows when I saw that it was Logan calling. Maybe it is time for me to pick up. "Hi."

"Jesus Christ—thank god."

The bitterness was evident in both my smile and tone as I mused. "Shitty feeling when your best friend's ignoring you, isn't it?"

Logan released a frustrated sigh. "Look, Kelsey—"

"No, Logan." I snapped, effectively cutting him off as I quickly glanced around, making sure no one was nearby. "You've been ignoring me for the past couple of days, and I have no idea why. I only ignored your calls so you knew what it felt like to be given the silent treatment. And because you know I can be real petty when I want."

The band then finished their second song before moving on to their third after having a brief pause to talk amongst one another. "Are you at a concert?" Logan questioned once they began playing again, completely derailing the conversation.

"No, I'm at their sound check. Now, why'd you call me?" I impatiently inquired, putting the topic back on track, not so subtly digging for an apology.

"Because you're my best friend, Kelsey." Logan sighed, sounding tired. "And I hate not talking to you. I was just pissed before."

I shrugged even though he couldn't see me, sinking a bit lower on the uncomfortable plastic seat screwed to the ground. "Why?"

"You're so far away, Kels." He explained. "You're all over Europe, and I'm sitting here without my best friend. I just miss you, and I miss hanging out, and now I'm seeing pictures of you with Cooper and his friends and—"

"Is that what this is about?" I cut him off yet again, this time sitting up on the chair and furrowing my eyebrows. "You're jealous because I finally have friends that aren't you?" That sounded a lot harsher than I intended, but that's what it sounded like. Back home, I had people I was friendly with that I invited to birthday parties when I was younger and vice versa, but not actual *friends*. Logan was the only person I'd hang out with on a regular basis, my birthday parties becoming birthday dinners the two of us would go on, either by ourselves or with our families. So from where I stand, me making friends with new people was a good thing—it was a welcome change.

"You seem pretty close with them—"

"Of course I am," I responded with a disbelieving laugh as my free hand ran through my hair, shaking my head in incredulity. "I practically live with them now, so I can't exactly ignore them, Logan." I paused before adding with a pointed laugh, "I'm with them every single day. So, honestly, you've got no right to be pissy with me because I'm getting along with the people I'm around 24/7."

"Do you like him?"

I rolled my eyes at his ridiculousness. "Of course I like him. Why would you—"

"No, Kelsey. Do you, like, *actually* like him?"

I stopped suddenly, my lips parting to speak, but no words came out. With the phone to my ear, my eyes flickered forward and, as if there was some sort of magnetic pull, landed immediately on Cooper as he ran ring-clad fingers through his dark hair, talking to Rafael with his guitar strapped to his body. As if sensing my gaze on him, Cooper turned his head and, despite being on opposite ends of the arena, I just knew his eyes were looking directly at mine. I thanked my parents for their amazing eyesight as I noticed a smile forming on Cooper's face as he lifted his right hand and sent me a two-fingered wave, which I absentmindedly returned with my free hand, not even noticing that I had done so.

I was pulled out of the sudden daze I had been thrown into as Logan's impatient voice asked, "Well?"

Licking my lips, I hastily replied, "That doesn't matter."

"I think you should figure it out," Logan returned shortly and, much to my complete frustration, ended the call right after. I stared at my screen, pressing my lips together in an attempt to smother the irritated yell that was threatening to curl pass my lips. *Why in the world were boys so goddamn infuriating?*

***

Cooper

When Kelsey walked through the connecting door to go to her own room to shower and I began surfing through channels on the telly in mine, I couldn't help but think of how strange Kelsey had been acting lately. It started when we were in Italy, and that was three and a half months ago. There would be days when she was herself and everything was great. But then there were days when she was quiet as if she had an inner conflict with herself.

Although our own friendship was progressing, I couldn't shake the helpless feeling at not being able to get her to talk to me for the past few months about something that was clearly putting her mood off every now and then. I sighed in mild frustration. I was watching a random news channel until the sound of a phone ringing prompted me to sit up. I picked up my phone from the bedside table and realized that it wasn't mine that was ringing. My eyes landed on Kelsey's phone at the edge of the bed, realizing she must have left it in my room before going to hers.

Turning it over, I read the caller ID and recognized Logan's name. My curious expression changed into one of annoyance as his name was accompanied by a picture of the two of them at what seemed to be their high school graduation. Glancing towards the open doorway leading into Kelsey's room, I knew the right thing to do was to just put her phone in there. I could still hear the shower running and wondered if I should just let it go to voicemail. But then I remembered that Kelsey had been off for a few days and the fact that she and Logan had been having some problems, so I swiftly accepted the call before changing my mind.

"Kelsey?" Logan's familiar American voice asked.

"Ah, no. It's Cooper," I replied, sitting back with my legs folded underneath me. "Kelsey's in the shower right now."

"Oh, alright." He paused briefly before suddenly saying, "While I have you on the phone—how is she?"

My eyebrows scrunched together in confusion. "She's good," I honestly answered. "Seems to be enjoying herself here."

Logan was silent for a brief moment before his low voice muttered, "She is, is she?"

I nodded and told him yes, eyebrows drawing together at his seemingly dissatisfied tone.

"What do you think of her?"

The frown only deepened on my face. I was unsure of where this conversation was headed. Leaning back against the pillows and spreading my legs in front of me, I kept glancing towards the doorway into Kelsey's room, only being able to see the bed. The shower was still running. "She's a wonderful girl," I replied carefully, truthfully. "Pretty funny as well. All the lads have taken a likin' to her."

A short, almost humorless laugh escaped Logan. "Yeah, I'm not surprised. She's amazing." He added quietly, almost under his breath, which only caused me to raise an eyebrow in suspicion. "Anyways, I, um, have to go. Tell Kelsey I called."

"Will do," I muttered halfheartedly as the line went dead, and I dropped her phone back on the mattress, frowning to myself once more.

Something about Logan irked me, though I couldn't place my finger on what exactly. One day he's the reason why Kelsey's in a bad mood, then the next, he's calling her up for a chat as if nothing happened. I supposed that was how close friendships worked—I know that's what it's like for me with the lads—but the way Logan's voice sounded when he spoke about Kelsey, wistful and faraway, wasn't how friends talked about other friends. My eyebrows raised and my eyes slightly widened as realization hit me like a drumstick: Logan fancied Kelsey.

My hands instantly clenched into fists.

Just then, the shower shut off, and I placed Kelsey's phone on the bed before leaning back into the pillows as if I was paying attention to whatever the telly was showing. I heard Kelsey step out of the bathroom moments later in her own room before appearing into my view, hair wrapped in her towel as she wore her favorite flannel pajama pants and a shirt with Charlie Brown on it. Against my will, my eyes watched every move Kelsey made as she stood in front of the vanity mirror in her room, her back to me, unwrapping her hair and using the towel to dry it as much as she could before draping it on the back of the chair.

"So." She began, making me blink as I met her gaze hastily while she wandered into my room. If she noticed me staring, she gave no indication as she sat on the edge of the bed, and I sat up, quirking my eyebrow. "Logan's been asking me if I'm going to visit Florida once this part of the tour is over, and I honestly don't know what to tell him."

At the mention of the man I just finished speaking to, my jaw tightened, feeling the muscle jump. The prickly sizzle that irritated my skin was jealousy, no doubt about it, and I knew it was unjustified, I didn't have any right to get jealous over Kelsey visiting her friend, but the tightening of my muscles didn't seem to care.

Kelsey turned her head to the left to look at me. Her lips pouted ever so slightly, and I had to make sure my eyes didn't get drawn to them too obviously. It was proving to be difficult because it was then when my brain realized just how full her naturally pink lips were.

But I managed to keep my integrity intact as I repeated the same sentiment I had told her months ago when she first told me about Logan wanting her to visit Florida. "It's a matter of what you want. If you think you're ready, then you should go."

Honestly, now, I wanted her to stay. Kelsey going back to Miami meant her spending time with Logan, and the very thought of that brought out an unjustifiably possessive and very primitive side of me that I did not like seeing. Kelsey was nothing more than my friend, someone I had grown to like as a person and someone to have around, and wanting to keep her away from someone was me completely overstepping boundaries that were drawn thickly. I couldn't tell her who she could or couldn't see—I couldn't tell her to do anything, period. She was her own person, and I was strictly against becoming someone who ordered other people around in any capacity in any sense.

But the possibility of this pretty blonde in front me spending time with someone that most definitely had feelings for her that went beyond the lines of friendship bothered me quite a bit.

A heavy, tired sigh escaped Kelsey as she leaned her head back, staring up at the ceiling. "I have some time until the tour's over to decide. I'll figure it out." She finally concluded, patting the bed once before standing up with a sigh.

I wanted to remind her that the tour would end in a few weeks or so and that I wanted to know what she would decide. Truth be told, I would support her decision no matter what, but her going off to Miami would be done with a fist shoved in my mouth to prevent me from saying anything to her regarding Logan. We were finally friends, but was it really my place to say anything in reference to Logan's possible feelings towards her? What if she already knew?

My jaw clenched as Kelsey bid me good night and went to her room, shutting the door behind her. I shook my head with a grunt, shutting off the TV and turning off all the lights. Darkness enveloped the room, which seemed to also spread through my mind.

Chapter 13

Kelsey

My sleepy eyes blinked open only for me to regret it. Sunlight filtering through the curtains almost blinded me briefly. A tired sigh escaped me as I reached up to rub my face before blinking up at the ceiling. Soft muffled snores could be heard through the door, Cooper sound asleep on the other side and a tired smile twitched at my lips. He was probably exhausted, since he only ever snored when he was particularly worn out.

Honestly, watching him perform his heart out every night was an amazing experience. Every night I was reminded just how talented he and his band were, performing for thousands of fans every night and giving it their all at each concert. They never complained, only ever excited about the crowd and looking forward to the next one. Hanging out with them backstage, I could see just how much they appreciated the life they live, the opportunity they were given to be able to do what they love and were good at with their best friends. I may not have known these guys long, but I couldn't help but feel proud of them every night they ran out on stage. And, not that I would let anyone know, but most of the time I just couldn't stop staring at Cooper when I watched Triage perform. Listening to his deep, smooth voice boom throughout the arenas seemed to bring a smile to my face, realizing I could listen to him all of the time.

Letting out a sigh, I forced myself to get out of bed and made my way towards the bathroom. It was still early in the morning, and we didn't need to be up for another few hours .During the past few months, I noticed how tired Cooper tended to get, so I figured he should get as much sleep as he could.

The European part of the tour was almost over, and we were currently in Lisbon, Portugal, where the last two shows were. The band then had about two weeks off until they started the North American leg. As far as I knew, all of the guys were heading back to London for their break—which, apparently, consisted of interviews and photoshoots they were scheduled for. Last time I checked, didn't a break mean some time off for relaxation? Poor dudes.

Speaking of guys, Logan had been acting off since a few weeks ago when he once again brought up when I would visit Florida. After that whole debacle of us ignoring each other's calls, I finally decided that the whole thing was stupid and I didn't want to unnecessarily fight with my best friend. So, I would try to call him whenever I could or whenever the time zone difference would allow. Sometimes our conversations sucked, especially when he did not contribute much to them. It made me feel like he did not want to talk to me at all. The last thing I wanted was for my best friend and me to grow apart, and I knew that the only way to fix this mess was for me to do it in person.

Honestly, I wasn't even completely sure if I wanted to go back to Miami, but Logan wanted me to, and I knew it would help improve our strained friendship. But while I was on tour with Triage, I couldn't help but acknowledge how much I missed London and the apartment. I had grown accustomed to my living in England despite not being there for the past four months. Going to Miami was bound to stir up painful memories, but maybe seeing my best friend and making him happy would make it worth it.

As I stared at myself in the mirror, face dripping with water after having just washed it, I pressed my lips together as I forced myself to make a decision. I mean, I had just spent the past four months visiting places all over Europe; what's so different about visiting Florida? A self-depreciative scoff escaped me; I knew exactly what was so different. Miami was where I grew up with my mom, but it was also where my mom had died. Since her death, my mind now just associated that place with Mom's passing instead of recognizing that was also where I made some great moments with her. The ever-present pain seemed to win out on the happy memories of the past.

Pushing my hair out of my face, I caught sight of my blue eyes in the reflection and gave a decisive nod.

***

Coming back to London felt a lot more like coming home than I had imagined. Stepping out of Heathrow Airport under the cloudy sky and avoiding the onslaught of paparazzi waiting for us there felt familiar and nice—except the paparazzi part, of course. When Cooper and I got back to the apartment and I entered the living room that was bright because of the natural light coming through the large windows, I felt instantly at peace—a far different feeling than when I first stepped into this place. The new sense of home I had developed wasn't lost on me.

Despite just getting back to London, my stay here would be short-lived since I had decided to go to Miami after debating the trip for so long. So, I sat on the floor of the bedroom, separating the clothes from my suitcase either to be washed, put away in my closet, or kept to take to Miami. Although we had just arrived in London two days ago, the boys were already busy today with some radio interviews. So, I spent the day sorting my things for Miami, my passport and ticket sitting in my bedside drawer. Cooper bought the latter after ignoring my protests.

My flight was booked for the next day, so I really didn't have much time to get my things together. When I told Logan about me visiting, he had been beyond happy. The excitement in his voice was evident, and I prayed that this meant things were looking up for the two of us.

Around four in the afternoon, hunger struck me, and I headed down to the kitchen and left behind my unfinished packing. I decided to make myself a grilled cheese. After I took out the pan, butter, and cheese, I looked around for the loaf of bread Cooper had bought yesterday. I couldn't find it—until my eyes wandered upwards. I saw the loaf sitting on top of the fridge.

I tried to reach up, even going on the tips of my toes. I muttered, "Great." I was too short to reach it, and mentally I cursed Cooper for even putting it up there in the first place. He *knew* I couldn't reach that high; maybe it was his way of making sure I didn't eat up all the bread with the Nutella sandwiches I was prone to making.

I was about to turn to grab one of the chairs in the corner of the room to booster myself when suddenly, an arm from behind me reached up and grabbed the bag. My eyes widened when the familiar scent of Mont Blanc cologne and something indistinguishably *Cooper* invaded my senses. I turned around and looked up to see the man in question staring down at me, mirth dancing in his eyes. "Bread?" He smirked, holding the pack in his hand.

My lips briefly pressed together as I took the package from him. My eyes were glued to his as I murmured, "Thanks."

Neither of us moved, though the proximity wasn't at all lost on us. Cooper and I stood staring at each other, my back pressed against the cool stainless steel fridge. I barely came up to his chin. "Have you finished packin'?" he asked.

His body heat was radiating off him, and my skin was warming up, and my heart was doing some crazy somersaults in the confines of my chest. At this moment, I realized that our unspoken rule of keeping a respectful distance was being thrown out the window. And I didn't even care as the nervousness I should've felt was replaced by sparks of excitement lighting up under my skin.

"Almost," I answered him quietly, afraid that if I spoke too loudly, I would scare this moment away—a moment I wasn't aware I wanted but wasn't running away from now that I was in it.

My gaze flickered from his green eyes to his pink lips. My throat dried at the sight of how inviting they looked, so kissable. A hot blush crept on my cheeks as that thought passed through my brain, and I quickly turned my gaze to the loaf of bread in my hands, hoping my curtain of blonde hair would cover my tomato-like cheeks.

The action was fruitless. "Y'know," Cooper said, forcing me to meet his intense gaze again, "you're bloody cute when you blush."

If that was his attempt at escalating the heat in my cheeks, he succeeded, as they instantly warmed again, the feeling stretching to the freaking tips of my ears. He was being every bit of the cheeky guy people claimed he was. And I was sure he could feel the warmth on my face when his left hand suddenly came up to cup my cheek, the metal of his rings starkly cool against my warm skin. The fluttery feeling in my chest and stomach returned as my lips parted in mild surprise, and my brain went into overdrive as it tried to make sense of what was happening. But all I could think about was Cooper—his bright green eyes, smirking lips, towering height, and the pleasant scent of him that I was enveloped in. We were *so* close, barely any space separating us save for the damn packet of bread I was holding in my hands.

And then Cooper began leaning in, his face inching closer and my heart rate speeding up excessively. I wondered if he could hear the pounding in my chest. He was getting closer, and I knew what was about to happen, and instead of asking myself if I wanted this to happen, if this was *actually* happening, I closed my eyes .All thought escaped my mind as nothing but anticipation took over me.

His lips barely brushed mine at first, so softly as if asking a question. It wasn't until I blindly reached back to deposit the loaf of bread on the counter and placed my hands on his biceps to push myself into him, my lips pressing against his once more—that he got the answer he was looking for. Cooper leaned into the kiss more as he pressed me against the fridge. I tasted the lingering flavor of his mint gum as my heart rate sped up faster than it had ever been.

It was unrushed and sweet, both of us taking our time to actually feel each other and savor this moment that I don't think either of us saw coming. *What the hell brought this on? Did Cooper actually feel for me what this kiss screamed of?* Questions that demanded answers swirled in my head, but I forced myself to ignore them and just enjoy the moment I found myself in—a moment completely dizzying and knee-weakening.

We parted moments later. His calloused thumbs drew circles on my cheeks as I felt his forehead press against mine briefly. He pulled away all too soon, and I opened my eyes, almost as if in a daze. "You should finish packin'." He pointed out in a husky voice, lips tugging upwards in a small smile. "I'll make your sandwich."

I bit my bottom lip, preventing my smile from blowing into a wide grin. I nodded, following Cooper with my eyes as he prepared my grilled cheese sandwich. Although standing there in a numb daze seemed inviting, I walked out of the kitchen. By the time I got back into the bedroom, I was breathless. Whether it was because I just ran up the stairs or because of that unexpected moment, I wasn't sure. Maybe both.

As I sank to the floor by my suitcase, my right hand came up to cover my mouth in disbelief—the mouth that had just been kissing Cooper's. My lips tingled as if they had been electrified, and I shook my head to clear it as the goofy smile returned to my face. I felt like a middle schooler who had just gotten noticed by her crush.

I pushed a pair of shoes inside my suitcase, and my eyes wandering around the bedroom that I had made my own since moving in here. I just kissed the guy who had begrudingly accepted me into his home because his family had told him to. Who hadn't wanted me to live her as much I didn't want to, only agreeing to it because of a request my dying mother had asked from us.

I bit my lower lip as I thought of my mother. *Had she wanted this?* Somehow she always knew what was going to happen. *Did she expect this?*

Focusing my attention on the task, I quickly finished my packing. I made sure to keep the Miami-appropriate clothes in the suitcase before zipping it shut .Deciding to do my laundry later, I began hanging the other clothes, and minutes later, Cooper walked in with my plate of grilled cheese cut in half.

I fumbled for a smile as I approached him, meeting his gaze briefly. His smile widened ever so slightly as I took the plate from him and said, "Thanks." My stomach was twisting this way and that in his presence, but I was surprised that the feeling wasn't completely unwelcome.

"Not a problem," Cooper replied, sitting on the edge of the bed as I sat on the floor next to my piles of clothes, enjoying the warm sandwich that he made for me. "Are you ready to go back?"

I shrugged as I swallowed the bite of my sandwich. "I guess so," I replied, looking up at him from my position on the floor. "I'm gonna have to go back at one point."

Cooper nodded, lips pursing briefly before he reluctantly and flatly added, "I'm sure Logan's thrilled to see you."

There it was—the same bitterness in his voice when he mentioned Logan could be heard in Logan's voice when he and I talked about Cooper. My eyebrows scrunched in both confusion and curiosity as I wondered aloud, "Do you two not like each other?" I just needed to hear at least one of them confirm this thought outwardly, even though I knew the answer.

The musician leaned back on his palms, shrugging indifferently. "I have a feelin' your friend isn't fond of me"—he informed me in his low British accent—"and truthfully, the feelin's mutual."

I finished off my sandwich—I had been so hungry—and stood up to place the empty plate on the dresser. "Oh, stop." I denied fruitlessly while walking into the bathroom to quickly wash and dry my hands. "I'm sure Logan doesn't...dislike you," I said once I returned to the room, only hesitating as I tried to think of the right word.

"I'm sure Logan doesn't like me," Cooper retorted with a pointed, knowing look.

"I don't like the fact that my best friend and my—"

I cut myself off as I pressed my lips together because I had no idea what I was about to say. We were friends. Hell, we were housemates who just kissed and now my mind had already taken the opportunity to fall into the dark pit of overthinking. *What had that kiss meant?*

I was going to refer to Cooper as my roomie, a term we both had coined for each other only to use it for joking purposes. We had been so annoyed when people used to call us that, for no reason other than petty bitterness for being forced to live together, but after kissing Cooper it just seemed teasingly flirtatious. Like calling him my *roomie* was giving him a title that meant something so much more.

Instead of finding weirdness in this situation like I did, Cooper prodded at it, seemingly reading my mind. "Your what?" He stood up, walking over to me as he added with a teasing smirk, "Come on, love. Say it."

The tip of my tongue pressed against the back of my teeth as I smiled at him disbelievingly, staring up at the tall man. He was still smirking boyishly, challenging me to say the word. Clearly, he was amused by this and wasn't weirded out by it anymore. So, with a roll of my eyes and a shake of my head, I got over my own mild discomfort and stated with a laugh, "My *roomie*."

Cooper raised his brows in triumph, his smirk widening. He rested his arms on my shoulders while linking his hands at the back of my neck. "Now, was that so hard to say?" He jested, tilting his head to the side.

I snorted. "You're annoying."

Grinning and shrugging casually, he said, "I know." Then he pressed his lips to mine in yet another kiss. I still had no idea what the hell was going on, but I found myself not caring—if it meant getting more kisses from Cooper and reveling in the feelings he suddenly stirred within me.

Chapter 14

"Did you get taller?"

"Maybe you just got shorter." I rolled my eyes at Logan's jab but chuckled, nonetheless, happy to see my grinning best friend in person. "Here, let me take this," he said, taking my suitcase from me and dragging it along himself.

The two of us stepped out of the airport and into the warm Miami air, a vast difference from London's cold weather. We crossed the street to the parking lot where his familiar silver Prius was parked. The drive to his house was short. His parents had offered for me to stay with them.

Logan asked, "How was the tour? See any interesting places?"

I nodded, smiling and glancing at him as we drove down the familiar streets. "We went to Spain, Italy, Denmark—so many beautiful places. Logan, you would've loved it."

Logan offered an absent nod as he made a left turn. "I'm sure I would've," he responded noncommittally. "How're things with you and Cooper?"

I bit my tongue, wondering if I should tell him how good things were between Cooper and me—or the fact that we kissed. Twice. What Cooper said to me rang through my mind—how him not liking Logan was probably a mutual feeling—and I was mildly frustrated. As my best friend, shouldn't Logan be happy that I was on good—more than good, actually—terms with the guy I had to live with? "Things are fine," I finally answered vaguely. "Cooper's great."

My friend only offered a nod to acknowledge that he was listening, which was fine because in a couple of minutes, we were pulling up in front of his family home. The familiar two-story house looked newer, and I realized it was because they repainted the exterior, giving it a fresh look.

The front door flew open before we even reached the porch, revealing Logan's mother, Julia, grinning with her dark hair tied in a bun. "Kelsey!" she all but exclaimed, pulling me in for a hug. "It's so good to see you, sweetheart." I grinned as we pulled away. Her hands cupped my cheeks in motherly affection. "Europe's been good to you."

I couldn't help but smile as we entered the house. In the living room, Logan's dad, Fletcher, stood up to greet me with a hug while Logan excused himself to put my suitcase in the guestroom down the hall. Logan's parents sat me down on the couch, asking me how my flight was, what my life was like in London, and how Cooper was.

"Do you like him?" Julia asked as she sat to my right, nudging my shoulder teasingly. I felt myself blush as she added, "You know—like *that*?" Sometimes I wondered if Julia was a teenage girl trapped in an adult's body.

I shrugged and let out a light, awkward laugh. Images of Cooper and I kissing flashed through my mind. "I don't know," I found myself saying. "He's a great guy, but it's complicated."

"Well, if nothing comes of it, you can just move in with his folks." Fletcher joked with a laugh, Julia saying his name in a jokingly warning tone.

I blinked in surprise. Somehow it had slipped my mind that living in Cooper's apartment was supposed to be just a temporary settlement. I talked to Cooper's mother every now and then, whenever Amelia called to check in, yet the topic of me moving into her home hadn't come up. Partly because I wasn't even in the country for the past few months, but I had assumed, before tour, that when I'd get back I would have to go to their home.

I surprised myself by realizing that I didn't want to leave Cooper's apartment. London was beautiful and I was already comfortable there, and the thought of leaving left a bitter taste in my mouth. No one had brought up the notion of me going to live with Cooper's family yet, and if I was being honest, I wasn't going to, either. I was finally used to this arrangement. Disrupting it seemed unnecessary at this point.

***

In the past few days in Miami, Logan and I visited all of our favorite places to eat and the beach where I brought my sketchbook. I hadn't drawn in a while, honestly, only here and there when the tour was going on. Sitting on the beach I used to frequent after so long, hearing the familiar crashing of the waves, and the Florida sun beating down on my skin felt really good. It was nice being able to go out and not having any paparazzi snapping pictures of me—most likely because I wasn't out with Cooper. It was perfectly fine with me. Much to my surprise, though, being in Miami wasn't as difficult or strenuous as I feared it would be. Being around Logan and his family had made things a lot easier and bearable.

On my fourth day, when Logan and his parents were both off at work, I grabbed the car keys that Julia had left for me and left the house with a specific destination in mind.

Before I got there, though, I stopped by a local flower shop and bought a small bouquet of purple dahlias. I made my way through the cemetery, feeling a chill run up my spine despite the warm breeze that blew by. I was nervous and even a little scared, my heart slowing down the nearer I got to the gravesite, but I pushed through. Not visiting my mother's grave when I returned to Miami was, in my mind, unforgivable.

I finally came to a stop in front of the familiar stone. My throat suddenly felt dry, and my grip on the flowers tightened.

Klara Abigail Ross
August 6, 1986–February 25, 2013
All human wisdom is contained in these two words: wait and hope.

I swallowed inaudibly as I looked over the words, her favorite quote from *The Count of Monte Cristo*. I released a breath and sat down with my legs crossed, feeling the grass tickle my legs. I propped the flowers against the headstone. Her grave was somewhat isolated. There were no other family member graves around because when Dad died, he was cremated, as per his will. So it was just her here. I felt my lower lip quiver as I thought of the fact that this was some of what was left of my mother, other than some of her belongings I kept. My fingers began fiddling in my lap as I took in a deep breath.

If I didn't talk, I knew I'd start crying. "Hi Mom. I miss you." I began, feeling somewhat awkward at first, since this was the first time I was visiting her—or anyone's—grave. Were you supposed to talk out loud when you were visiting someone's grave? I wasn't sure.

"Things have been different since you left." I made myself continue, keeping my breathing even as I looked over her headstone. "I actually really like living in London, and Cooper's company isn't as intolerable as I thought," I joked, offering a light chuckle. "Turns out, he's actually great. I went with his band on their European tour, and God, Mom, it was amazing. Every place we went to made me think of how much you'd love it there."

A breeze blew my hair over my shoulders .I tasted salt and touched my cheeks. I had started crying unknowingly. I wiped them away, thinking of how my mother wouldn't want me to be sitting here, shedding tears. She'd always hated seeing me cry.

"You know how you always said mother knows best?" I let out a short, breathy chuckle. "Did you just *know* that I would end up liking Cooper? Because that's what happening, I think, and I don't know if I wanna yell at you for meddling or thank you for doing what you did."

***

"How was it?" Cooper asked over the phone, "Visitin' your mum?"

I sighed, lying on the bed as my free hand toyed with the loose thread at the hem of my shirt. "Strange," I replied, eyes on the ceiling fan, watching the blades whir. "There were tears, obviously, but not a complete breakdown. That's progress, I guess."

I chuckled humorlessly, and Cooper sighed softly at the other end of the line. "It's good that you visited, Kelsey. You would've regretted it if you hadn't."

I mumbled my agreement, knowing he was right, before quickly changing the subject and asking what he was up to. The two of us hadn't been able to talk for a few days, ever since I went to visit Mom's grave, actually. The five-hour time difference came into play for that and because, as Cooper informed me, the band had been booked for photo shoots and interviews back and forth, talking about their tour and prepping for the third album that was going to drop soon. Little did he know that I started following some of those update accounts fans made for the band. Occasionally, I would go on Twitter and find out what Triage was up to while I was in Florida.

"Are you packed for your flight tomorrow?" Cooper then asked once he finished telling me about some weird blindfolding/tasting game one of the radio stations made them play.

I hummed out an acquiescence. "Yeah." I couldn't help but grin teasingly. "Why, miss me already?"

Cooper let out a rich laugh, deep and hearty. My grin instantly widened. "Maybe. I just need to know so I can restock on your Nutella. I may or may not have finished it."

"Cooper Shaw, I better see a brand-new king-sized jar when I get back, or I'm gonna hide your guitar where you'll never find it."

It was clear he didn't find me the least bit intimidating as he snorted. "Yes, ma'am."

A few hours later, I was in the living room with Logan, watching *Big Bang Theory*. Well, actually, Logan was watching while I was thinking about going back to London tomorrow and the newfound excitement I was feeling to be back in England. Even though Miami was where I was born and raised and I would always love it here, my newly discovered love for living in a different country was far greater. One of the things Mom said to me after she told me I'd be living in London was that it would be a new experience and adventure. She was right, as usual.

Plus, not hearing British accents everyday here was a weird change. I wasn't even *used* to hearing an American accent on a daily basis anymore!

Also, I kind of missed Cooper, but I kept that to myself.

"When are your parents coming back?" I found myself complaining as I leaned back on the couch next to Logan. "I'm starving." We were waiting for his parents to return with Chinese takeout for dinner.

He snickered at my impatience, checking his phone for the time. "They should be here soon. Hold your horses."

I rolled my eyes before looking back at the TV. Some sesame chicken from my favorite Chinese place was all I could think about at the moment. I tried to keep my attention on the show we were watching, but that was proving to be difficult when, from my peripheral, I noticed Logan staring at me.

So when I turned to look at him and ask if there was something on my face, imagine my surprise when I felt a pair of unfamiliar lips press against mine, sending a shockwave of incredulity through me. I dumbly stared at Logan. His own eyes were closed as he *kissed* me. I was sitting there, frozen as my mind tried to keep up with what was going on.

And when it did, when I finally realized what in the hell was going on, I pushed him away, gasping. I stared at him in complete disbelief, heart thudding. Logan's dark eyes met my blue ones, staring at me in both shock and horror, which was an expression that I'm pretty sure I was mirroring. The question was: was he in shock that he kissed me or was he in shock because I pushed him away?

"Kelsey—"

I didn't want to hear what he had to say. Not in this moment, at least. I just stood up and quickly made my way down the hall, ignoring Logan calling my name. After locking the bedroom door behind me, I pressed my back against it and brought my hands up to cover my face. *What the fuck is going on?*

The adult thing to do would be to go back out there and listen to what Logan had to say. But frankly, I wasn't ready for adult life, so locking myself in the room while Logan knocked on the door seemed like the better option. Even though *he* was the one to kiss me, I still felt embarrassment rush through my veins as my stomach churned uneasily. Was I really blind to not have seen this coming?

I must have been, because if *this* is the reason why Logan had been showing hostility towards Cooper, then everything just made so much sense. My fingers dug into my cheeks as I realized how complicated this just made everything. If Logan felt for me the way I think he felt—the way he just *showed* he felt—then I could honestly say he was going to be nothing but disappointed when he found out my real feelings.

"Kelsey," Logan's voice called through the door. "Please, open the door."

Part of me wanted to stay quiet until he went away, but I released a breath and shakily said, "Just go away, please."

He didn't say anything, though I did hear his footsteps retreating, and I inhaled deeply and rubbed my face. Taking a few steps forward, I fell onto the bed, stomach first, and folded my arms before resting my forehead on top of them. Not to be dramatic, but I could feel a headache coming on, and all I wanted to do was scream into the mattress because, shit, this was my life now. Within a span of a few months, everything had gotten so complicated and weird that I was failing to understand why this had to happen to me, why this had to happen at *all*.

Finding out Logan liked me beyond the way a best friend should was like having a bad dream. He was my best friend, someone I considered a *brother. How had he taken that friendship and thought of it as something more? How could he think kissing me was a good idea? We've been best friends for as long as I can remember. Why couldn't he be okay with being just that? Why did he want more?*

I huffed. I wouldn't feel guilty for not returning Logan's feelings. I wasn't obligated to. Kissing him, no matter how brief it had been, felt so wrong. Not just because I saw Logan as my brother, but after kissing Cooper, kissing anyone else didn't feel right. There was something *there*. Sure, we only shared two kisses so far, but I wasn't going to lie and say the attraction didn't exist. That, along with mutual respect and care and loyalty was enough for me to want to be with Cooper. Also, I *did* like him. Cooper could have any girl he wanted in the world—which was more true for him than it would be for any other guy since he's Mr. Rock Star—but he was out here kissing me, and I did not mind at all.

I don't know how long I stayed in bed like that, thinking over the millions of thoughts running through my mind and potentially giving myself a headache, but soon enough, there was a knock on my door that followed Julia's voice. "Kelsey, dinner's here, honey."

I looked up, about to tell her that I wasn't hungry, but I realized that would be incredibly rude of me. Not to mention, my stomach was growling like crazy, so I forced myself off the bed and opened the door. I forced myself to return Julia's smile and followed into the dining room. Fletcher and Logan were already seated and opening up containers of Chinese food.

I sat down on the chair directly across Logan, doing my best to ignore his gaze as I put some shrimp lo-mein, sesame chicken, and white rice on my plate. "You all set to head back tomorrow?" Fletcher suddenly asked me.

I swallowed before nodding and offering a smile. "Yeah, it's weird, but I miss London."

"It's not weird at all, sweetie." Julia smiled. "You've grown used to your new home. And you've grown close to Cooper so I'm sure you wanna get back to him," she added with a teasing wink. Fletcher laughed, and I blushed.

My eyes caught Logan clenching his jaw before shoving some food into his mouth, and I quickly looked away because he shouldn't be angry. *I* should. Just because I didn't return his feelings and he didn't get what he wanted, that didn't give him the right to all of a sudden develop an attitude. And so for the rest of the dinner, whenever Julia and Fletcher brought up Cooper, I was more than glad to go into a conversation about the green-eyed musician, just to childishly spite the guy who was supposed to be my best friend.

Was our friendship ever going to go back to the way it was?

***

Cooper

"How was your trip?" I asked Kelsey as I drove us back to the flat, after having just picked her up from the airport. I had been waiting for her with Dirk, dumbly hoping that a pair of sunglasses and a beanie would be enough for me to go unrecognized, though I knew it would be a long shot. By the time Kelsey and I were leaving the airport, dozens of fans and paparazzi had swarmed us, giving Dirk a run for his money as he safely guided us back to my car.

"It was…nice," Kelsey hesitantly replied.

My eyebrows shot up in curiosity. Glancing at her, I caught her nibbling on her bottom lip as she kept her gaze straight ahead, brows furrowing as if she was stressed or thinking about something conflicting. I looked back at the road before briefly looking over her once more, noticing the way she was playing with her rings on her finger absentmindedly, a red flag pointing out that she was nervous about something.

Whatever it was, it was bothering her, and instead of saying anything at the moment, I kept my eyes on the road until we arrived at the flat within a few minutes. The silence between us was comfortable as the only sounds came from the pebbles on the ground crunching under my shoes until we were inside the building.

Entering the flat, I watched as Kelsey take off her sunglasses and look around as if she was coming here for the first time. I saw the fond smile that tugged at her lips and felt a smile on my own face, knowing she was glad to be back. The two of us went up to her bedroom where I set her suitcase down. She dropped her purse and phone on the bed. "I'm gonna take a shower." She informed me, pulling out some clothes from a drawer before locking the bathroom door behind her.

I absently nodded, taking off my own sunglasses. When I was about to turn away to leave the room, Kelsey's phone lit up with a new notification. The shower was still running. It irritated me when I saw that it was Logan who had messaged her. Before I could stop myself, my eyes read the texts on her lock screen. My eyes narrowed.

Look, I know it was wrong of me to kiss you like that. But let me just explain, okay? Just call me and I'll give you an explanation. I screwed up, and I'm sorry.

I inhaled sharply through my nose. My teeth ached; I realized I was clenching them so tightly. *Logan kissed her?* Kelsey and I weren't together. We weren't in a relationship and the burst of jealousy I felt was unjustified because she wasn't *mine* to get jealous over. Yet I couldn't help but feel my jaw clench tightly at the thought of some other guy kissing her. Running my fingers through my hair in frustration, I left the room and went down to the living room. It was obvious now that the reason Logan wasn't fond of me was because he didn't like the fact that the girl he liked was living with some other guy, and I just knew something was off about him. I knew most of my anger towards him stemmed from the fact that I had feelings for Kelsey as well, and judging by his text, Kelsey hadn't reacted the way she had hoped.

No wonder Kelsey had seemed so withdrawn and nervous; she was probably in disbelief over this whole situation, knowing her. While I obviously didn't blame her for what happened—by the looks of it, she was giving Logan the silent treatment yet again—I wished she didn't seem so anxious about telling me.

I had been confused at first about my feelings for Kelsey, even when I had kissed her. I think a part of me was still trying to figure out if I truly did like her because of who she was and not just because she was *there*. But having her gone for a week, only being able to speak to her on the phone, made me realize that yes, I definitely did like her for who she was, for the person I had come to get to know and genuinely enjoy the company of.

Eventually, I heard footsteps descend the stairs and looked up to see Kelsey coming down. Her hair was still damp from her shower. She now wore a pair of leggings and a Florida Gators t-shirt. She offered a smile as she reached the bottom, which only disappeared when I found myself blurting, "Did Logan kiss you?"

Sick job, Shaw. What ever happened to subtlety?

Kelsey froze .Her blue eyes widened, and her lips parted. "How did yo—"

"I saw a message Logan sent you."

Her eyebrows scrunched together as a breath of surprise escaped her. "That's invasion of privacy, Cooper. You can't just—"

"The message popped up when I was by the bed, and I just happened to read it, alright?" I cut her off once again, watching as her lips thinned in annoyance. Standing up, I tilted my head and asked, "Were you even goin' to tell me about it? Or was I meant to be kept in the dark?"

Kelsey rubbed her face, muffling a groan. "Look, I don't know if I would've told you or not, okay? But I didn't kiss him back or anything. I don't like him like that." She took a step towards me as she tried to convince me of her words.

"Yeah?" I raised a challenging eyebrow, crossing my arms over my chest. "Because *he* does like you like that."

A short, incredulous laugh escaped Kelsey. "I don't care!" She shook her head. "And you shouldn't either."

I scoffed and rolled my eyes. "Oh, yeah, I'll just not care that some bloke is goin' around kissin' my—"

I cut off immediately, jaw clenching tightly because I didn't know *what* I was going to say. Kelsey's face scrunched up slightly in an expression I couldn't decipher. "Your what?" she repeated challengingly, cocking her head to the side. "I'm not your anything, Cooper. Just your unwanted roommate, remember?" She let out a humorless chuckle. "We both know you can have anyone you want, so you don't have to waste your time on me."

Her voice cracked at the last bit, giving away the fact that she, herself, didn't believe in the words she was spewing .My hands clenched into fists. What in the hell was going on in that head of hers? What made her think I wanted anyone else but her? What made her think, after all these months of getting to know each other and growing close, that she was still *unwanted*?

I shook my head and took the two short strides to get in front of her. Her blue eyes met mine in wide wonder as I said, "Shut up." I pulled her towards me and pressed my lips to hers.

The response was instant. I pulled her as close as I could, trying to convey just how much I wanted her and nobody else. That thought needed to be thrown out of her head immediately, and I was more than willing to make sure of that.

"Oh—fuck—holy shit."

Kelsey and I immediately, too soon, pulled away as her wide eyes looked past me. I turned around to see Rafael and Julian standing by the doorway, staring at us like some deers caught in the headlights. My lips pressed together, mentally cursing at myself for giving them keys to my flat. I glanced down at Kelsey, whose cheeks were now a dusty pink color as she stared at the two arseholes standing there.

None of my band mates knew about the fact that Kelsey and I had kissed twice before, which clearly changed the status of our relationship. I had been trying to make sense of things for myself before opening my already muddled mind to the opinions of my friends. So I'm guessing this was quite the surprising sight for the two of them.

I awkwardly rubbed the back of my neck and offered them a wave. "Uh, hey, lads."

Both Rafael and Julian were staring at us with raised eyebrows, looking unimpressed. Julian was the first to break out of it as he jibed. "You couldn't have gotten a room?"

I gestured to Kelsey and me wildly as I said, "This is *our* flat!"

Letting out a nervous, embarrassed laugh, Kelsey waved at the boys before saying, "I'm gonna go, uh, unpack." She swiftly jogged up the stairs. I didn't blame her.

My invading band mates smirked as they walked further into the living room, making themselves at home on the couch. Rafael mused. "So you and Kelsey, huh?"

I sat down on the other couch as I rolled my eyes. "Don't sound so surprised."

"Sorry, but"—Julian shrugged, playing with the telly remote as he shot me a sly smirk—"I didn't think she'd actually end up liking you."

"Fuck off."

"Are you two, like—" Rafael paused, eyebrows furrowing in confusion as he exchanged a look with Julian before looking back at me "—together now?"

I rubbed my hands nervously and shrugged. "I don't know, honestly. We'll see."

Julian chuckled as he turned on the television. "A bit strange, ain't it?" He grinned at me. "Datin' someone you're already living with."

I sank into the couch, taking a long and deep breath and nodding, gaze flickering towards the stairs Kelsey had ran up. "Tell me about it."

Chapter 15

Kelsey

It seemed like I couldn't catch a break. My head was spinning as I gripped my phone. I wondered if I should pick up the next time he would call. Yesterday, Cooper found out that Logan kissed me, which led to him admitting his feelings for me by kissing me. Julian and Rafael mortified me by walking in on it. Honestly, I'd be flattered with all of the kissing being thrown my way if it weren't for the fact that they were from my best friend and the guy I lived with, both of whom didn't like each other while I only liked, well, my roommate.

The next day, I got several messages from Logan after I didn't respond to the message that Cooper saw, and I realized that Logan's attempts at reaching me weren't going to stop like they had the first time. Cooper was at a meeting with his band and team, so as I settled in the living room, I finally grew some confidence and called Logan back.

"Kelsey, thank god." He sounded relieved, and I sighed, gaze focused on the shelf of awards Triage had won. "I'm so sorry for what I did."

My jaw clenched briefly. "You shouldn't have done it. You shouldn't have kissed me."

"I just—I'm sorry, Kels. I've had these feelings for so long, and I felt like I just had to act on it or else I would've lost the nerve."

I wish you had. "You didn't *have* to do anything," I retorted, furrowing my eyebrows. "You wanted to, so you did, and you shouldn't have when you know you and I can't be together."

Unexpectedly, Logan let out a short, humorless laugh. "Why? Because you live in London?" Before I could answer, Logan scoffed. "Come on, Kels. You and I both know if you really wanted to, you could just come back here." I frowned in annoyance. "You don't have to fulfill your mom's promise for the rest of your life."

My lips parted in incredulous hurt, taken aback that he would talk about breaking my promise to Mom as if it was no big deal. When in fact, it was. He probably didn't mean it that way, because for all our arguments and faults, Logan and I never set out to intentionally hurt each other. And while I was pissed at him for even thinking that I would break Mom's promise, I still took a breath to calm myself down.

"I like him, Logan." I finally admitted, telling him the one thing I knew he didn't want to hear but would have to anyway. If it made him back off and realize that his place in my life was just being my best friend, then so be it.

"What?"

I refrained from sighing impatiently. My knee was bouncing incessantly, and I was ready for this to be over. "I like Cooper." I repeated.

"Yeah, I heard you the first time." Logan snapped, and I blinked, taken aback by his change of tone but not entirely surprised. Annoyed? Yes. Was it unexpected? Not completely. Then he mumbled, so low and under his breath that I don't think I was supposed to hear, "Thought you were better than that."

He was being ridiculous and childish. "Sorry if I actually started getting feelings for someone I'm around all the damn time. You're just pissed that after years of being your friend, I never got those feelings for *you*." Then I promptly ended the call.

Fighting with my best friend was beginning to get extremely exhausting and repetitive, but it sadly seemed that was where our friendship was now.

***

"So I was wondering," Cooper mused, and I looked up from my laptop just as I submitted yet another paper for one of my classes. He wandered into the living room from the kitchen, a secretive smile on his face. "If you wanted to, y'know, go on a date with me?"

I blinked, feeling my heart swell happily as a smile spread across my lips. "Yeah, I'd love to."

"Brilliant! You've an hour to get ready. Dress casual. And bring a jacket."

Scrambling to my feet after shutting my laptop, I said, "This is way too short of a notice!"

Cooper's laughter was all I heard as I entered the room. I immediately began getting ready, mentally patting myself on the back for already taking a shower, so I didn't have to do so now. The first thing I did was my makeup, which would take the longest, though I didn't go overboard after hearing Cooper's statement of dressing casually. After French braiding my hair, I changed into a pair of black jeans and a purple button-down, tucking it into my shirt and putting on my favorite Converse. Glancing at the clock, I impressed myself to see I managed to get ready in about forty minutes.

I grabbed my coat and put on the bracelet Amelia had gifted me, I returned to the living room. Cooper was seated watching TV, and he stood up once he noticed me. His charming smile returned to his face as he sincerely said, "You look lovely."

My brief blush wasn't a surprise as I thanked him. We left the apartment and headed down to his car. As he started driving, I asked, "So, what are we doing?"

"I was thinkin' some ice skatin', and then we could grab some lunch." He shrugged, tapping his fingers on the wheel as he shot me a glance. "Up for it?"

I nodded. The thought of a casual date such as this excited me. Ice skating was always so much fun, despite the chance of me falling right on my ass. It was better than sitting at some overpriced restaurant that only rich people frequented. I think Cooper understood the fact that as nineteen/twenty-year-olds, we would have more fun at an ice skating rink than an expensive and fancy restaurant. Honestly, with a life as crazy as Cooper's, when it came to dates, the rule should be the simpler, the better.

During the fifteen-minute car ride, Cooper and I belted out to the songs that came on the radio, even when a Triage song came on. I grinned triumphantly when Cooper looked at me proudly as I happily sang out their words. Of course, I let him do most of the singing. I wasn't terrible, but I probably sounded like a dying seal compared to him. And it felt good, being able to be so comfortable and carefree around Cooper, a development in our relationship that occurred months ago on tour. Every time I thought about it, I couldn't help but smile because we seemed to come a long way from when we met.

We reached the rink soon enough. Cooper parked in the surprisingly empty lot. We got out, and Dirk followed us. Cooper and I stepped into the rink.

I glanced around, noticing there was no one else inside except the clerks. "Where's everyone else?" I asked Cooper as if he would know the answer.

Apparently, he did because Cooper didn't even bother looking up from his wallet as he pulled out some money. "I rented it out for now."

My eyes widened slightly as he handed the clerks money .His green eyes looked at me once more, and a smile tugged at his lips as he took in my incredulous expression. So much for casual. Nodding at the clerk, he asked me, "What size are you?"

Absently, I told him that my shoe size was a seven. I didn't let go of his gaze as I let out a disbelieving laugh. "Did you seriously rent the place out?" I asked, raising my brows. It was incredibly endearing, but then my eyes narrowed as I thought that maybe it was more about being logical and not wanting to be surrounded by people who could recognize him.

As he handed me my dark blue skates, Cooper looked down at me with a grin. "Just wanted some alone time with you."

Well, that answers that.

We sat down by the lockers, taking off our shoes and putting on the skates. We wobbled over to a shared locker to put away our shoes.

As I slid onto the rink, Cooper followed me and asked, "Have you done this before?"

A Taylor Swift song was playing throughout the empty rink as I glanced over my shoulder to see Cooper skating .He shoved his hands in the pockets of his leather jacket.

It was so cold; I could see my breath. "Yeah." We were skating leisurely now. We could hear the blades slowly sliding on the ice. "During the winter, there was an indoor arena that would become an ice skating rink, and in the summer, it would be a rollerblading rink. Mom and I used to go a lot." I smiled slightly at the memory.

I tried to push away the fact that I used to go ice-skating with Logan as well. Now was certainly not the time to stress over the status of our friendship.

Glancing at Cooper, I asked, "You?"

He nodded and smiled at me. "Yeah, my sister and I used to skate a lot when we were kids." He turned so now he was skating backward.

I grinned and quirked my eyebrow. "You showing off?"

Cooper shrugged and offered a smile that was more mischievous than innocent. "Little bit." He turned again and skated away much faster.

I laughed and rolled my eyes. I took my time, skating at my own pace, and he ended up coming to a stop next to me once more. A song by Imagine Dragons came on, and I felt Cooper's hand slide into mine. I glanced down as I interlaced my fingers with his. A smile grew on my face as I enjoyed the warmth of his hand.

"Anything else you did with your mum?"

Memories began flooding me as Cooper turned to skate backward again; this time, he grabbed both of my hands, pulling me along.

"We went out for ice cream every Friday afternoon when I was younger. It became sort of a tradition. And when I was in high school, she'd come home during her lunch break so we could go to the ice cream shop nearby our house. It was one of our favorite places." I hadn't even visited the ice cream parlor when I went to

Miami, knowing if I tried to walk in without Mom by my side, I wouldn't make it a single step.

I took in a breath, feeling Cooper squeeze my hands comfortingly. Suddenly, I felt a bit off for talking about my mother on my first date with Cooper. Not that I didn't love talking or thinking about my mom, but I don't think it was necessary for us to talk about this at the moment. The more I did, the more I knew my over-emotional self would want to start crying. Tearing up on the first date wasn't cute.

So I quickly changed the subject, bringing up Triage's tour in a few days.

"Are you goin' to be okay? Y'know, by yourself at the flat?"

I chuckled, staring up at him. "I'll be fine." I assured him with a roll of my eyes. "I'll probably hang out with the girls, and my classes will keep me busy."

Cooper pursed his lips. "I guess—I just hate to leave you alone, y'know?"

I pulled him closer and brought us to a stop. Stressed Out by Twenty-one Pilots came on. "I'm not a little girl, Coop." I giggled. "I'll be fine, I swear."

His concern was sweet but unnecessary; Cooper was a popular musician, and his occasional absence was just something I would have to get used to. Sure, it would be easier for me to go and live with his parents in Birmingham like the original arrangement was, but London had grown on me and now that Cooper and I were getting along, it just made sense to stay. Packing everything up for a second time and shifting sounded tedious especially when London already felt like home.

I didn't expect Cooper going on tour to have too much of an effect on me before because I didn't think I'd actually develop feelings for him, but here we were. I would probably miss him, but I would be fine. We both would be.

I pulled him down to capture his lips in a kiss, hoping that it was enough to ease any anxiety he might have been feeling at the moment. After all the comfort he had provided me, it was the least I could do for him.

Chapter 16

When I woke up on Thursday morning, two days after my date with Cooper, I expected to see him downstairs in the living room or in the kitchen preparing tea. Then it dawned on me that he had woken me up just a few hours earlier to say goodbye since he was leaving for the band's North American tour.

In the kitchen, I pausing right the fridge, noticing a note stuck on it. I smiled as I recognized Cooper's handwriting.

I've sorted for Dirk to stay back to drive you & such. See you soon, love. C xx

I was eating cereal in the living room when my phone rang. It was Cooper's mother. "Hi, Amelia," I answered.

"Kelsey, sweetheart, how are you?" she excitedly responded. Her kind voice brought a smile to my face.

"I'm good," I responded truthfully. "What about you?"

"I'm great; haven't spoken to you in a while and wanted to give you a ring, especially since Cooper's off for tour now."

Amelia asked me about the European tour, and I enjoyed the pleasant conversation that promised a good start to my morning. It was especially nice because Amelia, despite not being here, was a motherly presence in my life. She called me every now and then when we were on tour, and the two of us would talk about my mother most of the time. She would tell me stories about my mom that I never knew. Talking to Amelia brought me comfort, the type I knew only a mother could bring.

"Has Cooper been treating you well?" she then asked as I drank the last of my milk that had turned chocolaty due to the Coco Pops.

It was crazy how the mention of Cooper's name could make me blush. "Yeah, yes, he has." I assured her with an airy laugh. "He's a sweetheart."

Amelia sounded her approval of her son's behavior .Our conversation moved along pleasantly until she had to unfortunately leave. I ended the call after bidding her goodbye and promising her that I would call her soon.

***

"I'm so glad you called me." Dawn grinned as we walked through Westfield London. "Shopping is a definite cure-all for boredom in my book."

I smiled, humming my agreement. It was my third whole day without Cooper, and so I called Dawn. The two of us planned a shopping trip. Noelle and Heidi had also been invited, but the two of them were busy, so we promised to plan something with them another day. We walked through the mall, both carrying a couple of bags from the different stores we had visited so far.

As the two of us looked through a circular rack of clothes at H&M, I hesitantly spoke up, "Hey, Dawn, can I ask you something?"

The hazel-eyed girl met my gaze from the other side of the rack. She answered, "What's up?"

I twisted my lips to the side briefly. "How do you deal with Julian being away for months?"

Dawn stopped examining the pair of heels in her hands and turned to face me. A knowing expression crossed her face. "It's hard because, you know, the one person you care about isn't around as often as you'd like. It can get difficult."

I nodded and returned my gaze to the burgundy sweater I was holding.

"Are you missin' Cooper already?" she then asked with a sympathetic yet knowing smile.

I shrugged, chuckling nervously. "A little bit," I mumbled and sighed. "I mean, it's only been three days, and I'm not anywhere near getting used to him not being home." Dawn's smile widened, and I quirked a brow. "What?"

She shook her head dismissively, putting the heels back on the shelf before meeting my gaze. "It's nice to hear you thinking of this place as home. It's a vast difference from when you said you felt alone." She took a few steps closer to me.

My mind flashed back to that night in the bathroom at Garfunkel's. It was one of my first times hanging out with them .I had felt lonely then; I didn't know I would consider them as friends later on. Dawn had calmed me down and comforted me, and I was so grateful to her for that because she didn't have to.

I then smiled at Dawn's words, unable to properly voice my gratitude towards what she had done that night. She then went to look through the sweaters that I had been observing. "You know, I called it from day one, you and Coop getting together. I'm so glad it's finally happened." She giggled.

I rolled my eyes and shook my head, feeling the warmth spread across my cheeks. Cooper and I had only been on one date before he left, but sharing multiple kisses and already living together really did play a part in helping us establish the foundation of a newfound relationship. "Tell me about it."

***

Cooper

"Kelsey should be here, don't you think?" Julian asked as we passed the highway sign that read Miami. We were currently on the tour bus, having left Sunrise and entering Kelsey's hometown.

I was just on the phone with my realtor. I was looking into buying a new house in London. Kelsey didn't know this nor did I want to mention anything until it was finalized. Moving out of my flat had always been the plan, but things had been put on hold for a bit when Kelsey moved in and I didn't want to complicate an already difficult change for her. Now I was finally starting them up again.

I looked at Julian as I sat on the couch, crossing my arms over my chest. "No. Last time she came here, Logan kissed her," I said flatly.

Julian winced as if to say *yikes*. "My apologies."

I snorted.

We eventually pulled into the spacious parking lot of the American Airlines Arena. We had a show tonight, and we didn't bother to book a hotel since we were immediately heading for Louisville afterward. We would sleep on the tour bus.

We greeted everyone helping us out tonight and rehearsed for tonight's show. We tried on new clothes thanks to our stylist, Pamela. A few hours before the concert, I found myself craving Dunkin Donuts, specifically a chocolate glazed doughnut.

So, with Paul accompanying me, I drove to the nearest Dunkin Donuts, which only happened to be a five-minute drive from the arena. The sunglasses on my face did nothing to keep my identity a secret, which was unsurprising. There were only a handful of teenage girls around, and I took off my sunglasses and happily took some pictures with them. I got enough doughnuts to feed my band and Brick City, as well as our security teams.

Paul and I stepped outside, and I bumped into someone. I took a step back as I apologized. "Sorry about that, mate."

When I saw who it was, I couldn't help but release a breath of disbelief. Out of all the people in Miami, how was it possible for me to bump into *him*?

"What're you doing in Miami?" Logan asked, raising an eyebrow.

My jaw clenched. I knew that he and Kelsey weren't on speaking terms at the moment because he kissed her, and I was still pretty bothered about the whole thing. "Band's on tour," I simply replied. I placed the sunglasses back on my face and continued in a tone that clearly depicted I'd rather be anywhere else but here. "I'd love to stay and chat, but I have a show to get to."

That obviously irked him. His gaze flickered behind me as if he was looking for something. "Is Kelsey here?"

My eyes narrowed into a glare he couldn't see. "No, she's in London. You'd know that if you hadn't taken a piss on your friendship with her."

Logan scowled and took a step towards me. It wasn't going to do much since I wasn't at all threatened by him. Paul shuffled forward, ready to intervene if he had to. Logan didn't even spare him a glance as he said indignantly, "She's my best friend. She'll talk to me sooner or later."

I shrugged, though I knew it was true; no matter how mad she was at Logan, I knew Kelsey valued her friendship with him and would try to make amends soon enough. That in itself didn't bother me because it certainly wasn't my place to tell Kelsey who she could or couldn't be friends with. Still, I would continue to show my contempt for the bloke until he truly proved that he wasn't going to run around kissing other people's girls, or that he didn't try to ruin his friendship with Kelsey every chance he got. It was pathetic and wrong.

So I also offered him a smile, which only caused him to bristle where he stood. "Good luck with that. Gotta go. See you around, mate."

I didn't even wait for him to reply. I felt holes being burned in my back as I walked to the car.

Paul asked, "What was that about?"

"That guy kissed my girl."

***

Kelsey

"Have a lovely day." The bookstore clerk grinned, handing me the bag of books I just purchased. I had just bought a handful of books to keep me entertained for a few days.

As I stepped out onto the sidewalk, I was hounded by flashes. My eyes widened in astonishment before narrowing, and I raised my free hand to shield them. Paparazzi were calling my name, and my panicked mind wondered about two things: why were they taking photographs of me when I wasn't with Cooper, and where the hell was Dirk?

As if he heard my prayers, the burly man in question suddenly appeared, easily pushing his way through the crowd. He placed his hand on my upper back while his other arm held out and pushed me through. Of course, the shouts and flashes continued, and I kept my head lowered. This was insane, and facing this without Cooper by my side was making my stomach twist uncomfortably. I didn't understand why the paparazzi were after me when I was only friends with a couple of celebrities, and not even with any of them at this time.

Once at the car, Dirk helped me get in the back, and I let out a breath as the door shut, muffling the shouts of the paparazzi.

"Are you alright?" Dirk asked, and I nodded. I was definitely shaken, not having anticipated a bunch of middle-aged men to swarm me outside of a bookstore. I wanted to do nothing more but be in the safe confines of my apartment.

As soon as we pulled into the complex parking lot, I thanked Dirk and practically ran inside the building. I entered the apartment and deposited the bags on the coffee table. I rubbed my face and dropped myself on the couch. My breathing at this point had steadied as the shock of paparazzis shouting and cameras flashing subsided.

This was only my first experience with some rambunctious paparazzi, and I wondered how Cooper and the guys dealt with it on a regular basis. They were so rowdy with me; I could only imagine how they would act around a group of guys. But seriously, had they no decency to stop and ask themselves if that's how you treat another person? And all for what? A damn photograph? The fact that they even came after *me* in the first place was utterly ridiculous because I was nothing but a celebrity's friend. What could they possibly get for snapping a picture or two of me? It didn't make any sense to me, and it probably never would.

To calm myself down some more, I wandered into the kitchen and made myself a cup of tea, a habit I picked up from

Cooper. He really fit into the British stereotype, and because he always made me a cup when he made one for himself, I had developed a likeness for the beverage.

I drank my tea and watched *Iron Man 3*.My phone rang, and a smile tugged at my lips when Cooper's name flashed across my screen.

"Hey," Cooper replied after I greeted him. "We just finished sound check, so I decided to *check* in. Ha. Get it?" I snorted at the lame pun, earning a chuckle from him. "You alright?"

I took another sip of my drink. "Yeah, everything's good," I responded, only partially lying.

"Really?" Cooper asked, and my brows furrowed slightly. "Nothin' interestin' happened?"

I shook my head even though he couldn't see me. "Nope, not really."

"Yeah? Then why'd I see on Twitter that you got *swarmed* by paparazzi today?"

I sighed and placed the mug on a coaster. "To be fair, it happened only a little while ago. I would've told you." I bit the corner of my lip.

I could practically *hear* Cooper raising his brow as he said, "Would've you?"

"No."

Cooper gruffly responded, "You have to, yeah? I don't want to have to go online to find out what's goin' on with you, Kelsey. If somethin' like this happens again, you've gotta let me know, yeah?"

I could tell the genuine concern and worry in his tone, and I smiled, feeling the airy sensation in my chest that only occurred when Cooper was particularly sweet. Nodding slowly, I assured him. "Yeah, yeah, I'll let you know. I'm sorry."

"Don't be sorry, love," he replied, his tone growing soft and soothing. "Just don't keep me out."

The two of us had made some real progress in being open and comfortable with each other, so I assured him that I wouldn't. The last thing I wanted was to push away the only person who seemed to understand me more than I thought possible.

Chapter 17

I woke up to the shrill ringing of my phone and groaned into my pillow. *Is this what a rude awakening is?* With eyes half closed, I answered with a hoarse "Hello?"

"Sorry to disturb you, Ms. Ross." I recognized it was Crosby, the security/doorman downstairs. He had our numbers if he needed to reach us, which was convenient but not when it was so early in the morning. "But there's a young man here who's claiming to know you. He says his name is Logan Waters. Shall I send him up?"

Fully awake now, I sat up, blinking in confusion. *What? Had I heard Crosby right?* I kicked the covers off, frowning. "Uh, yeah, send him up. Thanks."

"Right away, ma'am." Crosby acquiesced before hanging up, and I stared at my phone screen, wondering what the hell was going on. *What was Logan doing here? Why was he here?*

Hastily, I stumbled off the bed and grabbed one Cooper's sweatshirt. I wrapped my hair into a messy bun and quickly made my way downstairs. Logan was here. We hadn't spoken in a while. He caught me completely off guard.

Someone knocked at the front door, and I inhaled deeply before swinging the door open. Logan offered a sheepish smile as he gave me a small, awkward wave. "Uh, hi."

I stared at him in disbelief for a while. "What the hell are you doing in London?"

Logan raised his eyebrows, holding his hands out jokingly. "What? You're not happy to see me?"

I turned around, leaving Logan to follow me. "Not really, not after what you did the last time I saw you."

I crossed my arms over my chest and shot him a pointed a look.

"I'm sorry, Kelsey." Logan sighed, running his fingers through his dark hair. "How many times do I have to say it?"

I shrugged indifferently. "When you mean it."

Logan let out a breath. I watched as his eyes took in his surroundings. He scoffed lightly when his gaze landed on Cooper's shelf of awards. Just by looking at his expression, I was beginning to feel annoyed. "So this is your new home, huh?" He looked out the window that had a nice view of the city below.

"Mmm," I hummed absently, hands digging in the front pocket of my sweatshirt.

"Doesn't it get lonely? When he's not here?"

I shrugged, biting the inside of my cheek briefly. This entire situation felt tense—with Logan attempting to have things go back to the way they were while I was debating on whether or not to forgive him. He was my best friend, but he also shouldn't have kissed me, and on top of that, he just shouldn't be going out of his way to show his obvious dislike of Cooper. It was getting tiring.

"A little bit. But classes keep me busy, and I've made some friends to hang out with." I was referring to the girls who would occasionally come by or go out with me.

Logan nodded slowly as I said this, biting his bottom lip. "So, uh, when do you see Cooper next?" he asked, shifting his weight from one foot to the other.

I sighed impatiently. This wasn't the conversation we were supposed to be having. Not that I was keen to talk about him kissing me, but it was still something we needed to talk about, wasn't it? Wasn't that how we were supposed to move on from it?

"In a week," I told him. "He's flying me out to New York."

Cooper called me yesterday, telling me that Triage would be in New York soon. He thought that it would be fun for me to visit them. I hadn't been to New York before, and the city was a place I'd always wanted to see, so this was the perfect opportunity. Not to mention that I would get to see Cooper, which was already something I was looking forward to.

Logan nodded once again. We sat down opposite each other. His shoulders hunched as he leaned forward, his hands linking. "You know, I saw Cooper, like, a week ago when he was in Miami." This was news to me. I quirked my eyebrows. *Why hadn't Cooper told me?* "He was a total dick."

I blinked. "Excuse me?"

"I'm just saying"—Logan shrugged nonchalantly—"said some shit about me pissing on our friendship?" He frowned. "And then got all high and mighty on me by mentioning the concert he was putting on and left like he was better than me or some shit."

My jaw clenched as I listened to him. Despite being in the biggest band today and constantly having people express their love for him, Cooper always made it a point to remain humble—that was one of the first things I noticed about him when I actually began getting to know him. He was a sweetheart, so Logan's words contradicted Cooper's personality.

Then again, Logan could be a little biased.

So, I released a breath to calm myself down. "That really doesn't sound like him."

Apparently, he didn't like what I said because he scoffed. "You're taking his side?"

My patience was starting to get thin. I groaned. "Logan, I'm not having this fight with you again. Not when it's eight in the morning."

Logan licked his lips, leaning back on the couch as his gaze met mine. He stared at me so intently that I bristled where I sat. "You really like him, don't you?"

I just nodded and thought of his familiar green eyes, his hearty laughter, and his smooth British voice. I found myself smiling fondly. Logan already knew this, though. I had blatantly told him that I liked the Brit.

"I thought you were better than falling for some rock star."

His words immediately wiped the smile off my face. My shoulders slumped as I said, "Why can't you just be happy for me?"

Something in my tone must've prompted the way Logan's own expression turned into one of defeat. Maybe he realized that he may, in fact, be wrong. But to my displeasure, it vanished from his face as quickly as it came. "I just think you're making a mistake."

I glanced away before looking back at Logan and shrugging halfheartedly. "You're supposed to be my best friend. What happened to being there for each other?" Leaning forward, I narrowed my eyes and asked, "If this does turn out to be a mistake, does that mean you're not gonna be there to help me through the heartbreak you're so convinced I'm gonna face? You aren't gonna be there to say I told you so?" Maybe I was being overdramatic with my words, but I didn't know how else to express how I was feeling. Whatever Cooper and I were trying to start, I wanted it to work out;

I didn't want to think of any potential heartaches. But apparently Logan was convinced that was inevitable.

Logan simply shrugged, and I would've thought my words had no effect on him if it weren't for the fact that his Adam's apple was bobbing. He *knew* he was being a jerk, but his stupid machismo and contempt of Cooper were getting in the way of him being a good friend. "Yeah, if you want, I will. But the more you get into your feelings for him, the more world of hurt you're in for."

***

"Not goin' to lie. Logan bein' there doesn't exactly bode well with me."

I sighed and sat on the couch, propping my feet up on the coffee table. "It's not like I saw this coming, Coop," I said with a light, tired laugh, "but he's gone now, so it's done."

"But he could've tried some—"

"He didn't though." I assured him, knowing what he was going to say as I lowered the volume of the television. Cooper wasn't at all thrilled about knowing that Logan had shown up in London while he was in America, but I knew I should tell him. Besides, Logan had only come for a day, wanting to hash things out with me. We didn't get anything done, really, because our friendship was still strained and he still wasn't happy about Cooper and me. Honestly, it was a waste of flight fare on his part, but I wasn't going to tell him that. That would just be uncalled for on my end, and Logan's chalked up enough of that in our friendship. Even our damn goodbye hug in the complex parking lot was awkward and tense.

It was sad, the more I thought about it. Logan and I used to be inseparable, but ever since Cooper came into the picture, Logan adopted a whole new condescending attitude directed strictly towards Cooper, and it was exhausting being stuck in the middle of it all. Why were guys seemingly stuck in a perpetual masculinity and superiority contest? The problem was, I knew, mostly Logan because of his tendency of picking fights; he could be really hotheaded, and that had come out extremely in the past few months. Honestly, I think it's because he feels some sort of threat when he sees Cooper, because if he likes me, then my relationship with Cooper was setting him off—especially now that actual feelings between Cooper and I were coming into play. Logan obviously wasn't handling that well, and instead of accepting it, he was—as Cooper put it—pissing on our friendship.

Cooper huffed on the other end of the phone. "Can never be too careful with that bloke."

I chuckled unexpectedly. "Cooper Shaw, are you jealous?" I mused knowingly. My grin widened when he was silent for a while.

Then he stated solidly, "Yes."

I blushed, feeling giddy. It was incredible—halfway across the world and Cooper still had the ability to make me blush. I knew Cooper had *some* type of feelings for me, but him actually being jealous was pretty endearing. "You don't need to be." I assured him.

He let out a breath before murmuring his acceptance and then asking, "You excited for New York?"

My grin widened. I absently twirled a lock of my hair around my finger as I told him just how much I was looking forward to visiting the city.

"We can go wherever you feel like—Empire State Building, the museums, you name it."

My heart jumped in my chest. I found Cooper utterly endearing for wanting to go out with me in New York despite the fact that we both knew just how crazy paparazzi could be in a place like that. Still, I didn't want him to feel obligated to do all of that. "That's sweet, Coop, but you don't have—"

He immediately cut me off. "I want to."

***

Cooper

Knowing Logan had been in London, only if it was for a day and a half, while I was in the United States annoyed me to no end. It was all I could think about as I sat on the couch in the living room of our hotel suite. The lads around me kept themselves entertained, quite loudly, oblivious to the raging thoughts going on in my mind. I stared out the window where I could see the towering buildings of New York City.

The thing was—Logan *knew* Kelsey. He'd been a part of her life for years. She shared with him most of her childhood memories, and that, pathetically enough, made me feel uneasy. She didn't have feelings for him the way he did, and I had to keep reminding myself of that. Their friendship was strained. Not that I was glad she was having trouble with her best friend—I wanted things for her to be okay, but I also wanted Logan to back the bloody hell off and stick to being only her best friend. She would forgive him eventually, and I knew that.

Truthfully, I was afraid of their closeness. What if Logan was adamant about insisting that Kelsey and I would not work out? I would assume as her best friend, he'd want her to be happy, but the mildly paranoid side of me wondered if he would still try to interfere with our relationship. What if he talked her into not giving us a try at all?

I frowned, plucking my guitar absentmindedly. Honestly, I had to give Kelsey more credit. The two of us, over the past six months or so, had come a long way from since the first day we met. She went through a tragedy I couldn't even imagine, but she was still smiling, still laughing. And everytime she did so because of something I did, I felt a swell of pride for being able to cheer her up.

I might not have known Kelsey for most of her life like Logan, but that didn't mean I was any less worthy of being in her life.

"Dunno if you're thinkin' hard or just constipated." Spencer interrupted my thoughts, joining me on the couch.

I rolled my eyes and leaned back. "Thinkin' hard."

"About?"

I shrugged, not exactly wanting to disclose my thoughts about my insecurities when it came to the whole Kelsey-Logan debacle. I knew outside opinions, even if they came from my best friend, would probably only complicate my mind. I felt pathetic about obsessing over this. They already knew of Logan's feelings towards Kelsey but not their full extent. I didn't want to hear their thoughts on the matter.

So, I just opted to say, "Kelsey's comin' today." A smile grew on my face.

"I know." The only blonde member of the band nodded. "You goin' to take her out?"

I released a breath, nodding. "Fingers crossed we don't get mobbed when we do."

Spencer nodded, rolling his blue eyes. "Don't count on it, mate."

We then watched the other lads who were busy playing video games on the Xbox. He, Julian, and Miles were shouting profanities at each other as they played a football game. I shook my head and thought about Kelsey again. Before I could help myself, I quietly blurted, "She deserves the best, y'know?"

Spencer's gaze returned to me. I could feel it, and from my peripheral, I could see him furrowing his brows, not understanding what I was trying to say. "And you what? You don't think you can give her the best?"

Sometimes my best mates knew me better than I cared to admit. So I stayed silent.

Spencer let out a deep sigh and turned to face me. "Coop, you seriously aren't thinkin' that Logan bloke can give her the best and you can't, are you? That's bloody ridiculous."

I shrugged, suddenly feeling stupid for worrying. Honestly, I wasn't usually concerned with this stuff. Girls had never been an issue before. If I saw a girl I liked, I'd ask her out if I wanted something long-term, and if not, the occasional hook-up was enjoyable as well.

"I don't know, Spence. I feel like I'm out of my league here."

Spencer patted my shoulder comfortingly. "It's only a matter of spending more time together, mate," he told me, offering a smile. "Honestly, the two of you got, like, together faster than I thought, and I'm happy for both of you. Don't start doubtin' it. Just…go with the flow." He laughed lightly.

His words brought a small smile to my face. Spencer was right; it was all about getting to know each other more, just like any other couple would do when they start to get together. Kelsey and I were just in the beginning stages of becoming a real couple, and while we had become friends, it's only a matter of us moving forward from there at our own pace. Maybe if I just stopped stressing myself out over things that weren't completely in my control—especially since I already had to deal with the everyday stress of our job—I could finally fucking relax a bit.

***

"Mmm, what was that for?" Kelsey grinned after pulling away from the kiss I couldn't hold myself back from. She peered up at me as I felt her fingers loosely link with mine.

We were standing in the middle of her hotel bedroom. The door was closed to give us some privacy from the other lads, since we all were staying in a large suite with multiple rooms. Kelsey had just arrived from London. When the lads and I got back to the hotel after doing an MTV interview, she was there waiting for us. One of the security details had gone to the airport to pick her and Dirk. When Kelsey finished hugging all of the guys, I selfishly pulled her into her room and kissed her then and there.

I smiled down at her, shrugging. "I'm just glad you're here." Her smile widened as she glanced away to most likely hide the blush on her cheeks. I chortled softly before asking, "You hungry?"

Her gaze met mine once again, and she offered a sheepish grin. "I could kill for some pizza."

As her wish was my command, the two of us left the hotel with Dirk and Paul. We headed to the pizza place I frequented whenever I came to New York. As soon as we stepped out of the lobby and onto the sidewalk, we were instantly greeted by a plethora of fans.

Kelsey squeezed my hand briefly before allowing Dirk to guide her to the SUV parked along the sidewalk. I stopped to take pictures with as many of the girls that were there. After taking a number of selfies, giving out hugs, and signing phone cases and such, I thanked the girls for being there and bid them goodbye.

Before the door the SUV slid shut behind me, I heard some of the girls shout, "I love you, Cooper!" and I happily shouted my love back for them.

Leaning back in the leather seat, I looked at Kelsey, who was smirking at me. I asked what she was looking at, laughing lightly, and she just shrugged and smiled knowingly. "Nothing, Mr. Rock Star," she said in a secretive tone before turning her gaze out the window. I snorted and shook my head.

For the next hour or so, Kelsey and I filled each other in on things that had been going on while we were away from each other. She told me about all of the assignments and exams she was taking, as well as the new books she was beginning to read and the shows she had started. I filled her in on how the new album was progressing and how Rafael and Julian would have hoverboard races through the floors of the arenas we performed in and kept score on who won each time. So far Rafael was beating Julian by two arenas.

The conversations continued as we entered the pizza parlor, Joe's. We ordered our pizza slices and sat down at a small round table in the back corner of the place. Dirk and Paul sat a few tables away to give us our privacy, enjoying their own pizzas. Kelsey and I paid no attention to the one or two people amongst the other patrons of this place that were throwing glances of recognition our way.

Honestly, our conversation got rid of all the worries I had concerned myself with lately.

"You comin' to both shows?" I asked Kelsey as we threw the paper plates and napkins in the garbage. I made it a point to thank the guys behind the counter as we left.

Kelsey snorted, rolling her eyes as if I had asked her something ridiculous. "Obviously."

When we stepped out of the parlor, I wasn't surprised when we heard shouting all around us. My hand instinctively grabbed Kelsey's as Dirk and Paul guarded us. My jaw clenched as I felt the familiar annoyance that always came when the paparazzi swarmed us. They always reminded me of vultures.

They shoved us as we tried to make our way to the parked car. The middle-aged men tried to get as close as they could to us while shoving their huge cameras in our faces. They were more or less blocked by Dirk and Paul who demanded everyone to keep their distance. Obviously, no one would listen to both.

"Cooper, over here!"

"How's the tour?"

"Smile, you two!"

"Are you together?"

"Kelsey, is it true you cheated on Cooper?"

Kelsey squeezed my hand in discomfort, and my jaw clenched tightly. My head snapped up, ready to say something, but Paul shot me a look while squeezing my shoulder. Inhaling sharply through my nose, I allowed our security details to guide us safely into the car. It wasn't until the door was shut behind us that Kelsey let out a breath. She let go of my hand and rubbed her face.

I looked at Kelsey worriedly, knowing that she wasn't used to or comfortable with the hounding of paparazzi. Unfortunately, no matter how much I hated it, she would have to get used to this lifestyle. It was something I had to warn my mum and sister about because it happened to them quite a bit too, just because they were related to me. Kelsey has become someone known within the fandom, consequentially a person of interest to the paparazzi as well. And now that we were together, she was suddenly more interesting to them. I knew this wasn't something someone should have to get used to, but she unfortunately would.

I also knew that the last question bothered her. Someone had spotted Logan and Kelsey when he was leaving London and she hugged him goodbye.

There were times when some paparazzi hid in front of the gates of my flat complex. It was something I had grown used to and didn't think twice about. I had forgotten to mention it to Kelsey, and of course, someone had caught a picture of her hugging Logan goodbye. It had stirred some rumors up on Twitter, but no one really paid it much attention because thanks to Kelsey's existing social media posts, they knew he was her best friend. They obviously didn't know, though, that they had been fighting lately. Some nosy gossip websites tried to make something out of nothing, but it went away fairly quickly and without any trouble, so we didn't think anything of it. Clearly, the paparazzi outside didn't get the memo, and for the first time, I wished this part of being famous didn't exist—not for my benefit, only for Kelsey's.

Chapter 18

Kelsey

New York was everything I imagined and more. My time out with Cooper and the guys was short because the paparazzi would get rowdy. We mostly just drove to wherever we wanted to go. Just like he promised, Cooper accompanied me to the places I wanted to see like the Museum of Modern Art and the Empire State Building. Of course, I couldn't help but think how Mom would love all the beautiful art pieces, and how she'd be terrified of being at the top of the Empire State because of her fear of heights. Missing her was like an ever-present ache in my chest, never gone but intensifying when I actively thought of her.

But Mom didn't like sadness. So I smiled, because she would want me to.

Along with our touristy activities, we even had dinner one night at the Sugar Factory with the guys. There were even times when I brought out my sketchbook and sat on the balcony of our hotel room and drew the New York skyline.

We were only in the city for about two days, but in that amount of time, we had gotten lots of things done. Cooper took me to some places, kissed me some, and we both were just enjoying each other's company, honestly. I had almost forgotten the thrill of being around the guys while they were on tour, always hyperactive, always doing something, and the concerts were amazing. It was so exciting, seeing them perform after about weeks of not seeing them on stage. I hadn't realized I missed this so much until the first New York show. The crowd was wild, and each show ended with fireworks and confetti.

As I exited the bathroom and entered the room, I heard the ending of Cooper's phone conversation. He had a habit of hanging out in my room. "Yeah, with the black bathroom tiles." He paused, shooting me a smile as I wandered to the dresser next to the TV. I brushed my hair as I shot him a curious look. "No, that's brilliant, actually. The sooner it's ready, the better. Alright, cheers."

"Who was that?" I winced slightly as the teeth of the comb got caught in a small knot of hair.

"That—" Cooper grinned "—was my real estate agent. He was lettin' me know when the new house was going to be ready."

I stopped, eyes widening. "The new house?" *Was he serious?* "When did you buy a new house?"

Cooper chuckled. He explained to me that he had wanted to move out of the apartment before I came. He put it on hold when everything between us happened and I moved in. He had found the perfect house but didn't want to move just yet because I was adjusting to my new life in London and he didn't want the news of a house to disrupt me anymore, or make me feel as though I was interrupting something. I sucked in a breath at the kindness behind that gesture. But if he didn't sign the lease soon, the previous owners might give it to someone else offering more money, so he had to think fast.

I continued to stare at him in silence, and a worried expression washed over Cooper's face. He hastily got to his feet. "I know you've already adjusted to so much by movin' to London and all, but I want you to know that I want you to keep staying with me. You don't have to go live with my—"

"Cooper, it's fine." I cut him off and offered him a reassuring smile because, really, it was totally okay with me. Besides, I didn't want to be the reason why he passed on buying his first house. It was a significant milestone in any person's life, and I would've felt so guilty if he didn't do it because of me. And his offer of still wanting me to live with him brought a fire to my cheeks. We were a bit backwards, weren't we? Already living together and then starting a relationship. But it worked. Somehow, it did. "That's so exciting."

He looked at me with a quirked eyebrow. "You sure?"

I laughed and nodded, hoping he believed me.

"Great, and, really, it's not too far from the shopping centers, and there's also a book cafe nearby as well," he said. I raised my eyebrows, wondering if that was in his criteria when he was first looking for a new house.

He laughed sheepishly. "I may have double-checked for your benefit."

"You've thought this whole thing through, haven't you?"

"Basically." Cooper shrugged, looking quite proud of himself with that boyish grin on his face. He leaned forward and kissed me. I melted into him as I wrapped my hands around his neck. I felt flutters in my stomach as I took in his familiar scent blissfully.

When we pulled away, I tried to fight the smile on my face. "What was that for?" I whispered.

His answer ignited a fire within me that I didn't feel the need to put out. "I'm happy."

***

Please, Kelsey, just talk to me.

My phone beeped again, and I sighed.

Come on, Kels. You're being a little ridiculous.

My eyes narrowed. If he thought that would make me call him, he had another thing coming.

We have to talk. You need to hear me out.

I held my phone and wondered if I should call Logan or not. This whole situation was getting out of hand. Every time we spoke, he would spew out some condescending remark about Cooper or my growing relationship with him, and it was so exhausting. I mean, I hadn't even told Cooper that I liked him—we kissed and all but never actually *admitted* our feelings for each other—yet Logan was already judging me for confessing to Cooper.

Wasn't that how friendships worked? You would tell your best friend about the person you liked before you confessed to them? Logan was making the whole process so much more complicated than it needed to be.

After chewing the crap out of my lower lip, I decided to give Logan the benefit of the doubt.

He picked up on the second ring. "Kelsey, hey."

"Yeah, hi," I responded, unable to even feign a casual or friendly tone. "You texted?" The bitchiness in my tone was clear as day yet I couldn't hold back from it.

"Texted? I also called and tried to reach you on Twitter. Your skills at ignoring someone are on the professional level."

I refrained from rolling my eyes even though he couldn't see me. "I think it's a fitting response towards you being rude to Cooper and your overall shitty attitude."

"Kelsey—"

"I mean, you've been rude to him to his face and mine. You're supposed to be my best friend, Logan. I know I was against moving to London and living with him, but you should be happy for me for getting over it and actually getting along with Cooper. How can you—"

"Because I love you."

I froze, and the phone almost slipped from my hand. *He what who now? I couldn't have heard him right.* He just threw us into the oldest cliché in the book. My stomach churned violently, feeling my heart quicken its pace in panicked incredulity.

Shit, shit, shit. Part of me was hoping that this was some sort of joke. I wouldn't believe it, though, because it was the side of me that believed Hogwarts was real.

He loved me.

Never in my life did I see him that way. I only ever saw him as a friend or a brother, yet here he was—confessing his feelings to me over the damn phone. I could feel a headache coming on.

"Logan." I honestly didn't even know what to say. I was absolutely floored. "I don't—I'm not—"

"I know you're trying out this new relationship with Cooper." He cut me off. "But do you genuinely like him or are you just projecting because of your living situation? I mean, you and I both know you can, like, find somewhere else to live. Maybe even move back here and—"

"Oh my god, stop." I snapped. "Are you serious? I literally can't believe I'm hearing this." I shook my head. "For your information, I *do* like Cooper, okay? More than you think. And let me remind you that my living situation was something my mom wanted for me before she died." Bringing my mother into this wasn't fair, but I didn't know how else I could get through Logan at this point. He kept blatantly telling me to completely disregard what she asked of me, and while I knew she had initially wanted me to live with Cooper's family, she was more than happy about my staying with just Cooper. She had wanted this for me and Logan telling me to just go back on it felt like he was asking me to spit on her grave. "So you suggesting that I just leave London, leave *Cooper* is basically you asking me to break the last promise I made with my mother. How fucking dare you?"

I ran my fingers through my hair. Honestly, I always tried to be civil with Logan every time he made a remark about Cooper, but this was too much.

"I'm not going to apologize for not returning your feelings the way you want me to. I'm *not* going to feel guilty for not feeling the way *you think* I should feel. Don't call me again, Logan. There was a line, and you've crossed it."

I hung up, tossing my phone to the other side of the bed. I wondered what in the hell was going on and how did things get so screwed up so fast. And I wondered if this was it, if I had officially lost the one person who'd been my best friend for as long as I can remember.

***

Cooper

Something was wrong. We had reached that point in our friendship—partnership?—for me to pick up hints when something was bothering Kelsey. She barely contributed to the conversations in our past few video chatting sessions and phone calls. I told her all about tour life and that the making of our album was at its end stages. She just seemed off, and I didn't say anything in hopes that she would tell me herself. It had been days now, and not a word about what was bothering her had come up. Not to mention, the past day or so, she hadn't texted or called like she normally would. Kelsey was an open book, I had come to learn, and every time something upset her, she would withdraw into herself. Those who didn't know her might just think she was generally a reserved person, but I knew something was up.

I opened FaceTime on my laptop, taking a breath as I clicked on her name. In the distance, I could hear the laughter of the lads who were outside having a match of football in the parking lot of the arena we were going to perform in later tonight.

The video call finally connected. Kelsey was sitting on the couch. Instantly, I recognized my black Nike sweatshirt, her smaller frame practically swimming in it.

"Hey, stranger. Long time no see," I greeted, trying to sound playful though my words held some truth.

"Hey, sorry," she replied, her tone hinting at some tiredness. "I've had lots of assignments to work on."

I was about to call out her lie since it was mid-July and summer holidays were starting, but then I remembered she had signed up for some online summer courses.

"Is that all?" I asked, furrowing my brows. "Everythin' else is alright?"

Kelsey ran her fingers through her blonde hair as she gave a tight-lipped smile. "Yeah, everything's great. Why do you ask?"

A bit unsure that I read this situation wrong, I shrugged just as I heard Julian very loudly call Spencer a *fucking shithead*. "I dunno—you seem a bit…off."

Another forced smile appeared on Kelsey's face, and I wondered if she honestly thought that would fool me. I mean, I like to get some credit here. "Don't worry about it, Coop. It's nothing."

That just meant it was *something*. I silently stared at her on my laptop screen, trying to read her through the pixels and wondering what could possibly set her mood off. Only one thing—one person—came into mind, and realization dawned on me. "Is it Logan?" I blurted.

Kelsey looked taken aback. Something undecipherable flashed in her eyes, and she briskly responded, "I'm not talking to him right now."

Was she ever? It seemed like they were more strangers than friends at this point. "Did somethin' happ—"

"I said it's nothing, Cooper." Kelsey cut me off, and I blinked in surprise. She squirmed slightly, looking riled up as if something was incessantly bothering her and not giving her a second to breathe. "Look, I've got an essay due in a couple of hours, and I haven't started it yet. I'll talk to you later, alright?"

She didn't even give me the chance to say goodbye before disconnecting the call.

Chapter 19

Kelsey

Ignoring Logan had become a sort of habit. It was sad to admit that, but it was true, what with the constant arguments the two of us were getting into. The distance made the feat easy to do so.

Ignoring Cooper, however, was more of a challenge than I had anticipated. I had gotten so used to talking to him whenever the time was right that I just felt out of balance when I didn't do so. So I stuck to sparingly texting him, if only for the sake of communication, and I managed to avoid any phone calls.

I knew if I talked to Cooper, I would blurt out what had happened with Logan. That was not something I wanted to tell Cooper over the phone—if at all. It wasn't like I was going to act on Logan's confession. Telling Cooper would only serve to bother him, I knew. He needed to focus on his tour.

I wondered if it would be better if I just told Cooper, though. We were progressing in *some* ways relationship-wise; we both had made it obvious the feelings between us were worth figuring out, worth acting upon. Being honest with each other would only help us out in the end.

I groaned and rubbed my face.

What's more cliché than a person falling in love with their best friend? A goddamn love triangle no one asked to be a part of. Just my luck, I was involved in both.

I was heating up the leftover vegetable stew I made last night. As I waited next to the microwave, I felt a random surge of guilt for snapping at Cooper two days ago. I wasn't fully ignoring him, only avoiding physically speaking to him by just texting him whenever I could. The conversations were dry and awkward, but at least there wasn't a total loss of communication.

Doesn't mean I didn't want to slap myself for causing the hurt look on his face right before I had disconnected our FaceTime call.

Restless for some reason, I ate my lunch by leaning against the counter in the kitchen. I sighed after taking a few bites. The two weeks I'd been back in London felt lonely, but I tried my best to entertain myself by spending time with Heidi, Dawn, and Noelle. The girls didn't know about my situation with Logan but were more than willing to gossip about my progress with Cooper. And for someone who didn't really have girl friends before, I milked it for all its worth.

I went into the living to look for my phone. I figured that it was probably in between the cushions. As I dug my hand between them, I heard a familiar voice ask, "Missin' something?"

I jumped and swiveled, finding Cooper. *What the hell was he doing here?* He was supposed to be on tour. His facial hair had grown a bit, covering his jaw and a bit of his neck. He dropped his black duffel bag next to his feet. "Cooper," I dumbly said, blinking once, "what're you doing here?"

"We have some time off"—he took a few steps forward—"before we head off to Canada."

I chuckled breathily. Even though I was tense, he was still a welcome sight. "I wasn't expecting to see you so soon."

He shrugged off his beloved leather jacket, revealing his tattooed arms. "A simple 'I missed you' would've sufficed." He smirked.

I smiled as I walked closer to him. Forgetting my stresses for a moment, I placed my hands on his biceps and said, "I missed you."

I pressed my lips to his, and he instantly returned the kiss. His growing beard scratched against my skin, though it wasn't by any means unpleasant. This was what I was yearning for—Cooper's kisses, his touch, that familiar woodsy scent, *him*. All of my worries melted away as I realized that he was what I needed to relax.

When we pulled back, Cooper smirked cheekily. "Now that's a welcome home kiss."

I laughed and pushed him back. "Are you hungry?"

Cooper's smirk widened as he raised his eyebrows. "I'm actually cravin' some grilled cheese if I'm bein' honest."

I ignored his protests of making the sandwich himself and prepared it. Seeing Cooper back so soon was unexpected but not totally unwelcome. I felt my stomach churn .Having him here, what happened with Logan would slip sooner rather than later. I wouldn't be surprised if Cooper found out before the end of the night.

I took the plate into the living room where he lay on the couch, shoes off while watching an episode of *MasterChef*. He sat up when he saw me walk in and chirped his thanks. I lay on the other couch, watching the television show with Cooper and feeling comforted by his presence alone.

It was funny; the silence that had dawned on us wasn't tense until Cooper finished his sandwich and asked, "What happened to you a couple of days ago?"

Logan's words instantly echoed in my head, the words I didn't want to hear. My hands clenched into fists. "I told you; nothing happened," I said firmly, grabbing the empty plate from his hands and walking into the kitchen. While I knew this conversation was coming up, it didn't mean I was ready for it. Suddenly, I wished I was at the bookstore with Dawn; she had a newfound love for crime novels.

Of course, Cooper followed me as I approached the dishwasher. "Do you honestly expect me to believe that, Kelsey?"

Putting the plate in the dishwasher, I muttered, "I was hoping you would."

"I don't," Cooper unhelpfully said, crossing his arms. He looked intimidating as he stood there, but I knew he was anything but. "Please just tell me what's been bothering you."

I stayed silent, pressing my lips together in contemplation.

He said, "I know it probably has somethin' to do with Logan. So you might as well tell me before I end up calling the bugger myself."

The blood in my veins froze. Cooper had already brought up Logan during the video chat. I hoped he would forget about him for a moment, but of course, Logan was the first person Cooper would assume had something to do with setting me off. He had every reason to, to be honest. Cooper obviously had an idea that something was wrong between us, so it *should* make telling him somewhat easier. I mean, the two of us weren't in a real relationship yet, so why was I being so overdramatic about things?

I wished Mom was here. I just knew that she would make confronting my problems seem easy; her encouragement would definitely help in this moment.

Cooper stared at me expectantly with raised eyebrows. I sighed and scratched the back of my neck awkwardly. "Look, Logan's just been…confused…lately, and I'm sure—"

"Confused about what?" Cooper narrowed his green eyes suspiciously.

Oh goddamn. "Uh, you know—his, um, feelings?" In reality, I knew *exactly* what he was feeling.

"Feelings about what, Kelsey?"

I rolled my lower lip into my mouth. The way he was asking these questions made me wonder if he already knew the answer to them. "Me."

Cooper inhaled deeply, and I could notice the muscle in his jaw tightening. "Why would Logan be confused about his feelings for you?"

There he goes again asking questions he seems to know the answers to.

When I wasn't quick enough to respond, Cooper tilted his head ever so slightly. "What did he say to you?"

Oh fucking hell, I might as well just come out and say it.

The tension was building up, and it was doing nothing but churning up nerves and awkwardness. I finally confessed. "He said he loves me."

Cooper was still as my words hung in the air, heavy over our heads. It felt suffocating. The silence was almost agonizing. He stared at me with slightly scrunched eyebrows.

"I'm *honestly* going to sock him in the fuckin' face."

My eyes widened. He clenched his fists at his sides as if he was actually prepared to punch Logan at that moment. Yeah, because violence was definitely the answer to this situation.

"Come on, Coop," I said and laughed nervously. "You know I don't think of Logan that way."

"Don't you?" Cooper retorted icily. "You two have been best friends for God knows how long. Are you tellin' me it's a complete impossibility for you to return Logan's feelin's?"

Where the hell is this coming from?

Cooper was usually the one to keep his cool, so this was coming out of left field for me. I stared at him incredulously. "Yes, Cooper, I'm telling you it's impossible for me to have feelings for Logan," I said firmly, hoping that he understood. "I've only ever seen him as a brother, okay?"

Cooper shrugged.

I wondered how I ended up in this mess. For once, couldn't things be simple?

"Clearly somethin' went on for Logan to see you as somethin' other than a sister."

"I can't speak for Logan—" I chose my next words carefully so he would realize that I really did mean them "—but I like *you*, Cooper."

***

Cooper

"I like *you*, Cooper."

As soon as those words escaped Kelsey's mouth, it was like all of the tension, unease, and anger I felt previously had disappeared in the blink of an eye. She looked at me with her bright blue eyes, silently saying that she hoped I understood exactly what she meant. All I could do was stare at her.

Having Kelsey actually *say* that she liked me instead of just going around with the thought unconfirmed in my mind felt like a weight was being lifted off both my shoulders and heart. The two of us had been kissing, and I think a part of us never actually said anything about it because it may have been a conversation neither of us were sure how to have. I think both of us were hesitant on officially labeling our relationship because we already lived together, and dating someone you were living with could have some complications. Normally you date someone and *then* move in together, but mine and Kelsey's circumstances were backwards. It didn't help that neither of us had been in a relationship serious enough where moving in had ever been a step to consider taking. And we wanted to stay living together, especially after I told her about the new house and we had a conversation about if she wanted to go to Birmingham to live with my parents, But Kelsey wanted to stay here, and I was glad.

We got along perfectly fine as housemates, but that had always been as strangers slowly becoming friends. Would things change once we were in an established relationship?

Or was I just worrying myself by over thinking?

Our circumstances were vastly different and strange than that of a normal couple. And maybe because of that, there had been a part of me that had this fear stemming from the insecurity that Kelsey may not feel for me the way I felt for her. She completely proved me wrong.

She liked me and didn't feel that way about Logan. While this wasn't any good on Logan's end, I couldn't help but be happy and relieved.

The reassurance her words brought spread a comforting warmth through my chest while the prickling annoyance I felt towards Logan disappeared as my gaze met Kelsey's. She stared at me expectantly as she waited for me to speak. I took two long strides towards her, cupped her face in my hands, and pulled her in for a searing kiss that I hoped would convey my feelings. Words couldn't possibly do justice to my emotions.

The force had her stumbling back as my left arm wound around her waist, holding her in place. Her lips moved against mine, and heat spread through my body.

We pulled away, her hands against my chest as she tried to even her breathing. She stared at me with the most beautiful blue eyes I had ever seen. "Going from being my housemate to my girlfriend is quite the development, huh?" I smiled as she laughed.

"I don't think this is what my mom had in mind when she planned this." She grinned, wrapping her hands around my torso, and it was a relief to see the happiness in her eyes outshine the longing she felt for her mother.

I pecked her nose. "I like to think she wouldn't mind."

Kelsey's grip around my waist tightened as she earnestly agreed, "I don't think she would."

Chapter 20

Kelsey

The rest of the day following Cooper's arrival was spent in pure peace. We ate food that we cooked for dinner together, watched movies, snuggled under the blankets on the couch, and of course, kissed. Our time was spent in what I liked to call *soft moments*—lots of cuddling and touching and basking in the comfort the other's presence. It was after we *officially* got together when I realized the little things he did. Like when we were cuddling on the couch, he winded our legs together comfortably and kept an arm around me. As we watched TV, Cooper would rest his cheek on the top of my head, and sometimes he would also interlace our fingers together. It was excitingly wonderful.

Triage was on a mini break from their North American tour. When they would get back on the road, they would finish the rest of the tour. Cooper had also taken this opportunity to inform me that the house that he had bought for us was ready, and it was only a matter of us packing our things here—including kitchen appliances and things—and bringing them over. The new house was fully furnished. Cooper had picked out some of them. We could wait until he got back from tour to move in, but the prospect of moving had suddenly gotten me really excited.

It gave me something to do other than sitting around and doing my coursework and reading books. Cooper was hesitant, saying there's no way he'd be able to unpack things before going back on the road. I managed to convince him by saying that I could do it. I *wanted* to do it. After telling him I didn't want to see the house until it was moving day—I wanted to be surprised—we began packing.

Cooper had managed to bring up lots of boxes. I was in the middle of packing the plates in the kitchen when someone knocked on the front door, the sound barely heard over the music we were playing. Glancing up briefly, I saw Cooper run across the living room to answer. "What're you two doin' here?"

"Oh yeah, cheers, mate. Nice to see you too," Miles's unmistakable and sarcastic voice responded. I chuckled lightly as I wrapped up a plate in newspaper before putting it in a box.

Just then, Noelle wandered into the kitchen, grinning excitedly. She announced in a singing tone, "We're here to help you pack!"

I groaned in relief. You never realize how much stuff you have until you need to pack them all. Noelle and I worked in there as the guys did who knows what. We listened to The Weeknd and caught up. We had last seen each other about four days ago.

When I taped the box of plates and labeled it, I heard Cooper's voice shout from somewhere in the apartment, "Kelsey, what do you want me t'do with your makeup?"

My eyes widened briefly. I wondered why the hell he was touching any of that.

Noelle hissed. "Get up there and don't let him touch any of it!"

I passed Miles, who had taken it upon himself to pack up Cooper's awards, and ran up the stairs two steps at a time. In the bedroom, Cooper had cleared out most of his side of the vanity table, leaving only a few things out. My side, however, was cluttered with my things. "Don't touch anything." I demanded, extremely territorial over my makeup. Cooper raised his hands in defense, watching with mirth dancing in his eyes as I approached the table. He may be gentle with his guitar, but there was no knowing what he'd do to my makeup.

He began to clean out the closet, mostly focusing on what to do with his shoes. I put away my makeup, save for the products I used on a daily basis. We had been at this for hours now, and my hands were cramping from packing and taping boxes up, but my excitement for this move kept me going.

Hours later, we had finished packing, more or less. There were still some things here and there that we needed to pack, but for the most part, it was over. I guess the extra hands Miles and Noelle provided really helped. By eleven at night, Cooper and I were exhausted from packing. We haven't had dinner yet. We didn't have any leftovers nor did we want to cook anything. A couple of plates and utensils had been left unpacked for us to use, but then Cooper had the great idea of going to McDonald's. So we got into the car and drove. There were no security details with us because it was a Wednesday night and who was going to be around a McDonald's to spot Cooper?

When we arrived at the twenty-four-hour fast food joint, both of us were relieved to see that practically no one was there. The employees—all middle-aged women—didn't spare Cooper a glance as we ordered. While he paid, my eyes trailed over to a couple of old ladies sitting at a table near the door. One of them, as she ate her

French fries, was staring at Cooper in adorable surprise while saying something to her friend, and I laughed.

As Cooper stuffed his credit card back in his wallet, he shot me a questioning look. "What's so funny?"

I smiled as the cashier handed us cups for our sodas. "I think that lady over there's a fan of yours."

Cooper's brows furrowed as he glanced over his shoulder, and he chuckled. "Oh God." He looked down, and from his expression, I could tell that he was wishing he wasn't blushing. It only widened my grin.

When we got our food and sat down at a corner booth, I delved into my meal of a chicken sandwich and fries. I groaned in satisfaction as Cooper ate his Big Mac.

"Can we go in the play place after?" Cooper asked.

I stopped eating midway. He stared at me innocently, and I scoffed bemusedly. "You're kidding, right?"

Cooper shook his head, looking dead serious. "I'm actually not. It makes me feel like a kid again."

This time, I laughed in disbelief. "I don't think those places are meant for twenty-year-olds."

"Please?"

"We'll literally get kicked out."

"So?" Harry shrugged and sipped his drink before smiling boyishly. "I'd hate to do so, but I can always pull the 'I'm famous card."

I snorted after swallowing a bite of my sandwich and wiping my mouth with a napkin. "Aren't you modest?"

He offered a pleading look, lips pouting. I groaned, giving in. When he saw my agreement, he grinned and whispered an excited yes. I shook my head in amusement.

Cooper and I threw away our trash. Since the play place was towards the back and was obstructed from the view of the workers behind the counter, we were able to sneak into it. It had colorful slides, tunnels, and netted bridges. I hadn't been in one of these things since I was nine, and I wasn't going to lie, it was kind of exciting when we kicked off our shoes.

As I placed mine in a cubby, Cooper shot me a wolfish smirk before running up the green tube slide, disappearing from my view. I heard the thudding of his feet against the plastic followed by his excited laugh. I laughed, feeling like a kid again. I glanced back at the restaurant area, double-checking to make sure no one was looking.

"What're you waitin' for?"

I looked up. Cooper was looking down at me through one of the corner tunnels.

I snorted in amusement before climbing up. Unlike Cooper, I took the actual plastic platforms that made it all the way to the top. The nets around them prevented anyone from falling off the sides. On my hands and knees, I crawled into the tube. When I couldn't see Cooper through any of the three tunnels that it led to, I called out, "Where the hell are you?"

"You gotta find me!" His singsong voice echoed throughout the empty arena, and I rolled my eyes.

I crawled and climbed, looking down the multiple tubes and dead ends for the six-foot-tall singer. Could he really fit through any of these places? "This is ridiculous," I muttered. I couldn't stop myself from laughing lightly even though my palms and knees had begun hurting.

After a couple more seconds of crawling, I finally found him. He was in the little portion that had the exterior of a helicopter. It had a steering wheel that moved the plastic propeller. He was sitting against the wall, knees brought up and arms resting on top of them. I sighed in relief when I caught sight of him. "I see you've found me." He grinned as I crawled inside. I sat against the wall across from him, which didn't put that much of a distance between us.

"Mmm." I hummed, crossing my legs and resting my hands on my lap. "Was all of this necessary?" I glanced around the inside of the green playpen. The bright color was slightly reflecting on our skin.

"It's fun," Cooper answered softly and smiled. "Doin' childish stuff like this sometimes is better than bein' famous."

I tilted my head to the side, waiting for him to elaborate.

"It's what we get reduced to, y'know? We're doin' what we love, and I'm so grateful for that, don't get me wrong."

I nodded.

"But because we're famous, we're supposed to act a certain way because we've got young and impressionable fans. We're under this pressure that if we make one wrong move, then everythin's gonna blow up in our faces and everythin' we've worked for is gonna be gone." Cooper shrugged.

"Sometimes I'd rather be the weird twenty-year-old who likes to play in a McDonald's than someone who's been reduced to nothing but…being famous."

I pulled my lower lip into my mouth. Honestly, I had never thought of it that way or that this was how Cooper felt when it came to his career. He was always so upbeat about his life—except when it came to the paparazzi hounding him—that it never crossed my mind that there could be times when Cooper was afraid it'd be taken away from him. I never thought that he just wanted to be *normal*.

"Your fans don't see you like that, though." I tried to soothe him, offering a comforting smile. "And that's what should really matter. You're not some famous person to them; you're an inspiration, one of the people they look towards to make themselves feel better because they support your band, your music, and you."

Cooper's green eyes remained on my blue ones. He was silent as he took in my words that I hoped did mean something to him. I smiled in relief when his eyes mirrored mine. "Thanks, love."

He stretched his legs out on the floor into a V and reached forward to grab my hands. He suddenly pulled me towards him, and I effortlessly slid across the smooth surface of the playpen until I was sitting comfortably between his legs. He pressed his forehead against mine.

"You know just what to say, don't you?" His gaze dropped to my lips. As our noses brushed together, the nest of butterflies residing in my stomach stirred.

I didn't try fighting the smile from my lips as I shrugged. "It's a gift."

Cooper rolled his eyes good-naturedly, muttering a soft, "Yeah, yeah." He then pressed his lips to mine, and I kissed him back.

The sweet moment was cut short when a loud, manly voice interrupted us from down below. "Oi, you two up there! This place is only for kids ten and under! Get out!"

Chapter 21

"Holy shit," I muttered under my breath as I looked up at the flat-roofed, white two-story house in front of me.

Multiple windows lined up the front of the house on both stories, and down the end of the driveway was a gate that a security guard was in charge of opening and closing to let people drive in. The black metal gates were pretty tall and thick. It was good because unlike at the apartment complex, the paparazzi wouldn't be able to capture sneaky pictures through them.

Once Cooper was out of the car, he wiggled his eyebrows at me and dangled the keys enticingly. He nodded towards the door, and I followed him in. Excitement bubbled up inside me as Cooper unlocked the door and we stepped into the foyer. A staircase to the left led up to the second floor. To the right was a wide doorway into the living room with brand-new beige carpeting, and there was a dark blue suede couch shaped like an L. In front of the couch was a TV and stereo system. On the other side were two floral design chairs and a glass coffee table. There was also a white recliner matching the chairs in the corner that looked incredibly comfortable to just sink into. Only one room in and I was already in love.

Behind the couch, from where we entered the living room, was a long black wooden table. To the left was a wide doorless entryway that led into the dining room. It had the lightest blue walls that appeared white if you stared at them long enough. Inside was a wooden rectangular dining table with eight chairs, and a modern chandelier hung above it. The window on the other end of the dining table allowed for sunlight to glint against the crystals of the chandelier.

We walked through the secondary entryway in the dining room that led back out to the foyer. I let out a breath, overwhelmed by the beauty of the house. We went past the staircase and into the kitchen. It was kind of similar to our apartment kitchen except there was a stainless steel fridge built into the wall. A marble counter was on one side, and on the other were black cabinets. It was simple and beautiful, and I was excited to cook in here.

"This is gorgeous." My gaze wandered around the kitchen as I smiled in amazement. I couldn't believe that this was our new home—that *I* would be living here. I opened the fridge door randomly, stopping short when I saw what was inside. "How the hell is there beer in here already?" I asked, facing Cooper as I shut the door behind me.

He chuckled, running his ring-clad fingers through his hair. "The lads are comin' over to get a jump start on unpackin'." My eyebrows shot up. "I know you said you wanted to do it all by yourself after I go, but they're just helpin' unload the boxes. Nothin' too crazy."

I smiled, nodding in appreciation as we wandered out of the kitchen and back towards the living room. We hadn't been up to the second floor yet, but I had no doubt that it was just as amazing as the first floor. "I personally like the couch," Cooper commented, plopping down on the long couch with his arms folded behind his head.

Laughing down at him, I nodded as I placed my purse on the coffee table. I couldn't get enough of this place; the white walls were pristine, and the large windows allowed for natural light. Cooper and I had talked about getting some plants to place around the house. "I have to hand it to you—you did well." I praised him honestly.

Cooper grinned proudly, and suddenly, I heard the front door fly open, followed by Spencer's deep voice ringing out, "This place is sick, guys!"

I turned around just when the four guys wandered in. They gave me hugs and kisses—a greeting that I always adored. Rafael, folding his sunglasses and hanging them on the neckline of his shirt, said, "The movin' truck is outside."

Cooper stood up from the couch, cracking his knuckles as he nodded at his friends. "Oi, one of you come help me with the suitcases."

Miles offered himself as a volunteer, and the two of them disappeared out of the house. The other three boys stared at me expectantly, and I rolled my eyes and jutted my chin. "Beer is in the fridge."

The three men—children, really—cheered and turned to run off towards the alcohol, but Julian swiftly stepped forward and pressed a quick kiss to my cheek. "This is why we love you," he said before turning around and disappearing in the direction of the other guys.

I then went outside. Miles pulled a box out of the back of the truck while Cooper talked to the driver and headed to his car. The trunk was unlocked, so I pulled out our duffel bags and walked back into the house. I was only halfway up the stairs when Miles and

Cooper entered the house carrying boxes. Miles held a box labeled *books*. "Who has this many books?" he asked.

Snorting, all I said was "I love reading. It's not a sin."

Miles huffed. "It is when I'm the one carryin' the box."

Upstairs, I heard Cooper's voice in the distance. "Oi, stop drinking and help with the boxes!"

One door opened to reveal a nicely sized bathroom. I stopped in at the end of the hallway, remembering Cooper telling me that my bedroom was there. It was pretty big. The walls were a nice mixture of beige and gold. The window had a view of the driveway out front. There were doorways to the bathroom and a walk-in closet. There was also a dark wooden vanity and dresser that matched the queen-sized bed.

Although I wanted to stay and revel in the room, I just left the duffels on the bed before heading back downstairs. I came just in time to see Spencer enter the house carrying a box labeled *plates* in one hand and drinking his beer with the other. I jogged down the last few steps, exclaiming, "Spence, jeez, hold the box carefully!"

Of course, my statement backfired because Spencer, taken aback by my loud voice, suddenly let go of the box. Fortunately, Rafael, who had been walking out of the kitchen and was right next to Spencer, immediately caught the box only seconds before it hit the ground. I gripped the banister, sighing in relief.

"Holy shit," I muttered under my breath. I smiled gratefully at Rafael, who called Spencer a *fuckin' dumbass* before taking the box into the kitchen.

As the guys emptied out the boxes on the truck, I pulled out my suitcases from the car and dragged them up the stairs, ignoring the protests of the boys who said they could do it for me. Admittedly, I was proud of myself for being able to do so.

When all of the kitchen boxes were in the appropriate room, the guys went off to get the other stuff, and I went in there to begin taking out the plates and utensils, kind of really excited. If I got at least one of the boxes unpacked even halfway, I would be satisfied.

I grabbed the Swiss knife Cooper brought and cut through the tape of one of the cardboard boxes. The utensils were all placed in wooden cases. I opened up one of the drawers that already had stainless steel flatware storage caddies and began placing them there.

I was in the middle of placing in all of the spoons when I felt an arm loosely slide around my waist. It was Cooper. I smiled at the warmth his body immediately provided and his familiar scent.

I saw the beer bottle he was gripping. "Shouldn't you be unpacking instead of drinking?" I asked, picking up some spoons from their wooden cases and putting them in the drawer.

"I'm awardin' myself a break." Cooper chuckled and kissed my temple.

I nudged him with my elbow, causing him to jerk slightly. I said in a singsong tone, "Lazy."

Cooper squeezed my waist, his lips trailing from my temple to my cheek, scratching my skin with his beard. It was impossible to fight the smile from my face.

"You're a jerk," I said.

"I like to think of it as honest."

***

I blinked blearily as I tried to rid of the sleep in my eyes. The clock read 10:24. I let out a sigh because it was an appropriate time to wake up, no room for allowing myself a few extra hours of sleep. Sitting on the edge of the bed, I reached over for my phone and clicked the home button. My eyes landed on the date, and the bones in my body went rigid.

August 6.

The date was all too familiar. I felt a sinking sensation in my chest and my throat dry as if I hadn't drank water in ages. Phone tightly gripped in my hand, I padded out of the room and down the stairs. My stomach was queasy as if I wanted to throw up, but I hadn't eaten much, so there was no chance of that happening.

I was about to go into the kitchen to make myself some coffee until I realized I was in no mood to eat or drink anything. My empty stomach felt misleadingly full with dense grief. Instead, I walked into the living room and dropped myself on the couch, elbows resting on my knees and face burying into my hands as the thudding of my heart grew louder in my ears.

I could feel my lips quivering and the tears burning in my eyes. Memories of the woman who meant the most to me in the world played through my mind on a loop. Birthdays, holidays, the happy times, and the sad all flickered behind my closed eyes like a movie. All up until the moment she left me. It was like I was losing her all over again as the hot tears trailed down my cheeks and the first sob shuddered through my body. I tried to suppress any sounds with my hand covering my mouth.

"Kelsey?" Cooper's sleep-ridden voice asked. He lowered himself on the couch next to me and squeezed my knee. "What's the matter?"

I bit my quivering lower lip. It was like someone had reached inside my chest and was trying to rip my heart out from where it belonged. Emotional turmoil tricked me into believing it was physical pain, so I wrapped my arms over my stomach. It felt like my whole body was both sore from pain and continuously being inflicted with it as well.

"Hey, hey," Cooper's voice softened. His arm wrapped around my shoulders as he bowed his messy bed head, trying to meet my gaze. He looked so worried, staring at me with a pleading expression as he asked, "What's wrong, Kelsey? Talk to me."

I sniffled sharply, lips parting to speak but only letting out a small gasp, and his expression fell even more as his grip around my shoulders tightened. His other hand grasped both of mine. Swallowing did nothing to push down the massive lump that had formed in my throat. My cheeks and neck were wet from the onslaught of tears. Breathing was difficult. Cooper was patient as he stared at me, silently pleading with me to tell him what was going on as the panic in his green eyes rose.

"I-It's my mom's b-birthday today."

"Oh God, Kels," he murmured, not hesitating to pull me in. My temple rested against his chest.

I squeezed his hands. My eyes shut tightly as I whispered, "She'd be forty-five." Another sob shook my shoulders. Cooper rubbed his thumb over the back of my hand and held me in the comforting embrace I was in desperate need of. In all honesty, the only one who could comfort me, who could make any of this better, was my mother, but she was gone, and I could do nothing about it but cry.

Actually, no. I wasn't going to just sit here and weep on my mom's first birthday since her passing. If she could see me now, she would be so disappointed. She had always been big on doing nothing but smile on one's birthday, and me crying on the day commemorating her birth would have her rolling in her grave right about now. It hurt so much at this moment—didn't they say the first holidays or birthdays after one's passing were the most difficult?—a pain I couldn't possibly put into words because of the sheer magnitude of it, but I was going to push through. I had to.

So, sniffling sharply, I shook my head against Cooper's chest and pulled my hands from his grasp. I wiped the tears from my face, neck, and the bottom of my chin. "I'm not going to just sit and cry, not today." I sat up.

Cooper leaned back slightly and looked at me with raised eyebrows. I nodded, more to myself than him, voice shaky as I continued, "Today's a happy day. It's my mom's birthday. She wouldn't want me to spend it crying over her."

When he saw the determined expression on my face, Cooper smiled almost proudly, and I even managed to return it because I was adamant about following through. No more tears, not for today. Cooper's lips parted to speak, but the shrill tone of a phone ringing cut him off. He pulled his phone out from the pocket of his flannel pajamas. He checked the caller ID, shooting me a glance before answering, "Mum, hey."

I smiled as his face lit up while talking to his mother, the sight nothing but endearing even if I was missing mine. "You are? Really? No, that's great news." He shot me a glance, and I returned it with a curious one of my own. "Yeah, we'd be happy to have you guys. You can help with the unpackin'." He let out a laugh as I began to realize what they were talking about. "Alright, see you then. Love you too, Mum. Bye."

"What'd she say?"

"Mum and Alessandra are driving down here tomorrow, staying for a day or so." He explained, and I smiled, happy to be able to see the two women again. "Is that alright?"

I nudged his arm with my fist, laughing before sniffling, an annoying side effect from all of that crying. "Of course, it's alright with me. It'll be so nice to see them again."

Cooper grinned before pursing his lips. His Adam's apple bobbed as he swallowed. "D'you want to do anythin' today?"

My mouth closed softly before I shrugged half-heartedly. I said I wouldn't cry. I never said I would be up to actually do something. Of course, Cooper had a way of cheering me up. "How about the two of us go out? Have lunch somewhere and explore the city? I realize I haven't really taken you to any of the touristy places, and you haven't been anywhere much, have you?" I shook my head, and he grinned. "Why not today?"

My eyes widened slightly at his offer, feeling a small bubble of excitement, not enough to diminish the sadness this day inherently brought but maybe enough to get my mind off it. "Really?"

Cooper nodded, slapping his thighs and pushing himself to his feet. "Yes. Go on and get ready. I'll cook us some breakfast to get us started for the day."

I stood up as well. "Oh, I'm not hu—"

"It doesn't matter." Cooper cut me off, throwing me a pointed look, knowing exactly why I was refusing to eat. "You're eatin' French toast whether you like it or not, woman."

Clamping my mouth shut, I smothered a chuckle and nodded before grabbing my phone and heading up the stairs. After using the bathroom and washing my face, I quickly did my makeup to mask the fact that I had been crying earlier. I made myself presentable in some jeans and a shirt.

Once I was ready, I headed back downstairs as the sweet aroma of French toast invaded my senses. I wandered over to Cooper, overwhelmed with the sudden urge to hug him. When I reached his side, I wrapped my arms around his torso and felt his left arm instantly wrap around my shoulders. He pressed a kiss to the top of my head. The small gesture felt nice, comforting on a day that I probably needed it a lot. And while nothing would replace my mother's touch, I was lucky to have Cooper with me to cheer me up, if nothing else.

I pulled away moments later so he could finish making the food. I took out a tray from one cabinet before placing plates and utensils on it, as well as glasses so we could drink some orange juice. There were still some unopened boxes littered around the house since we hadn't finished unpacking, but most of the kitchen stuff was done, as well as the things to put in our bedrooms. It was only our second full day here, but we were taking our time with the unpacking process since the boxes didn't really bother us. Most of them were in the guest room upstairs and the spare room downstairs that would be converted into Cooper's in-house studio.

When Cooper was done with the French toast, he brought the plate over to the dining room as I followed with the tray. Once we were settled, we immediately began eating.

I chuckled as he sat across from me. The two of us began eating, and as soon as I took the first bite of the toast, I let out a groan of satisfaction. "This is so good," I said, nodding.

Cooper grinned proudly. *Seriously, was there anything this guy couldn't do?* He wasn't just all looks and musical talent, it seemed.

Once breakfast was finished, Cooper quickly got dressed before we left the house. I was unsurprised to see Dirk chatting with the security guard, Steven, at the gate.

Once we hit the road, I felt the cool blast of the air conditioner fan my skin. The radio filled the silence in the car. I tried to focus on the view outside rather than today's date.

But the only thought that kept running through my brain was how Mom would've loved London.

Eventually, we found ourselves at Kensington Gardens. Cooper's hand casually found mine as we strolled through the huge park. There were people lying on the grass, walking around, and biking down the paths. Chatter filled the air. With sunglasses on our faces, no one seemed to recognize us—well, mostly Cooper—and I was grateful for the privacy we were being granted in this public setting. It was so peaceful. My hand gripped Cooper's as I rested my head against his arm. We walked at a leisurely pace.

Memories of going to the park with my mom flashed through my mind, bringing a soft smile to my lips instead of tears in my eyes. She was such a hands-on and involved mother, always making sure to provide as much as she possibly could for me and never once making me feel like I was missing out on anything in life. The scales could've tipped either way when my father died, but my mother decided to be the best damn mom anyone could ever ask for.

Cooper and I walked past a wooden kiosk selling ice cream. He tugged my hand, turning to stand in line and eventually buying me a cone of chocolate ice cream and himself a vanilla.

There was a circle of green metal benches a few feet away. Surrounding them were bushes of colorful flowers. Cooper and I sat down to enjoy our ice creams while Dirk stood in line to buy one for himself.

As I licked at the sweet chocolate ice cream, I glanced at Cooper, who seemed to be staring at the flowers, and I smiled. "Thank you for today, Coop," I earnestly told him. He looked at me. "It's a lot better than, you know, locking myself up in the room."

Cooper reached over to hold my hand, squeezing it as he responded without hesitation, "Y'know I've got you."

Chapter 22

"I haven't even seen this entire place, but it's absolutely beautiful." Amelia grinned as she and Alessandra followed me into the living room. The two women looked around the area, impressed. Amelia's smile turned adorably excited as she gave me a sideways hug, squeezing me as she practically squealed, "I'm so excited for you both."

"Oi, Kelsey gets a hug and I don't?"

Alessandra and I snickered as Amelia huffed in amusement, turning around to see Cooper wandering into the room with an exaggerated pout on his lips. His mother rolled her eyes. "Come here, you baby." She shook her head before pulling her son into a hug.

We spent the next few minutes taking Alessandra and Amelia upstairs where the guest room was. Cooper carried their single suitcases up the steps. Once the women freshened up after the nearly three-hour drive they endured, we retreated to the living room. I prepped them some tea, which they took gratefully as we fell into easy conversation. I had to say, it was nice seeing Amelia and

Alessandra again; talking to them on the phone just wasn't the same as being with them in person.

Hours passed by as we lounged in the living room, talking about any topic that came up. I laughed every time Alessandra decided to tease her younger brother. It was adorable watching Cooper interact with his mom and sister because it was crystal clear how much he loved and respected both of them; it was also so obvious that he was a complete mama's boy with just his behavior alone. Cooper looked at Amelia as if she were a superhero, and that was a kind of sentiment I was all too familiar with.

I have no idea how long we had been sitting chatting, but soon enough, it was dinnertime. Cooper suggested that we go out to eat, so we all scrambled up the stairs and got dressed as he made a last minute reservation to that same restaurant the two of us had our first dinner. Apparently, it was Alessandra's favorite, and since the food was so great, it sounded like the perfect place to eat.

Once everyone was dressed, we got into the roomy SUV with Dirk. He drove us to the restaurant. The car ride, unsurprisingly, was full of lively chatter, only dying down when we pulled up in front of the restaurant's entrance. The obnoxious flash of cameras accompanied by shouting from paparazzi greeted us. "For fuck's sake," I heard Cooper curse, "someone must've leaked our reservations or somethin'."

Amelia, sitting behind him, reached forward and squeezed her son's shoulder. "It's alright, sweetheart; nothing we're not used to." She assured him. Cooper sighed.

We slid out, hands and clutches shielding our eyes from the incessant and bright flashes of the cameras that were strong enough to blind someone, their obnoxious shouting not any kinder.

Cooper grabbed my left hand, and I instinctively reached behind me, my other hand grasping Alessandra's. Dirk was able to push a number of the paparazzi away as we finally reached the entrance.

Glancing at Cooper, I noticed the way the muscle in his jaw was jumping, no doubt completely ticked off at what had just happened. He looked over the rest of us, checking to see that we weren't hurt. The expression he wore was kind of intimidating if I'm being honest. His normally kind eyes hardened in irritation, and his lips thinned.

"We're so incredibly sorry, Mr. Shaw." A middle-aged man in a suit hurried over. He was shorter than Cooper and had a balding head. "We hadn't expected for those photographers to be here."

Hadn't he seen them outside? I didn't voice the question, however, as Cooper merely nodded. Almost every patron was staring at him in wonder and shock. "It's alright," he said, his voice leveled. "Can we get to our table?"

The man nodded vigorously, hastily grabbing some menus from the host's podium before leading us towards the back of the familiar restaurant. The host just stood there without moving a muscle. The delicious aroma of food surrounded us as we sat down. The man—whom I assumed was the manager—handed us our menus and said, "Your waiter will be with you shortly." Then he scurried off.

A snicker left Alessandra as she opened her menu. Her dark green eyes twinkled as she looked at her brother from across the table. "I think you scared him, Coop." She joked, an attempt to lighten the tense atmosphere.

Cooper let out a breath, shoulders slumping as he looked at all of us apologetically. "I'm sorry that had to happen."

Déjà vu clicked in my brain as I remembered the first time Cooper and I came here, also getting surrounded by a group of paparazzi then. Cooper had kept apologizing for it, feeling guilt over a situation he had no control over. A small fond smile danced on my lips because it just spoke volumes of Cooper's character. No wonder his fans insanely adored him—other than just for his music, of course.

Amelia, quick to quell any guilt Cooper might have been feeling, smiled at him and squeezed his hand. "It's alright, love. We understand."

Cooper let out a soft breath, clearly still disgruntled, but dropped it as we looked over our menus. We decided what we wanted fairly quickly, so when the waiter came by for our drinks, we told him our food orders as well.

While we waited, Amelia took the opportunity to launch into some baby stories about Cooper, much to his displeasure and Alessandra's wicked entertainment.

Before Amelia could start, Cooper dropped his head and groaned. "Mum, don't—"

But she shushed him instantly and looked at me from across the table, grinning. "When Cooper was about four years old, I took him to his aunt's baby shower with me. Now, he didn't know how pregnancies worked, obviously, and was confused as to why everyone kept rubbing her big belly and asked her what was inside."

My eyebrows raised in curious amusement. Cooper mumbled an embarrassed, "Oh God."

Amelia ignored him. "So his aunt told him that her baby was in there, just like Cooper once was in my tummy." She laughed, and my lips parted. I knew where this story involving a young, innocent Cooper might be going. Cooper shook his head, looking just done with this.

"He was absolutely horrified. So, of course, he began screaming and crying, saying that I would never eat him, and I had to take him home because he just would not settle. He almost wet himself from all the crying he was doing!"

I couldn't help the laughter that bubbled up inside me. Alessandra joined in to further humiliate her brother. As I glanced at Cooper, my laughter intensified. He just sat there, head shaking and arms crossed over his chest. "I was *four*." He defended exasperatedly, lips pursing as his comment did nothing to ease our amusement.

Our conversations continued as our drinks arrived first, and I felt a hand slide into my right hand. I glanced at Cooper as his fingers interlaced with mine under the table. I smiled instantly, loving the feeling of his skin against my own. The only time we let go of our hands, albeit reluctantly, was when our food arrived, and we began digging in.

There was a lull in conversation as we ate, letting the low hum of the restaurant crowd takeover our silence. I was about halfway through my steak when Amelia spoke up. "So Cooper, Kelsey, I know you two are responsible in your own right, but I hope I don't have to give you a talking to for living under the same roof now that you're together? I'm afraid I'm a bit too young to be a grandmother."

Holy shit. What?

Upon hearing those words, my fork fell from my hand and landed on my plate with an obnoxious *clang*. I felt my face instantaneously heat up as Cooper quite literally began choking on his Coke. Alessandra stared at her mother incredulously, who was watching along in innocence as I patted Cooper's back while he coughed.

When he recovered, I snatched my hand from his back and stared at Amelia in dumbfounded disbelief, jaw slack as the tips of my ears burned. Cooper all but exclaimed in horror, "Mum, *what?*"

Alessandra now just looked amused, pressing her lips together. Amelia shrugged as if her words were the most casual thing in the world. "Well, I know how you kids operate. I didn't have to worry too much at first because I didn't think there would be a romance to come out of this—" My mouth dried in horror. Cooper was stunned, cheeks pink. "God, Mum!"

Amelia continued without hesitation, shooting us both pointed looks. "But now that you two are together, I trust you'll be careful, right?"

Okay, I adored Amelia, but was she *crazy*? Cooper and I only *just* started seeing each other in the romantic sense. We may have shared a bed, but *sleeping* together was on a completely different level, which was something I didn't necessarily concern myself with until I was ready. It wouldn't even be my first time having sex—just that sex with Cooper was something I never thought would happen when I first met him. Now it was a possibility, and I just knew if I worried myself over that, I would go crazy. I was a dramatic overthinker, obviously, and if I spent my time wondering if and when Cooper and I were going to sleep together, I would give myself a migraine. So, it was best not to think about that.

Clearly, it was something Amelia expected to happen and she had no qualms in bringing it up over dinner. In public.

I exchanged a mortified look with Cooper. He looked so incredibly embarrassed and in shock that his mother would ever bring this up—especially in a public place. I looked back at Amelia and cleared my throat. "I, uh, I don't—" I began, unable to stop myself from stuttering. My cheeks were on fire and I felt as though I was about to melt in my seat. "I don't think you need to, um, worry about that."

Throughout this interchange, Alessandra was covering her mouth with her napkin, trying to smother the laughter that was so obviously threatening to spill out. She was clearly enjoying this, while Cooper and I were bristling in our seats. Was it possible for a person to spontaneously combust? Because I had a feeling that was about to happen to me right now. This was so unexpected and embarrassing, and seriously? Definitely not dinner conversation. Cooper and I were taking our time with things, going our own pace.

Not to mention—we hadn't slept together! It's too soon for us, personally, in my opinion. We would get there when we get there, and Amelia already being suspicious of it just made me wish the earth would open up beneath me and swallow me whole.

"I would hope so," Amelia answered hummed with a raise of an eyebrow. "Like I said—I'm too young to be a grandmother."

Oh, fucking hell—kill me now. Cooper scratched the back of his neck nervously, clearly finding this whole topic uncomfortable as he glanced around, making sure no one was paying any attention. Our table was a bit isolated, but still. "Seriously, Mum, this isn't the time or place to have this conversation." He shot her a look that clearly told her to drop this humiliating discussion.

Amelia rolled her eyes, but thankfully, she nodded. "Fine, fine," she said before pointing at both Cooper and me with her fork, "but I'm serious—stay safe."

***

I fell on my back on the bed, laughing as Cooper's lean body fell right on top of mine. He kept himself up with his hands on the bed. Cooper silenced me with his lips, soft and welcoming. I reached up to cup his face, feeling the scratchiness of his facial hair on my skin. Being this close to him was something I was growing so used to. I reveled in his proximity and the taste of his lips from the head-spinning kisses he gave me.

I tangled my hands in his short hair, and Cooper groaned against my lips. He reluctantly pulled away, resting his forehead against mine. His warm breath fanned against my lips as he whispered, "I'm gonna miss bein' able to do this."

For a moment, I was confused, wondering what he meant until I realized that Triage was heading back on tour in a couple of days. Once again, Cooper would be gone, and I would be here by myself, this time, alone in a big house instead of the apartment. I would be busy, I knew, with classes and unpacking the leftover boxes, but that wouldn't make me miss Cooper any less.

"Don't remind me." I sighed as I peered up at him still hovering over me. With an exaggerated pout, I added, "I'm gonna be all lonely."

Cooper let out a breath and dipped his head, pressing his face against my collarbones, and I tilted my head back, laughing lightly as his hair tickled my neck. "You should come with me." He suggested, his lips brushing against my skin as he spoke, igniting a fire in their wake.

"You know I can't." I chuckled, hand on the back of his neck as I stared up at the ceiling.

Lifting his head, Cooper's green-eyed gaze met mine as he smirked lightly. "A lad can dream."

***

Two days later, Amelia and Alessandra had gone, and it was the day before the guys were supposed to leave for tour. And so, naturally, Cooper and I had all the guys come over, as well as the girls, to have a casual little get together. Cooper had gone out to pick up lots of Chinese food, and when Noelle and Miles came by, they had brought food from Nando's as well, so there was more than enough food for the nine of us.

It was fun, honestly, sitting with everyone in the living room as we ate the various food and watched movies back to back. We wanted as many Marvel movies, in order, we could fit in one sitting. Though with a group as talkative as this one, we were never once silent. I sat in between Cooper and Heidi. My plate consisted of shrimp lo-mein and fried chicken. I fought off Cooper's grabby fingers as he tried to take my chicken from me.

When dinner was over, I waited until we were halfway through *Thor* to slip back into the kitchen, where I had made chocolate mousse for dessert. With bowls of it set on a tray, I returned to the living room where the only source of light was the television. Spencer sat up from where he lay on the recliner at the sight of me entering the room. "What've you got there?" he asked eagerly, always having room for more food.

I wiggled my eyebrows, putting the tray down on the coffee table next to all of the containers and plates. "I made chocolate mousse."

Everyone reached forward for a bowl. I grabbed one and settled back in my seat, watching proudly as they took their bites and voiced their approval. I smiled, satisfied, as Heidi commented, "Best bloody chocolate mousse I've ever had."

My grin widened as I scooped up a spoonful, swallowing the chocolaty bite. I remarked, "You boys are leaving tomorrow, and I figured we could use some comfort food." I shrugged. "Well, at least it's comfort food for me."

Julian, who was failing to steal some of Dawn's dessert, pouted at his girlfriend as she turned away from him. "How come?" she asked.

A small fond smile danced on my lips as I leaned back on the couch, comfortable between Cooper and Heidi. "My mom used to make it for me whenever I got sad or whatever. Her mom used to make it for her, so she did the same for me."

Cooper pressed a kiss to my temple as the others smiled at the sweet memory. I thought of my mom for a moment. She had given me her special chocolate mousse recipe when I was seventeen so I could practice making it for myself, and it was one of my favorite gifts I'd received from her.

Hours later, the house was emptied out by one-thirty in the morning. They were reluctant to leave because we were all enjoying ourselves, but the guys needed to get at least a decent amount of sleep before their flight in the morning.

After starting up the dishwasher, Cooper and I retreated upstairs, where he had begged for us to sleep in the same bed before he was reduced to sleeping alone for tour. I found myself being unable to say no to his puppy dog eyes, and if he found out how much of an effect they had on me, I would be done for.

We climbed into his bed after I changed into my pajamas and turned off the lights. I didn't realize how sleepy I was until I got under the covers and my head hit the pillow. My eyes almost instantly drifted shut as I lay on my side, back faced to Cooper.

That's when I heard his tired, thickly accented voice gruff out, "Come *here*."

I smiled to myself, eyes closed and unmoving as I hum out, "No, I'm good on my side."

Cooper was silent for a brief moment before groaning, and I let out a light laugh when the mattress shifted under me. Cooper's arm slid around my waist under the cover, pressing my back to his chest, and he tangled our legs together. His lips brushed my ear as he murmured, "I win."

His deep voice sent light, pleasant shivers down my spine, his embrace nothing but welcoming as I found myself easily drifting off to a heavy sleep. It was so comfortable, lying here with his arm around me and breath tickling my neck. The butterflies in my stomach stirred while the familiar scent of Cooper helped me fall into a dreamless yet peaceful sleep.

Too bad in the morning, he'd be gone.

Chapter 23

One thing I failed to understand was why paparazzi felt the need to hound celebrities. Really, how much was a photograph of a celebrity doing grocery shopping worth? And, okay, maybe snapping pictures of celebrities I understood on *some level*, but what's the point of doing so to a celebrity's non-famous friend or family member? Like, really, I very much doubted that a picture of me loading my groceries into the trunk of the SUV was worth anything at all.

Yet when I was in the parking lot today at the local Whole Foods Market, there were a couple of photographers either snapping pictures from a respectful distance or having no shame in coming right up to me and doing so, all the while asking me questions about Cooper or my relationship with him. Dirk was with me, of course, but that didn't mean the constant yelling didn't hurt my head or make it spin dizzily. They had surrounded me, and I couldn't exactly keep my head lowered as I loaded the bags in the trunk. I hastily got in, letting out a breath as Dirk got in the front.

It was overwhelming; I wasn't going to lie, and each time it happened, I would feel bad for Cooper and the guys. They had to deal with this on a daily basis, every single time they went out, and so did the girls, I knew, if they were somehow recognized. It was ridiculous how taking pictures of the significant others of the members of Triage was almost as important as getting photos of the boys themselves. Triage had left for tour about a week or so ago, and I hadn't been out of the house much except to hang out with the girls or to the library to research for assignments, which only happened three times so far. But today, when I needed to do the weekly grocery shopping, somehow they found me and thought it'd be a good opportunity to take pictures of a nineteen-year-old girl just because she was involved with a famous musician. The way all of this worked was just ridiculous to me.

When we got to the house, I thanked Dirk for helping me with the groceries before telling him he could go home. I didn't plan on leaving the house today—especially after that. And so he left, and I was alone in the big house that felt extremely empty when it was just me in here. To busy myself, I emptied out the grocery bags, putting away the new purchases where they belonged, and I was only halfway through when my phone began ringing. I smiled slightly as Cooper's name and face lit up my screen.

I could barely get a word in when I heard Cooper ask, "Are you okay?"

I pressed the phone between my ear and shoulder blade as I put the apples in a glass fruit bowl. I furrowed my brows and confusedly responded, "Uh, yeah, I'm okay."

Cooper sighed. "So"—he stretched out the word curiously—"you're not goin' to tell me how paps found you outside of the grocery store?"

Wow, talk about déjà vu. Cooper found out about me being swarmed by paparazzi before I could even have the chance of processing it. He always ended up calling me, using the same knowing tone to get me to answer truthfully. Though, I never seemed to do so, whether it be intentionally or not. Oops.

I grabbed my phone, sighing. For someone who was supposed to be busy, Cooper somehow always found out everything online. Before I could defend myself, he added, "You need to tell me this stuff, Kelsey, rather than me findin' out on Twitter."

His concern was sweet but unneeded. It's not like Cooper could do anything about it, and telling him would just add stress to his life that could be easily avoided. I knew how demanding his career could be, so what was the point in piling on more on top of it? "In my defense, I got home just a little while ago." I tried to joke before adding, "Look, Coop, there's nothing we can do about it, and it's not a big deal. Dirk was with me, and everything was fine."

"I still like to know." Cooper disclosed as I took the carton of eggs and put it in the newly stocked fridge. "I get nervous knowing middle-aged men are followin' you around."

I smiled, my heart twisting adoringly at the twenty-year-old man living it up in Vancouver at the moment. It was in moments like this, when he was unfalteringly concerned and sweet, that overwhelmed me with how much I liked him. "I've got Dirk by my side. That's what he's here for, right?" I assured him, earning a reluctant agreeing hum. "I'll be fine, I promise. I don't tell you this stuff because I don't want to worry you, but I will if it'll make you feel better. But seriously, stop stressing; I can handle it."

He sighed. "If you say so."

***

Over the next couple of days, if I happened to venture out, I was able to handle it if some paparazzi found me, just like I had told Cooper I could. I just kept my mouth shut and head bowed, allowing

Dirk to make way for me. I wondered if he was paid enough to put up with this bullshit. But in all honesty, lately, there weren't that many paparazzi waiting around. I think it had to do with the fact that I saw Justin Bieber roaming around London for a while. Though, as per my promise to Cooper, I'd call or text him just to assure him that I was fine so he wouldn't have to go online and see for himself.

He was so sweet; it was unbelievable, though I felt bad that he always felt so nervous whenever I went out. It wasn't often that I did; only recently when I went out to lunch with Heidi or to that same bookstore to get some new ones because reading was such a wonderful source of entertainment. In fact, it's what I was doing at the moment when my phone began ringing, and I blinked in surprise when I saw that it was Julia, Logan's mom, calling.

"Julia, hi," I greeted as I put my book down, frowning in wonder as to why she was calling me.

"Hi, honey. Thank goodness you picked up." Her urgent tone deepened my frown. "Sweetheart, Logan got into a car accident; he's—his leg is broken, and he has a concussion, and I just—he's in the hospital, and I thought you'd want to know."

My heart dropped to the pit of my stomach as if it were made of lead. I expelled a shuddering breath that shook my entire body. Whether or not we were fighting, the absolute last thing I would ever want was for Logan to be hurt, and knowing he was in the hospital twisted my stomach and had bile rising in the back of my throat. We hadn't spoken in so goddamn long. The guilt of it suddenly made a startling appearance and began immediately eating away at me.

All of our fights and arguments suddenly meant nothing to me as my lower lip quivered. There was a staggering realization that, God forbid, I could've lost him. After Mom's death, if I lost anyone, I don't think I could've handled it, and other than my mom, Logan was the only other person I'd known for most of my life. It was in this unfortunate moment that I truly realized the extent of how our previous fights were petty and ridiculous and solvable and that our friendship meant more than enough to me to just let it die because of some dumb arguments. The disagreements might have formed over unrequited feelings, but they could easily be put aside in this moment.

Swallowing the lump in my throat, I reached out for my laptop with a shaky hand. Stammering, I said, "Hang on, Julia. I'm about to book the next flight out to Miami."

Julia sniffled and asked me if I was sure about this. I bit my lower lip, shaking my head in an attempt to rid of the guilt I was feeling for not speaking to Logan for so long. "I can't sit here while he's in the hospital. It'll feel so wrong if I'm not there for him."

***

"I honestly didn't think you'd come."

I looked up at Logan, who sat on the hospital bed against some pillows. A white bandage cloth was wrapped around his head while his left leg was propped up, a cast wrapped around the broken foot. According to the doctor, he had some internal injuries like fractured ribs that were nicely healing, but there were also some cuts on his face and hands from where the glass of the window had pierced him.

When I first saw him, my mouth had dried, and I visibly flinched. No one wants to see their best friend lying in a hospital bed with IV needles stuck in them and a heart monitor whose beeping sounds told you that they are still alive and breathing. It was a sight that shook my hands and brought tears to my eyes. Knowing that this could be so much worse, I was grateful that he was still here.

I had gotten to the hospital about half an hour ago, coming straight from the airport where Fletcher had picked me up, and I had yet to leave Logan's side. He had just woken up a few minutes ago, our greetings slightly awkward, though I just blamed it on the medicine he was under. I knew better, but whatever.

"Of course, I'd come," I replied, sitting up in the uncomfortable plastic chair as I offered him a small smile. "You're in the hospital, Logan; it was a no-brainer."

He returned the small smile gratefully. Logan hesitated before speaking up. "Look, Kelsey, I'm really so—"

"Don't worry about that right now." I cut him off, not wanting to hear an apology from my best friend while he was sitting injured in a hospital bed. Now wasn't the time for this. "All you need to focus on is getting better, alright? We've got plenty of time to talk about it later."

Logan let out a breath, nodding as he reached up to scratch his neck. He flinched slightly when he grazed a cut. I winced as well, just as Julia walked back into the room, and I squeezed Logan's hand before standing up. "I'm gonna go to the bathroom real quick."

I walked down the busy hospital hallway, the smell of medicine and disinfectant smothering my senses, and reached the bathroom. Logan hadn't been moved to a private room yet, so the bathroom down the hall was the closest. As I stepped into the pink tiled room, my phone began ringing. When Cooper's name appeared, I let out a curse. Everything had happened so fast and hastily that I failed to inform Cooper about my spontaneous trip to Miami, but he knew. When the plane had landed and I turned on my phone, I saw that Cooper had called and texted a few times because paparazzi had spotted me at Heathrow Airport. I just never called him back because I was too focused on Logan. I told him I'd call if anything happened, and I completely threw that promise out the window the next minute. And since I was aware of how Cooper wanted to make sure I was okay, I just hoped he wouldn't be too irritated.

Of course, there was a fat chance of that because when I answered the call inside the empty bathroom, Cooper instantly said, "You know what I hate?"

I stopped in the middle of the bathroom, looking at myself in the mirror. I reluctantly asked, "Uh, what?"

"How I have to find out *online* that you're in Miami because you didn't tell me, and that you don't answer my calls when I just wanna know what's happenin'," he answered, a hard edge in his tone that I wasn't familiar with but didn't like the sound of at all.

Biting the inside of my cheek, I feebly said, "I was gonna tell you." It just slipped my mind.

"Yeah? When?" he retorted, huffing out an aggravated breath. "When you were back in London?"

Not wanting us to fight about this, I ran my fingers through my hair as my grip on my phone tightened. "Cooper, Logan was in a car accident, okay? I had to visit him, and it all just happened so fast. All I could think of at the moment was getting to him. I'm sorry."

"No, don't—don't apologize," Cooper said and sighed deeply. I rolled my lips into my mouth and stood with my legs crossed. I really had to pee. "I just wish you took out two seconds to just text me what was goin' on. Is Logan okay?"

A rush of guilt coursed through me, knowing that he was kind of right. I could have easily texted him when Dirk was driving me to the airport, telling him about Logan's situation and that I was headed to Florida instead of letting him find out online. Even though I mostly was just focused on Logan, I was partly at fault for not keeping Cooper in mind, even if a little.

"His leg's broken, and he's got some fractured ribs and a concussion, along with a few cuts."

Cooper swore. "I hope he feels better," he earnestly responded, and I nodded absently, chewing my lower lip. It was silent between us for a few seconds as I heard the distant sound of a toilet flushing. It was the men's room next door. "I know he's your best friend, Kelsey, and I'm obviously not, like, mad that you went to visit him. I just wish you'd keep in mind that I only wanna make sure you're okay, yeah? I don't wanna sound like some controlling dick because I'm just concerned for your safety whenever you go out. I know Dirk's there, but it's just, like, a matter of peace of mind. And the fact that you didn't find it important to tell me you were goin' to Florida gives me the idea that you don't trust me enough or that you don't find it important to let me know."

Cooper sounded defeated and disappointed as he spoke, and the part of me that had made it a conscious decision to just not tell him about this felt guilty. I was concerned about Logan, and I don't feel guilty about that, but Cooper was right in some sense. I could've made an effort to not leave him out of the loop. He made it a point to let me know whenever they're headed out to a new city or something. I could've easily just told him I was leaving the country. And because Cooper was one of the most genuinely nicest guys I'd ever met, having him be even the slightest bit upset with me sucked.

"Coop, I was just so worried about Logan, you know? It slipped my mind," I said, partly lying but also kind of telling the truth. "You know trust isn't an issue. I *do* trust you." Hell, this had nothing to even do with trust, rather than more so with my unfortunate ability to only have tunnel vision when it came to certain things.

"It kind of feels like you don't, Kels," Cooper said, and I frowned, pulling my lower lip into my mouth. I knew Cooper felt responsible for me in some way—hell, that's what my mom entrusted him with, isn't it?—but this kind of seemed a bit extreme.

When I opened my mouth to say something, I was cut off by a beep, telling me that Cooper had hung up without saying goodbye. My heart sank a bit, and I groaned. I didn't need Cooper to be upset with me while my friend was in the hospital. Why were things always going sideways for me? For once, I wished life could be easy.

***

My stay in Miami was coming up to a week or so, and I was glad that I had only bought a one-way ticket, since the date of my return wasn't a solid fix. Ever since my conversation with Cooper at the hospital, we didn't really speak much. I mean, we did; we texted each other as he would let me know where the band was headed, and I'd fill him in on Logan's progress and such. The texts were dry, but at least we weren't straight up ignoring each other. Not like the radio silence that existed whenever Logan and I were fighting. Plus, I kept texting Cooper in an attempt to get back on his good side; I wasn't sure if it was working, though.

Logan had been discharged from the hospital yesterday. He used crutches to get around, though his parents and I would rather have him stay in one place, since his ribs weren't fully healed.

Currently, I was sitting in their family living room, finishing an assignment online since I brought some of my textbooks with me. Logan hobbled over after returning from the bathroom and sat down on the couch next to me, releasing a breath of relief.

He looked at me as I submitted my assignment. I quirked my brow, and he said, "I think it's about time we talked."

I watched as my assignment submitted, nodding. "I guess so."

I put my laptop aside and turned to face him. I tried to ignore the fact that the last time I sat here, Logan had kissed me. Yikes. This time, though, Logan sighed as his eyes wandered around the room as if he was pulling his thoughts together.

"I was a douche." He looked at me. "I shouldn't have said any of what I did about Cooper or your feelings for him, and I definitely shouldn't have kissed you or gotten mad that you didn't return my feelings. It was uncalled for, and I was being a jealous asshole, and I'm so sorry about that. I had no right."

"No, you didn't." I agreed without hesitation, propping my elbow up on the back of the couch and leaning my head against my hand. His words were genuine, I could tell, but I still said, "It made Cooper and me really angry; you hurt my feelings, Logan."

The regret was evident on Logan's face as his expression fell, shoulders sinking as he nodded. "I know," he admitted shamefully, glancing down as he wrung his fingers together. "Believe me, hurting you was the last thing I wanted. I can't be angry at you for who you like, even if I wish it was me. I can't change that, and I know that, and I'm fine with it."

I gave him a small sad smile, so incredibly glad that we were finally coming to an understanding after months of being strangers instead of best friends. Logan's actions, at the moment he had done them, seemed unforgivable, but after worrying myself over his recovery and acknowledging the fact that I could've lost him forever, I was beyond ready to bury the hatchet. At the end of the day, he was my best friend, and while I couldn't love him in the way he wanted, I still could in the way I knew best—as my family.

Wanting to show that I forgave him and to lighten the situation, I poked his arm and joked. "You think you can get over me that easy?"

Logan instantly snorted, rolling his dark eyes. "I think I can manage," he responded. I laughed, and he grinned as well. "So, are you gonna fill me in on what's really going on with you and Cooper?"

And just like that, we were back to being friends. I guess we were both exhausted and stressed from this ridiculous argument being dragged out for so long. I guess a near-death experience puts things into perspective. Though it sucks that that's what got Logan and me to finally get our shit together.

I was a bit hesitant to answer him because even though we were moving past this situation, was it really a good idea for me to tell him about my growing relationship with Cooper? I didn't think so, but the expression on Logan's face showed genuine interest, so I hesitantly said, "It's…nice. I mean, it's kind of weird because we're together, but we've been living with each other for a while so it almost feels backwards. But I really do like him. He's just…He's amazing."

Completely aware that I sounded like a blissfully wistful idiot, I pressed my lips together as I felt heat spread across my cheeks. It didn't help when Logan quirked an eyebrow as he knowingly asked, "Why do I get the feeling that you like him a lot more than you're saying?"

I stayed silent, staring at him with slightly widened eyes, and Logan huffed impatiently with a roll of his eyes. "You obviously like him more than you're leading on, Kelsey. Just admit it."

"I literally just did!" I tried to cover up with a laugh, though it was pathetic how awkward it sounded. No way was I fooling Logan.

My best friend smirked, shifting slightly to face me while keeping his broken foot propped up on the coffee table in front of us. "Kelsey," he began, his tone sounding as if he was speaking to a child. "If you love Cooper, then I think you should tell him."

I gasped, staring at Logan with widened, disbelieving eyes. I was rigid in my seat as I took in the knowing expression on his face, wondering if he was right. Love was definitely a strong emotion, and I hadn't felt it for any of my previous boyfriends because the relationships didn't last long enough. But Cooper and I had only been together for a few months or something like that; wasn't it a bit too soon for me to be in love with him? Didn't that thing take some time before reaching that kind of level?

The fact that it was Logan who was telling me this, someone who had hated the idea of Cooper and me being together, made it even crazier than it already was.

Holy shit. Do I love Cooper?

The question brought his face to my mind—bright, kind green eyes and the most handsome smile I'd ever seen on anyone's face. Cooper was a sweetheart with everyone around him—whether it be his family, me, the boys, and especially the fans that dedicate their time and money to support him and his band. He was appreciative of everything life had given him, never once taking anything for granted even when the paparazzi got too much and interviewers got too personal. It was no secret that the mere thought of Cooper brought a smile to my face and picked up my heart rate exponentially, spreading a comforting warmth through my chest

But was that what this was? Was I actually in love with the guy my mother had basically blindsided me into living with?

Both life and fate had a damn funny way of working out.

"It was only a matter of time until you did fall in love with him." Logan's voice pulled me out of my thoughts. My gaze flickered back to him. He flipped nonexistent long hair over his shoulder as he said in an obnoxiously high tone, "He's, like, totally dreamy!"

I chuckled incredulously at his depiction of a teenage girl, and he grinned. I sank my teeth into my lower lip, still trying to figure out my feelings. I was certain that my feelings for Cooper were stronger than I had thought, but I was confused as to when that even happened. "I'm just—I don't know."

"Well, you can figure your feelings out on the plane." I stared at him with raised eyebrows, since I wasn't planning on going back to London for a few days. Logan rolled his eyes. "Find out where your boyfriend is and fly out and surprise him or some shit. I'm guessing things are still a bit tense between you two?" He knew about Cooper's reaction when he found out I had flown to Miami.

I offered a tiny smile. "Just a bit."

Logan raised his eyebrow, jutting his chin towards my laptop. "What're you waiting for? Channel your inner hopeless romantic and buy a damn ticket."

Chapter 24

When the hotel room door swung open, revealing Cooper on the other side, I felt my heart skip a beat or two. He stared at me for a dumbfounded moment and chuckled disbelievingly. "What're you doin' here?"

He was genuinely pleased and surprised, no sign of the irritation I had feared. I smiled nervously and shrugged casually. "Thought I'd drop by and visit," I answered, gripping the handle of my carry-on suitcase.

Cooper stepped aside to open the door wider, allowing me to come in. I smiled to myself as he pressed a quick kiss to my cheek. Shutting the door, Cooper followed me further into the room, and I looked at him, watching as he rubbed his hands together. He asked, "How's Logan?"

I dropped my purse on the bed. "He's good," I answered carefully. "He's on crutches, but he'll be fine."

He nodded, leaning against the wall, hands in the pockets of his black jeans. "That's good," he replied. The awkwardness in his tone was evident, and I sighed in defeat.

"Are you still mad? Because I'm sorry that I didn't tell you, Coop. You know I didn't mean it." I shot him a pleading look, wanting us to get past this stupid misunderstanding. "It has nothing to do with trust, okay? I was just being forgetful."

This time, Cooper sighed, running his ring-clad fingers through his hair. He offered the smallest of smiles. "I know you're sorry, and I am too, honestly. I overreacted." He pursed his lips.

I shrugged, knowing he was right but also knowing I was partly to blame for this issue. "I should've told you what was going on, and I especially should've told you about going to Florida. I'm sorry you had to find out online instead of hearing it from me, again. It shouldn't work that way."

Cooper nodded, glancing away for a brief moment. "Yeah, but I still did overreact on you goin' to Miami. Logan's your best friend, and I'm not anyone to stop you from visitin' him—especially if he's in the hospital."

I took a step forward, smiling because I was glad that we were at least communicating this through. That's how things worked. "We're both at fault here. I'll promise to let you know if something with the paparazzi or me flying off happens again, and you can promise not to freak out over little things."

He grinned, pushing himself off the wall and making his way towards me. I looked up at him the closer he got. His arms slid around my waist, and my heart did a somersault at the sight of his smile. He promised, "You've got yourself a deal, love. I still am sorry if I came out lookin' like a controlling arsehole. And I'm glad Logan's okay."

I wanted to tell him to stop apologizing, but I knew it was because he still felt guilty, and it was his way of exorcising it out. "It's fine, Coop." I assured him, my arms winding around his neck. "I mean, the worse you could do is not care at all. It's nice to know that you do," I grinned cheekily, gaze locking with his.

He pressed a sweet kiss to my lips, short enough to leave me wanting more. "Don't ever doubt it."

***

"Can we just stay like this?"

Cooper's hoarse morning voice brought a smile to my face as we rested on the bed. I was on my stomach, cheek pressed against the soft mattress as Cooper lay next to me, fingers tracing random shapes on my back through the material of my shirt.

"That's the plan," I murmured, his actions making me feel surprisingly sleepy.

He then shifted our positions, pressing my back against his chest. I felt his toned torso through the flimsy material of his shirt. His lips brushed the spot where my neck and jaw met. Cooper intertwined our legs under the sheets as he murmured, "When are you goin' back?"

Snorting, I teased him. "Wanna get rid of me already?"

His arm around me squeezed in protest. "Course not. Want you here as long as you can stay."

Before I could respond, someone knocked on the hotel room door. Rafael's deep voice called out, "Cooper! Let's go, mate. We've a radio interview!"

Cooper let out a loud, protesting groan that I'm sure Rafael could hear. I chuckled. "Alright," he called back, making me flinch slightly as he yelled right by my ear, "let me just piss real quick."

My face scrunched up in disgust as Cooper climbed off the bed, hurrying over to the bathroom. He was already dressed for the day. The toilet flushed, and the faucet ran, and then moments later,

Cooper walked out of the bathroom and slipped into his shoes. He kissed me and said, "I'll see you in a few hours." He hurried out the door just as my phone rang.

"Hey, Logan," I greeted after reading the caller ID.

"Did you tell him?" was his way of greeting me, and I rolled my eyes as I sat up on the bed, knowing exactly what he was referring to. "Did you tell Cooper you *lo-o-ove* him?" he asked, stretching the word out.

"No, Logan," I answered with a sigh, leaning my head against the headboard of the bed. "Why are *you*, of all people, so impatient about this?"

"Because you're obviously really happy with them, and as your reestablished, non-douchey best friend, I want what's best for you. So, when are you gonna tell him?"

This was ridiculous. The complete 180 in his attitude towards Cooper and me was still making my head spin. I was glad that he was supportive now, no matter how difficult it may seem to be, but now I was just being hounded by him the way the paparazzi tended to do. "Logan, I'm not even sure if I *do* feel that way about him."

Logan scoffed in sarcastic disbelief. "Yes, you do," he said, the seriousness creeping into his voice. "Look, Kels, I've seen the way you talk about him, and all those damn paparazzi pictures make you two look like you're in love. Stop doubting your feelings for him because it's obvious that's how you feel about him, even if you can't see it."

"I can't tell Cooper that I love him when I'm not one hundred percent sure about it myself, Logan." I sighed, running my fingers through my hair. "I mean, yeah, I get what you're saying, but I don't wanna say it to him until I've come to terms with it myself, you know? It's a big damn deal."

My best friend was silent for a few moments before I heard him huff. "You take the fun out of everything."

I laughed and shook my head in amusement. "Piss off. I'll do it when I'm ready, and sure, when I do, you'll be the first to know. After Cooper, of course."

Logan chortled, satisfied. "Good. Now, if you'll excuse me, I need to have lunch. *Adios, amigo.*"

"It's *amiga.*"

"Shut up. You know I failed Spanish."

***

"So where exactly are you kidnapping me to?" I asked as Cooper drove the car, one of the SUVs that he had decided to steal. It was around one in the morning, just a couple of hours after the boys' concert had ended. Cooper had announced that the two of us were going on a drive after convincing his security team that we didn't need anyone to come with us. We were in South Carolina. Did he even know the roads well enough to be driving us somewhere?

"I want some ice cream." Cooper didn't spare me a glance as we drove. It was dark out, obviously, and there was little to no cars in the streets, as it was late and it was a Tuesday. "Been cravin' some cookies and cream since we got off stage."

We drove with the radio playing some old throwbacks, enjoying music ranging from the eighties up to recent years as the streetlights we drove under provided a ray of light for brief moments at a time. Cooper and I sat in silence, comfortable in the music and presence of each other. My left hand loosely gripped his right, atop the center console as he drove with one hand on the wheel. Almost absentmindedly, he traced circles on the back of my hand with his thumb, the gentle action gluing the fond smile on my lips.

Eventually, after almost forty minutes of driving, Cooper pulled the car into a deserted parking lot that was lit up only by two lamps. I looked out the windshield to see that it was some sort of town plaza. The parking lot was empty, save for a car or two parked here and there, and I realized that it was because the Baskin Robbins next to the twenty-four hour CVS was also open.

Unbuckling his seatbelt, Cooper told me that he would be back with our ice creams after I told him what I wanted, and I watched as he got out into the cold November night and jogged towards the ice cream parlor. I had told him I would go inside, since the workers most likely wouldn't recognize me, but he insisted. Though, I don't see how leaving me by myself in a car in the middle of a nearly deserted parking lot was any better.

The radio was still on, playing an old Pink Floyd song as I nodded to the beat. Then Cooper walked back out a few minutes later. With my oversized Nike sweatshirt drowning me, I got out of the car, relieved that it wasn't as cold as it could be. He held two cups of cookies and cream ice cream and shot me a confused look as to why I got out. I hopped up on the hood of the vehicle and left the door of the car open so we could hear the music from the radio. Cooper handed me the ice cream before sitting right next to me, both of us enjoying the cold treat in the slightly cold weather. "So—" I swallowed—"is there any particular reason why we're sitting in the middle of an empty lot eating ice cream?"

"It was a spur-of-the-moment kind of thing," Cooper said, his plastic spoon scooping up more ice cream before turning his head to smile up at me. "Plus, I wanted to spend some alone time with you."

His words brought a smile to my face and warmth to my cheeks. I glanced down at my plastic cup. We could've easily had alone time in the hotel, but actually going out on this mini adventure was a lot sweeter and so much more endearing. It was little things like this that sent my feelings for Cooper into overdrive.

As we finished off the rest of our ice cream, a new, unfamiliar song began playing on the radio. I placed my empty cup next to me and listened to the music playing. Tilting my head back slightly, I looked up at the sky blanketed with stars and an airplane flying by as its wing lights blinked red. The radio was playing some cheesy love song, and I bit my lower lip, eyes flickering over to Cooper as the lyrics about being in love practically taunted me about my feelings.

He was looking up at the night sky too. A cool breeze blew by, ruffling our hair. Goosebumps raised on the back of my neck and legs, despite the fact that I was wearing jeans. The silence between us was comfortable, but my mind was so loud because all I could think of were the continuous love songs playing on the radio and Logan's words.

My gaze was glued to him, though he couldn't tell, since his own was to the sky. I swallowed inaudibly as the mere sight of him stirred a completely pleasant and welcoming sensation in my stomach. Tearing my eyes from the guy I was with, I glanced down at my wrist and looked at the diamond bracelet his mom had given to me, a small gift to welcome me into the family so after my mom, I would feel as though I still had one.

The bracelet hadn't been a gift from Cooper, just his mother, but it still reminded me of him. Reminded me of my mom's passing, of how kind his family was to me, how far Cooper and I had come. It reminded me that we were two people from two completely different lifestyles brought together because our mothers knew best. Despite this, we were still capable of finding feelings we didn't think we could have for the person we were essentially forced to live with, the person we ended up *wanting* to live with. Who knew the friendship we had taken a while to establish could become deeper than we ever thought?

It was an overwhelming conclusion in the middle of a South Carolina parking lot under the stars that I was so lucky my mom did this one last thing for me before she left. My mom may not have intended for me to end up falling in love with her best friend's son, but it was not at all surprising that it was because of the woman I loved the most that I found the man I love.

I inhaled sharply at the realization, eyes widening slightly. Suddenly, Cooper was in front of me, looking at me curiously. "Alright, love?"

Love. Love, love, love.

I didn't answer, opting to let the silence envelop us. I stared at Cooper's ridiculously perfect face. His green eyes were dark, and he had shaven a few days ago, but there was some growing stubble along his sharp jaw and his mouth. Cooper gazed at me, wondering why I was looking the way that I was, and I just reached up and cupped his face in my hands, ignoring the gloriously prickling sensation of his stubble. I captured his lips in a searing, heart-stopping kiss.

He was taken aback for a second but recovered almost instantly, returning the kiss just as heatedly as his hands found my hips. Standing in the space between my legs, he gave me warmth. My heart was pounding wildly in my chest, threatening to break my ribs, and giddiness twisted my stomach in the best of ways. It was overwhelming and terrifying and so incredible, and I couldn't wait to let Cooper know about my feelings.

We pulled away moments later, both gasping for air as our breath intermingled and chests moved rapidly. My hands were still on his face, and I smiled as I opened my eyes. I almost shook with excitement because holy shit, I loved Cooper, and just coming to terms with that was a stunning realization.

Cooper's green eyes met my blue ones, his gaze never wavering. He took my hand and brought it between us. I stared at him curiously and impatiently—wanting to know what he was doing but also wanting to tell him that I freaking loved him before I lost my confidence. The familiar boyish smirk tugged at his lips as he pressed a kiss to the back of my hand. "You know, usually, a lad tells the girl first that he loves her and then gets a house or whatever to live with her in, but obviously, we're not normal enough for that."

My breath hitched in my throat. Was this going where I thought this was going? I stayed silent, desperately and impatiently wanting to know what Cooper was about to say. His other hand rested on the hood next to me, practically trapping me in. As if I would want to be anywhere but here.

His expression turned soft, adoring, and my heart skipped a beat. "I love you, Kelsey," Cooper finally said, his voice nothing but a low whisper as if he was telling me the greatest secret in the world. "So much," he added with a light nervous laugh.

I laughed too as I, unsurprisingly enough, felt tears burn in my eyes. With a small yet charming grin, he added, "I love you and I wish your mum was here so I could thank her for bringing you into my life."

His words lifted a weight off my chest, utterly wiping out the previous nerves and fear I had felt for finally letting my feelings known. I knew now that I had nothing to be anxious or afraid of because, once again, I had Cooper here to make everything easier for me.

Pressing my free hand against his chest, I fisted the material of his sweatshirt and felt the tears drop from my eyes. I felt ridiculous for crying, but I was just so happy. The kind of happy I didn't think I could be for so long. "I love you, too, Cooper."

He grinned, and I wondered if his cheeks hurt like mine were beginning to, though I didn't care a bit. All I cared about was the guy standing in front of me, the way he made me feel, and the way I made him feel. I was in love with him—the unadulterated, head-spinning type of love that I certainly hadn't expected finding myself in. My life seemed to be full of those, didn't it? Unexpected events that called for tears of both sadness and joy? They shaped my life into what it was today. And it was well worth it.

My mother had wanted to leave this world knowing that I was happy and loved. She had blindsided me by throwing Cooper into my life, and I wondered if she just knew that something amazing would come from this.

She must've. Mothers know best, after all.

Epilogue

Cooper

Three years later

Being forced to open my home to a stranger was the closest I had ever come to hating my mother. I was twenty years old, for god's sake, with a career that had me constantly moving about and just called for the bachelor lifestyle with the appropriate home. Being in the biggest multi-platinum-album-selling band in the world, I had to have my own place for the single lifestyle and enjoy my dream career, but clearly, my mother had thought differently. And if my mother had put her mind to something, she would see it through—that's one thing we had in common. She was as stubborn as a mule, and that's why no one on my band's management team or record label had argued with her when she had ultimately decided my fate. Whatever happened to record labels wanting an uncomplicated frontman who seemingly sold more records than a damn twenty-year-old who suddenly had a new roommate and the whole world knew about it?

Kelsey Ross wasn't happy about this arranged living situation either, but her mum had cancer and was dying and had asked this of her. I couldn't entirely blame Kelsey for going along with it. Who were we to deny a woman her last wish? And then Klara Ross passed away and my home was suddenly someone else's too.

There had been ups and downs and so much more confusion as Kelsey and I tried to make our way through this unwanted circumstance we were in. We tried to figure out how to act around each other, tried to get to know each other. Sure, people lived with strangers all the time at university, but knowing this was more or less permanent sat heavily on our shoulders.

So we tried to figure it out, together, losing our balance along the way but eventually finding our footing. Then I fell in love with her. Shit, I fell in love with her so hard and so unexpectedly. It bloody terrified me, realizing I was in love with her during one of our sound checks as she sat in one of the middle rows, watching my best mates and I joke around on stage. But when she returned those same three words, it was like being able to breathe again. I didn't think I could know a love like this.

And then I met our daughters.

They were born right after Triage's fourth worldwide tour, a year and a half after we got married. We were young, we knew, but we were in love and ready for a new chapter in our lives. Our girls helped in that—twin daughters by the names of Klara Amelia Shaw and Abigail Leah Shaw, the most beautiful girls I had ever laid eyes on, both named after the two women Kelsey and I owed our love and lives to. It was like throughout the entirety of Kelsey's pregnancy, I couldn't breathe, but once my girls were in my arms, my lungs were finally expanding and my heart was soaring in my chest. I didn't know I could love this much.

My eyes trailed over to Kelsey, who was finally asleep after hours upon hours of labor, utterly spent and exhausted and getting a much-deserved rest. Her blonde hair was still tied messily as she slept, but I couldn't help the smile on my face as I excitedly thought: *She's the mother of my children.*

Her bed was surrounded by congratulatory balloons and stuffed animals, all given by our friends and family who were adamant about staying in the hospital throughout the whole ordeal of Kelsey's labor. On the single bedside, where a glass and jug of water were kept, was Kelsey's mother's old copy of *The Count of Monte Cristo*, the book Kelsey had been reading during labor to distract her when the commotion of our friends sparked her temper, shortened drastically while she was pregnant. The book served well in both relaxing her and making her feel like Klara was right by her side during this moment. She, unfortunately, couldn't be here, but she definitely wasn't forgotten.

I walked over to the cribs near the bed, since we had decided that we wanted the babies to sleep in this room for now. Peering down at them, I felt an airy sensation in my chest as tears began gathering in my eyes. I still couldn't believe that Kelsey and I made *this*—two perfect little human beings, sleeping soundly and peacefully, making me feel a depth of love I didn't know existed.

The hospital room door quietly opened. I glanced over my shoulder to see my mum gently close the door behind her. She had been lingering in the waiting room that was full of people that had refused to leave since the moment Kelsey had been admitted—my band mates, their girls, my family, and even Logan, who had flown in from Florida with his fiancé. I wasn't surprised that Mum couldn't stand being outside for too long.

She whispered, "She's quite a warrior." My gaze followed hers to my sleeping wife. "Just like her mother."

I smiled, agreeing with her statement with no doubt in my mind as my mum hugged me sideways. My own arm wrapped around her shoulders as we both looked down at the sleeping babies that were only a few hours old. "You did so well, sweetheart," Mum murmured, leaning into me as she smiled down at her granddaughters. Her green eyes glimmered with joyful tears. The sight tugged at my heart. "There aren't enough words that describe how proud I am of you."

She gave a watery smile, and I chuckled softly, pulling her back in and kissing the top of her head. "Come on, Mum. Don't cry."

"Sorry, sorry," she responded and laughing sheepishly, quietly as she wiped at her eyes. "It's just amazing, honey. You're only twenty-three and you've accomplished so much. I've only ever wanted the best for you, and your hard work's paid off."

I squeezed her frame, lips rolling into my mouth as her words resonated deeply in me. I blinked back the tears that were blurring my vision while pressing my nose to the top of my mum's head. Gathering my wits, I spoke up again. "It's all because of you and Klara." I looked at her as I spoke so she could see just how much I meant my words. "It was because of you two that Kelsey and I ever met, and if that pipe in your house hadn't burst, none of this would've happened." We both chuckled at the reminder of the reason why Kelsey had to move into my apartment as opposed to my parents' house. "All the hard work and accomplishments come from you, Mum, and I can't ever thank you enough for everythin' that you've given me. Including your granddaughters."

The tears in Mum's eyes only increased tenfold as she hugged me properly this time, burying her face in my chest. I wrapped my arms around the woman who had given me four more incredible women in my life—my sister, my wife, and my daughters. I meant every word. If my mother hadn't pushed me into living with Kelsey, getting to know her, I wouldn't have been able to experience a startling new adventure of falling in love with someone. First, I met Kelsey, then I became friends with her, and then I fell in love with her. Our love and our lives had been unconventional in more ways than one—ranging from the heartbreaking loss of a parent, feuding best friends, to the crazy career and rowdy paparazzi—but it was ours. Our love and our lives. And I wouldn't change a damn thing.

The End

Can't get enough of Kelsey and Cooper? Make sure you sign up for the author's blog to find out more about them!

Get these two bonus chapters and more freebies when you sign up at *summer-nawaz.awesomeauthors.org*!

Here is a sample from another story you may enjoy:

STOLEN KISSES

Kerttu-Liis Kiili

Chapter 1

To survive four years of high school in Grant High, one must follow three very simple steps.

1. Stay away from Seth Lee as much as possible.
2. Don't become friends with Seth Lee.
3. Avoid engaging in romantic activities with Seth Lee.

So why is it that in a span of six months, I managed to ignore all the rules previously set by my friend Kelly and me and broke all of those three rules? I guess I can say something stupid like "You can't control who you fall in love with," or "He just came to me." I had nothing to do with this, but in all honesty, this was sort of my fault as well.

You see, not only was my brother in the popular group, but his best friend just happens to be the previously mentioned delinquent, Seth Lee. Therefore, as much as I am trying to ignore the guy, it just isn't physically possible. He is always around, hanging out with my brother and annoying me. I've spent three years of my high school life ignoring him as much as possible, but one evening, my brother decides it is the perfect time to ruin everything.

Here I am, sitting on a bar stool behind the kitchen counter, messily doodling on the edge of my essay paper and procrastinating as much as possible. That's when I hear my brother skipping downstairs—minor detail: he never does anything like that—and head straight toward my mother, who is sitting on the couch and watching a stupid reality show about some housewives.

"Mom, if I ask you a favor, promise me you'll say yes," River murmurs, making my head snap toward his direction. His elbows are placed on the edge of the couch as he's leaning down toward my mother.

"Depends on the question." Mom chuckles.

"My friend Seth needs a place to stay—"

"I swear to God, River, if you're going to ask Mom if he can stay here, I will chop off your arm!" I hiss, making River look at me with a mischievous grin, and then a small chuckle escapes past his lips.

Seth Lee is the most arrogant guy ever. He thinks that just because he looks like a Greek god, he can get anything he wants in life while others sweat their butt off to reach their goals. He doesn't even realize that in the real world, good looks won't get you very far. You have to work hard to achieve your goals.

River chuckles nervously. "I'm not going to ask that. What're you talking about?" He then proceeds to walk up close to Mom and whispers something to her.

"Oh, honey. Of course, he can!" Mom exclaims. "Seth is such a wonderful guy. I'd be happy to have him living with us for a while."

My mouth drops open as I hear those words leaving my mother's.

Crossing my arms over my chest, I glare at River. "I'm sorry. What part of 'I will chop off your arm' don't you understand?"

River walks over to me and messes up my hair. "Ella, chill. It's not like he will steal your lip balm collection."

The minute he says that, I feel my heart drop. My lip balm collection is the most precious thing to me, and if something happens to it, I will not survive. I need my lip balms to keep my lips soft for my non-existent boyfriends.

"Don't say that, River!" I yell. "He might do that." Before River can reply, I grab my laptop and run upstairs. I lock my door behind me and walk to my dresser, which has my lip balm collection on top. I'm sure I have over a hundred lip balms by now, and I keep buying more and more every day. You can find possibly every flavor in my collection, starting from banana and ending with peanut butter.

I grab my favorite flavor, cherry, and put it on my lips. One thing weird about me is that I never let anybody into my room, not even my mom. Maybe I'm afraid of them stealing my lip balms, or maybe I'm afraid of them judging me because of my obsession. Either way, I'm not letting anyone in besides my best friend, Kelly.

Kelly and I have been friends since our diaper days. We met in kindergarten; there was an instant connection between us, and we've been inseparable ever since. Some people even say we're like Siamese cats since we do everything together. That's half-true.

After my five minutes of alone time with my lip balms, I walk downstairs and straight to the kitchen where I can smell brownies—Nutella brownies to be specific. My mom loves baking, and considering how Nutella brownies are everyone's favorite, she makes them almost every day.

"Mom, why did you let Seth—"

"I'm home! Did you guys miss me?" an obnoxious voice yells, and I roll my eyes. Of course, Seth Lee would come here now when I'm just about to eat all the brownies. "River, get your fat ass downstairs. I'm here."

"Seth, honey, I made brownies," Mom yells back. "Come eat some before Ella eats them all."

As she says that, the hallway fills with Seth's laughter, and I feel a blush creeping onto my cheeks. Everyone knows about my love for sweet things, and the constant teasing about it is getting tiring.

Seth walks through the kitchen door, his eyes landing on me. He gives me a small smile as he drops a duffle bag on the ground. "Hey, Ellie, did you miss your hunk of a friend?"

"Call me Ellie and I will castrate you."

"Awe," Seth answers and walks over to me, pinching my cheeks. "I love you too, babe." He gives me a quick peck on the forehead, and I gag. Many people might even think that Seth and I are dating since he acts as if he's my boyfriend, but in reality, he just likes annoying me.

"For fuck's sake," I mumble. "Will you ever stop annoying me?"

"The minute I stop annoying you is the minute hell freezes over." He chuckles. "So that's never going to happen. Besides, you're River's baby sister. It's my job as the best friend to annoy the crap out of you."

"Fuck you, Seth Lee, fuck you."

"We'll do the fucking later, don't worry." Seth winks, and I look over at my mom who's just smiling at the both of us. She wipes away an imaginary tear and leaves the kitchen, smiling like an idiot.

Wow, what a great mother, I think to myself and grab a plate full of brownies before walking upstairs. I close the door, and shortly, Seth walks in and lies down on my bed.

I glare at him. "Would you mind leaving?"

"Ellie, if we're going to be sleeping in rooms next to each other, you might as well be nice to me. I can take a lot of time in the washroom in the morning, and I'm sure you'd like to shower too." He smirks.

"Say what?"

A wide grin appears on Seth's face. "Ellie, I'm going to be staying in the room next door, and we're going to share a bathroom."

Kill me now.

If you enjoyed this sample then look for
Stolen Kisses.

Acknowledgements

First and foremost, I want to thank Wattpad for giving me the platform I didn't know I needed. *Bound* was one of the first stories I posted at fifteen years old, full of mistakes and plot holes yet one of my most popular works on there. If it weren't for Wattpad and the readers I've gained on it, this opportunity would never be possible.

I would like to thank my best friends, Sabrina Hussaini and Veronica DeJesus and my cousin Salma Khan. These three women have constantly listened to me complain when it came to writing yet were always encouraging me. They even let me bounce ideas off them and were there if I needed help in any way. They've been supporting me since day one, and I can't ever thank them enough for it.

Lastly, I would like to give my utter gratitude to Doug DePice, my eleventh grade Creative Expressions teacher. He was someone who, from the first day of class, always praised my way with words. He made me want to write when I didn't think I could anymore, was always encouraging and was convinced that someday I would get a book published. I'm so grateful that I can tell him someday is today.

Author's Note

Hey there!

Thank you so much for reading *Bound*! I can't express how grateful I am for reading something that was once just a thought inside my head.

I'd love to hear from you! Please feel free to email me at summer_nawaz@awesomeauthors.org and sign up at summer-nawaz.awesomeauthors.org for freebies!

One last thing: I'd love to hear your thoughts on the book. Please leave a review on Amazon or Goodreads because I just love reading your comments and getting to know YOU!

Whether that review is good or bad, I'd still love to hear it!

Can't wait to hear from you!
Summer Nawaz

About the Author

She grew up in Pakistan and moved to New Jersey at the age of eleven, only to develop an intense love for reading and writing. She joined Wattpad in 2012 and have been writing ever since, honing her skills while taking inspiration from books she reads, shows and movies she watches, and music she listens to. Writing is a form of escape, and she hopes that someday the stories she creates in her books can become an escape for the people reading them.